The SEVEN STRATEGIES of MASTER PRESENTERS

BY

DR. BRAD McRAE
author of *The Seven Strategies of Master Negotiators*

DAVID BROOKS
Toastmasters World Champion of Public Speaking

FOREWORD BY TED CORCORAN
President, Toastmasters International 2003—2004

CAREER PRESS

Franklin Lakes, NJ

THE SEVEN STRATEGIES OF MASTER PRESENTERS
Cover design by Brill Graphic Design Inc.
Printed in the U.S.A. by Book-mart Press

To order this title, please call toll-free 1-800-CAREER-1 (NJ and Canada: 201-848-0310) to order using VISA or MasterCard, or for further information on books from Career Press.

The Career Press, Inc., 3 Tice Road, PO Box 687,
Franklin Lakes, NJ 07417
www.careerpress.com

Library of Congress Cataloging-in-Publication Data

McRae, Bradley C. (Bradley Collins), 1945-
　The seven strategies of master presenters / by Brad McRae & David Brooks ; foreword by Ted Corcoran.
　　p. cm.
　Includes bibliographical references and index.
　ISBN 1-56414-744-4 (paper)
　1. Public speaking.　I. Brooks, David, 1952-　II. Title.

PN4129.15.M387 2004
808.5'1—dc22
2003069597

Brad dedicates this book to his three lifelong friends John Loback, Terrye Perlman, and Carolyn Flynn; and to his beloved children, Andrew and Katie McRae.

David dedicates this book to his wife and son Beth and Matthew Brooks.

A portion of the profits from this book is being donated to Lara's Hope to find a cure for Huntington's disease.

ACKNOWLEDGMENTS

One of the best ways to make the material in this book come to life is to illustrate the strategies through interviews with Master Presenters. The 28 Master Presenters we interviewed freely shared the wisdom that they had painstakingly gathered through countless years of experience. Their insights significantly broadened and deepened our understanding of *The Seven Strategies of Master Presenters.*

Brad would like to express his heartfelt thanks to his corporate clients. Being able to teach *The Seven Strategies of Master Presenters* throughout such organizations as Saint Mary's University at the World Trade Centre; London Life; Maritime Life; Great-West Life; CO-OP Atlantic; Credit Union Central of Nova Scotia; Michelin North America; and the Governments of Nova Scotia and Canada was invaluable.

We want thank our colleagues Pat Lazaruk, Betty Cooper, and Fraser McAllan for their insightful suggestions regarding both the content and the style of this book, and our home editing team of Katherine Coy, Mary-Beth Clark, Joan Homewood, and Lawrence McEachern, without whose help and encouragement this manuscript would have remained partially written forever. Glenn Sutherland kept the computers and the software running when they didn't really want to, and Alain Godbout helped get all of the figures in the right form and resolution. The staff in the reference departments at the Halifax Regional Library and at Dalhousie University Library had the grace and wisdom to track down and ferret out the most obscure references.

We were also greatly assisted by our editor, Mike Pye, our eagle-eyed editorial director, Stacey Farkas, and all of the staff at Career Press for turning our manuscript into a book. Their professional guidance and personal encouragement were invaluable. We would like to add a special note of thanks to Jeff and Deborah Herman for writing the book *Write the Perfect Book Proposal*, and to Jeff Herman for being the perfect agent.

Lastly, Brad would like to thank his children, Andrew and Katie, and close friends for their support and understanding throughout the research, writing, editing, and reresearching, rewriting, and reediting of this book. David would like to thank his wife, Beth, and son, Matthew, for their unflagging support and encouragement.

Brad McRae
Halifax, Nova Scotia

David Brooks
Austin, Texas

April, 2004

CONTENTS

FOREWORD

Ninety-eight years ago, William Jennings Bryan wrote:

> The age of oratory has not passed; nor will it pass....As long as there are human rights to be defended; as long as there are great interests to be guarded; as long as the welfare of nations is a matter for discussion, so long will public speaking have its place.[1]

It is irrefutable that public speaking shall always have its place. However, it is indisputable that in the ensuing century since William Jennings Bryan wrote those words, the "age of oratory" has experienced significant change. Bryan also wrote, "The press, instead of displacing the orator, has given him a larger audience and enabled him to do a more extended work."[2] Yet, it is precisely because "the press" has changed that oratory has changed as well. The press that Bryan referred to was solely a print medium; in 1906, radio was still in its infancy and television would not arrive for another four decades.

As radio, television, and other media evolved, so did oratory. Today's orators, who frequently depend on the media of electronic mass communication, must speak differently than orators of a century ago. Today's orators must be more concise. Though clarity was, and still is, a primary communication goal, today's orators must include an added dimension: brevity. As author Roger Ailes wrote, "Today we're all tuned to receive information much more quickly, and we get bored in a hurry if things slow down. The video age has sped up our cognitive powers."[3]

Unquestionably, today's audiences listen differently. Therefore, today's oral communicators must speak differently. In the pages that follow, Dr. Brad McRae and David Brooks have written a definitive guide for 21st-century speakers. This book will serve as an invaluable reference for those who wish to understand the techniques, methods, and strategies that enable today's orators to be effective when speaking to today's increasingly impatient listeners.

As an Irishman, I come from a land steeped in a history of eloquence. As a Toastmaster, I respect those who speak with precision and purpose. Consequently, I revere those whose finely framed words delight the ears, challenge the intellect, and stir the soul. With *The Seven Strategies of Master Presenters* you will learn what Mark Twain meant when he wrote, "Lord, what an organ is human speech when it is played by a Master."[4]

Ted Corcoran
President, Toastmasters International 2003–2004

PREFACE

More than $6 billion dollars is spent on training and presentations in North America every year—and this figure does not include the indirect costs of paying employees while they attend training and presentations. This is an enormous investment of time and resources. Sadly, many of these presentations are poorly designed, poorly delivered, and poorly received. However, when a presentation is exquisitely designed and masterfully delivered, the audience members are moved to see the world differently than they ever saw it before and is inspired to achieve more than they ever thought possible.

If we spend this much time either giving or attending presentations, why is the return on investment (ROI) so low? The answer is that most of us have had very little formal training in how to improve our presentation skills. The good news is that there are dozens of excellent courses available to improve presentation skills. At the same time, there are many excellent books to help us learn to develop and enhance our presentation skills. However, there is an area that has not been fully addressed by any of these books. None of them address the skills and strategies necessary to be a Master Presenter. That is the focus of this book: how to develop the strategies used so effectively by Master Presenters.

The emphasis of this book is on development and practical application of presentation skills and strategies. These skills and strategies can help you become a more effective presenter, regardless of whether you are giving a one-on-one presentation, a presentation to a small group, or a presentation to an audience of a thousand or more. This book is designed to be highly interactive. It contains many exercises, each one carefully constructed to help you develop and enhance your content, delivery, and presentation style. You will learn how to make your presentations more memorable, actionable, and transferable to the workplace so that they have both an immediate and a lasting impact. You will also learn how to obtain salient feedback so you absolutely know what is working and what needs to be improved. By actively involving yourself in these exercises, you can watch yourself improve and grow as a presenter.

—Dr. Brad McRae and David Brooks

INTRODUCTION

People are the common denominators of progress...
no improvement is possible with unimproved people.
— *John Kenneth Galbraith,* The Affluent Society[1]

Why are presentation skills so important to the progress of organizations and to the careers of individuals who give them? The following examples answer this question especially well.

Rudolph Giuliani became the face of despair and the symbol of determination after the tragic events of September 11, 2001. In fact, he spoke so well that he became known as America's mayor. In his book, *Leadership,* Giuliani's presents strategies for making and delivering a dynamic presentation. Five of those points follow.

"Develop and communicate strong beliefs"

Mayor Giuliani communicated his beliefs about reducing crime, welfare reform, improving education and police protection every chance he got. As a result, everyone knew what he stood for and what he stood against.

"Don't save your best argument for last"

Giuliani states that the first five minutes are the optimal opportunity to get the audience's attention. He advises us to not save the "...best argument for last, when maybe only a third of them are listening."[2]

"Use facts to build your case"

There are many instances when presenters need to use facts and objective criteria to make their case. During his tenure as mayor, Giuliani wanted New Yorkers to know that progress was being made and that more progress would be forthcoming. Among the facts that he used to demonstrate that progress was being made were that crime fell by 57 percent, shootings fell by 75 percent, the murder rate fell by two-thirds, funding for the New York school system increased by $4 billion, and the economy created more than 485,000 new private-sector jobs.

By reading Giuliani's book *Leadership*, you will see that the mayor used facts, statistics, and objective criteria every chance he got to build his case for what New York needed and for what New York had accomplished. Building a strong case and building a strong presentation are both based on facts.

"Be able to explain and simplify"

Mayor Giuliani is a master at explaining and simplifying. He combined this skill with his ability to develop and communicate strong beliefs in economic prosperity for the City of New York and in the welfare of its citizens.[3]

"Challenge the audience and challenge yourself"

Mayor Giuliani believes that the purpose of the annual State of the City address "...wasn't simply to report whether the city was in good or bad shape [but] to produce a blueprint for what I hoped to achieve[—]...the idea behind the speeches was to set a direction for the city." His goal was to challenge the people who worked for the city, the citizens of New York, and, most of all, himself.[4]

The second example that illustrates how important presentation skills are is seen in Lee Iacocca. Through his superb presentation skills, Iacocca saved the Chrysler Corporation. Iacocca became the pitchman on television for Chrysler, telling all who would listen: "If you can find a better car than Chrysler, buy it." He made presentation after presentation to the dealership network convincing them to stay with a Chrysler. Likewise, he negotiated wage concessions with the unions and negotiated loan guarantees with the United States Congress to keep Chrysler afloat. The loan guarantees were repaid seven years ahead of schedule. Iacocca was being paid only one dollar a year in salary with stock options as an incentive. He used his presentation skills to turn around a failing company. In the process, he turned himself into a multi-millionaire.

In his book, *You've Got to Be Believed to Be Heard*,[5] Bert Decker compares Lee Iacocca and Lawrence Rawl. Lawrence Rawl was the president and CEO of the Exxon Corporation during the *Exxon Valdez* environmental disaster. In 1989, that ship ran aground and spilled more than 11 million gallons of Alaskan oil in the straits of Prince William Sound. In countless media interviews, Rawl steadfastly refused to acknowledge the seriousness of the problem, either for the people of Prince William Sound or for Exxon's business. The oil spill blackened more than 1,300 miles of pristine Alaskan shoreline.

When asked about the cost of the clean up, Rawl said that the impact on Exxon's bottom line would be minimal. By the fall of 1992, the company had spent $2.1 billion on cleanup efforts. The $5 billion it had to pay out in punitive damages was the largest ever awarded in a pollution case![6] After the *Exxon Valdez* spill, thousands of Exxon customers mailed their Exxon credit cards back to Rawl. Ten years after the *Exxon Valdez*, consumers still had a negative view of Exxon based on how poorly the crisis was handled at the highest level in the company.

In his book, Decker asks a most interesting question: "What do we think would have happened if Lee Iacocca were president of Exxon and Lawrence Rawl were president of Chrysler during the time of their respective crises." Decker's question makes an exceptional point. These men probably had similar IQs. However, their EQ (emotional intelligence), which includes their ability to communicate and present during a crisis, were as different as night and day.

This example illustrates that how we present ourselves and our messages can have a powerful impact on how well we are perceived and how well we perform. Whether speaking to one person, to two or three in a meeting, to hundreds in an auditorium, or to tens of thousands through mass media, presentation skills matter. The ability to present clearly, credibly, and confidently is important to us individually, and to our organizations and communities.

This book is devoted to understanding and mastering the Seven Strategies of Master Presenters and it will show you how to take your presentation skills to the highest level possible.

The Seven Strategies were developed by carefully reading the literature on effective presentation skills, by interviewing 26 of the top presenters in North America, and by interviewing some of the top speech coaches.[7] It was further developed in the classroom, by teaching these strategies and skills to people from all walks of life who attended our courses on the Seven Strategies of Master Presenters. Through instruction and testing, people in our classes improved dramatically, progressing from average to good and from good to great.

In this book, we look at the critical differences between Master Presenters and their less successful counterparts. We explore the importance of gaining an audience's trust and establishing credibility as a presenter in the first few minutes of any presentation. We then examine the power of the "slight edge technique" and illustrate incremental improvements that will make it easier to develop these most important skills. We also look at why most people fail to develop this critically important skill set, leaving their more presentation-savvy counterparts' careers to soar while theirs do not. Lastly, we provide a means for you to survey your current presentation skills and determine your developmental needs.

Determining What Matters Most About a Presenter

Most courses that teach High Impact Presentation Skills ask the participants to do an exercise in which they list the qualities of the best and worst presenters they have ever seen. This is a good exercise and one that we have used ourselves. Recently, however, we learned how to ask a much more powerful question that goes to the foundation of successful presentations. That question involves looking at some of the presenters who have had the most impact on us and determining what accounted for that impact.

Just as astronomers look closely at the light from distant stars to try to figure out historically how the universe was formed, Master Presenters look to the past, in particular at their favorite and/or most influential elementary school, junior high, high school, or university teacher in order to determine *why* those teachers were so influential.

For example, when one of our seminar participants thought back, he realized that one name stood out from all of the rest: Mrs. Goltz. His description of Mrs. Goltz follows.

I have spoken to as many of my old high school friends as I could find. One of the most amazing things about these reunions is that after everyone catches up on what has happened to all of their friends, frequently the conversation turns to one particular teacher—our junior-year English teacher—Mrs. Goltz. She taught with a passion and intensity that is hard to describe in words. And it wasn't just about English literature. It was much deeper than that. In addition to reading some of the best English literature, her classes were a voyage of discovery.

Somehow we all ended up with literary nicknames in Mrs. Goltz's class. Sometimes she chose the name; sometimes other classmates gave us the name. I became so taken with Steinbeck that one of my classmates started calling me Steinbeck. After reading The Grapes of Wrath, *I became interested in social justice, and Mrs. Goltz gave me a biography of Gandhi to read. Another student, who eventually became a psychologist, was called Freud. If you have seen the movie* Dead Poet's Society, *that's the type of influence Mrs. Goltz had on her students and that is the type of culture we had in our classroom.*

In the exercise that follows, we ask you to think of such a teacher from your past. Yes, we know it is out of the ordinary to jump right into an exercise while still in the Introduction, and we expect that many of you will be tempted to skip it. However, it would be a mistake to do so. This exercise will help you to determine the teachers whom you found most influential and, more importantly, why you found them so effective and memorable. You will find that the teachers you list were memorable or influential for a specific reason. That reason was important at that time in your life and that reason may still be important now. That reason may be a message from the past—a vital suggestion as to how you should change or enhance your current presentation style.

Note: For all the exercises presented in this book, please use a separate notebook.

EXERCISE INTRO-1

Think about your favorite, most memorable, and most influential teacher from elementary school, junior high or middle school, high school, and college or university. What were the characteristics that made that teacher so outstanding? Why do you remember that teacher more clearly, more fondly, and more intensely than all of the others?

Write down your recollections for each of the following headings. You do not have to fill in all of the categories, only the ones that stir intense and fond memories.

- Recollections of my most memorable/influential elementary school teacher(s).
- Recollections of my most memorable/influential junior high or middle school teacher(s).
- Recollections of my most memorable/influential high school teacher(s).
- Recollections of my most memorable/influential college/university professors/teachers.

EXERCISE INTRO-2

Which aspects of your favorite or most influential teachers do you most wish to emulate, and how will you do it?

Through analyzing our students' examples, our own observations of expert presenters, and from reviewing the literature, we found that five factors were consistently used to describe these Master Presenters. The five factors were:

1. Credible
2. Competent
3. Compatible

4. Caring
5. Dynamic

One way to help remember this is to think of 4 Cs and a D, or 4 CDs.

1. Credible

Keynote presentations are at the pinnacle that is the very top of the presentation business. Very few get there, and even fewer survive. They are paid large sums of money for usually very short presentations. Master Presenters know that they have a very short period of time to establish their ABC's, which stands for Authenticity, Believability, and Credibility.

—Warren Evans, Certified Speaking Professional

Likewise, Edward R. Murrow said:

To be persuasive, we must be believable.

To be believable, we must be credible.

To be credible, we must be truthful.

Among the factors that contribute to credibility as a presenter are honesty, authenticity, and accurately telling the audience what you will cover and sticking to it.

Being honest as a presenter means that we have to present the most accurate, up-to-date material possible. If a question is asked, and we don't know the answer, we should say we don't know the answer, and will do our best to find out.

We must **be authentic** in that we must practice what we preach. In talking to meeting and event planners about their war/horror stories, one factor that audiences will absolutely not forgive is an inauthentic presenter. High on the list of inauthentic presenters are the egotistical know-it-alls, who not only think they know everything, but who also let audiences know how lucky they are that these speakers have taken the time to speak to a group of lesser beings. A second, but equally unforgivable, authenticity sin is when a presenter gets caught not practicing what is being presented, such as the stress management expert who becomes inordinately stressed because something isn't working in the session, the detail management expert who does not end the session on time, the technical expert whose information is blatantly out of date or just plain wrong, or the high-tech presentation expert whose equipment won't work.

We must **be absolutely clear as to what we will and will not cover**. In training and workshop situations, most presenters rightfully ask for the participants' expectations. The presenter can very effectively use this information to align his or her presentation with the audience's expectations. It also affords the presenter the opportunity to negotiate what can and cannot be effectively covered. For example, in Brad's negotiation course, he does not specifically cover union/management negotiations, because the purpose of the course is using negotiating and influencing as personal and interpersonal effectiveness tools. He does, however, cover strategies and skills that can help in the effectiveness of all negotiations. If the participant is specifically interested in union/management negotiations, other courses and books are recommended.

It is equally important to encourage people to pass if their expectations have already been covered. If you, as the presenter, are respectful of the participants' time, you increase the likelihood that they will be respectful of your and each other's time.

2. Competent

As a presenter you have two minutes to demonstrate that you are competent. If you don't demonstrate it within the first two minutes, you can still do so, but it will require much more time and effort. Master Presenters establish their competence in numerous ways:

- Based on their experience.
- Based on their research.
- Based on synthesizing the research of others.
- Based on their dedicated study and in-depth understanding of their material.

One of Brad's techniques is to use the participants' expectations of what they want to learn in the session to explain some of the most interesting research on the negotiation process. This is effective for two reasons. First, it is unexpected and we have never heard other presenters present some of their in-depth material during the time that they are gathering the participants' expectations. Second, the research that he presents is so well thought out and so powerful, it gives him instant credibility. For example, when Brad teaches *The Seven*

Strategies of Master Negotiators course, invariably, one participant will mention that he would like to be more confident in his ability to negotiate. At this point, he presents research on the "Eight competencies that differentiate effective senior managers from their average counterparts." Because one of the competencies is self-confidence, he demonstrates how Master Negotiators developed their self-confidence by developing the other seven competencies. Brad also gives the participants a newsletter that summarizes the scientific research on the eight competencies so that participants can concentrate on the material rather than try to take copious notes.

The act of presenting the material and then supplying a copy of the material in the form of one of his *Negotiation Newsletters* enhances Brad's credibility. A third way Brad establishes his credibility is by handing out a copy of his annotated bibliography that lists more than 125 books and films.[8] Likewise, if you have written an article or a book, this is the time to have it on hand.

EXERCISE INTRO-3

Part 1: Master Presenters establish their competency as early as possible in the presentation. The material that is presented must be incredibly clear, powerful, and purposeful. In your notebook, please list any techniques and/or tools that you have seen Master Presenters use that established their competency early in their presentation.

Part 2: List one or two tools or techniques that you will use to establish your competency at the earliest point possible in your next presentation.

3. Compatible

I think when you are "up on stage" you are not delivering a message. Rather, you are establishing a contact between soul and soul. The listeners want to know who you are, and what you are like, before they will hear, really hear, anything you have to say. They want to know what you have in common with them, and what you have that is unique to you, from which they may learn. Both strands are important. "Who are you?" is the foremost question that every listener brings to your presentation. Therefore, if you think in your head that there is some role you should play, some other presenter that you should "be like," some style of another that you should emulate, then you are ducking the foremost question on their mind. The key style of your presentation should be that you are just yourself.

—Richard Bolles

One of the most efficient ways to learn is to learn from the experience of others. This process is called modeling. We watch how "the model" does something and we incorporate that behavior into our own repertoire. Psychological research on modeling demonstrates that we feel more comfortable with and are more likely to model behavior of people who we feel are more similar to us. Therefore, you need to establish your compatibility with your audience within the first two minutes.

Master Presenters do everything within their power to be, or at least appear to be, compatible with the audience members. One way Brad does this, after being introduced as the author of several books on negotiating and influencing skills, and having studied negotiating skills at the Harvard Program on Negotiation, is by remarking, "You would think that someone with all that training could get his kids to clean up their rooms." First, it is true. Second, it makes him human, and third, it demonstrates that all of us have some negotiations that are more difficult than others. As this example demonstrates, one of the best ways to demonstrate compatibility is with self-depreciating humor. Likewise, David is often introduced with the following: "David has spoken in all 50 U.S. states, every Canadian province, and 12 countries." Then, in his opening remarks he says, "I need to clarify one point you heard in my introduction. It's true that I have spoken in 50 states, 8 Canadian provinces, and 12 countries, but I have to be honest with you. In eight of those 12 countries, it was just to ask for directions."

In the same vein, Master Presenter Harold Taylor establishes his compatibility with his audiences by explaining that he had to develop time-management skills because his business was failing, his marriage was failing, and he had bleeding ulcers. Harold's droll and dry sense of humor makes it easy for anyone to identify with him. Contrast this with a well-known presenter whose introduction makes him or her sound like a superman or a superwoman: the person who overcame everything and, in addition to raising six children, has adopted 28 others, is on the board of every charity, and is an Olympic athlete. Unlike the superman or superwoman presenter, people in the audience can identify with Harold.[9]

Master Presenters make sure that they are seen as being compatible with the members of the audience. This is especially true if we are from different ethnic and/or professional cultures. Our intuition, when it is on, can help us form a bond of compatibility with our audience. For example, Brad had the privilege of presenting *The Seven Strategies of Master Negotiators* to a Native Band Council. During the session Brad told the story of an eye accident that happened to his daughter along with his efforts to reduce the likelihood of this type of accident happening to other children. For this session, Brad told this story much earlier than usual. Because most North American aboriginal cultures are so strongly child-centered, his story helped him form an early bond of compatibility with the course participants. However, when our intuition is off, it can have the opposite effect.

4. Caring

I think that the very first thing that a Master Presenter does is that he or she doesn't think about teaching or presenting, but about learning and connecting. And so that the very first thing that they do is focus on the individuals in their audience rather than focusing on themselves. They do not seek to tell, they think to influence. They do not seek to communicate, they seek to connect. They don't believe it is something you do to an audience, but something you do with an audience. They understand that their purpose is not to speak, but to serve.

—Nido Qubein, *Certified Speaking Professional*

Nido is talking about the old maxim that, *"People don't care how much you know until they know how much you care."* Although presenters may be able to fool their audiences in the short run, they can never fool their audiences in the long run. It is also true that excellent presenters, who did care at one point in their career, can become so enamored and burdened by their success, that the caring has been worn out of them. One way to find out how caring you appear to your audience is to ask several people who have seen you present to rate you from one to 10 on how caring you appear to be. You can also ask someone who has seen you present in the past if you come across as more or less caring in a current presentation. Lastly, you can also ask this question in a more formal way by including it on a presentation evaluation form.

5. Dynamic

In an economy of more—more ads, more e-mail, more meetings—the only scarce commodity is attention. If you want to get people's attention, whether during a formal presentation, a casual conversation, or a chance meeting on an airplane, you have to offer a compelling performance.

—Curtis Sittenfeld, Fast Company, *September 1999*

Audiences want to see a presenter at his or her best. That means, were you to momentarily think of yourself as a log, they want to see you when you are burning most brightly, and when your energy lights up your whole being. That always comes from one thing, and one thing only: and that is, from speaking on a subject that you care passionately about. A presenter willing to speak on "any subject"—say, one that a committee assigns to them—whether or not they feel passionate about it, is a presenter who is willing to appear at their worst. "Best" comes from energy, and energy comes from passion that lights up your whole being. There is no way around that fundamental truth.

—Richard Bolles

Master Presenters bring hope, motivation, and energy to audience members. The people they are presenting to can feel the energy level in the room increase. They also find it difficult not to pay attention. If you want to hear some of these Master Presenters in action, you can order copies of their audio and videotapes from Convention Cassettes Unlimited.[10] Several of the tapes that we highly recommend are *Motivational PEG Session* by Mark Victor Hanson (co-author of *Chicken Soup for the Soul*) NSA National Meeting, July 2001; *Presentation Magic by the Motivator* by Les Brown; and *Crafting Magical Moments* by Jeanne Robertson, NSA National Meeting, August 2000. The amazing thing is, you can feel how powerful these speakers are by listening to their tapes.

Part of being dynamic is being forward-looking. It is extremely unlikely, no matter how good a presenter you may be, that you will deliver a real barn burner by asking the participants in your audience to maintain the status quo. Master Presenters, on the other hand, give their audiences both the hope and the means to move themselves and their organizations up the performance escalator to the next level.

Now that we have established that Master Presenters are credible, competent, compatible, caring, and dynamic, we have to find out how they got to be that way. One of the secrets to becoming a **Master** Presenter is the "Slight Edge Technique."

The Slight Edge Technique

One of Brad's favorite sayings is, "Real change, like aging, **takes** place slowly." Using the Slight Edge Technique helps ensure **that we** make the changes we want to make, and reinforces the power **of in-** cremental improvements.

The slight edge is a matter of presence of mind—knowing what you are doing at the moment you are doing it.[11]

—*Kenneth Wydro, author*

The Slight Edge Technique involves both developing a particular skill and being able to use it intentionally. In other words, the **Slight** Edge Technique means being a student of the game, and gaining **enough** experience to know exactly what to do and when to do it. Studies **of** elite athletes, musicians, and actors demonstrate intentionality **in ac-** tion. Master Presenters have attained that same high degree of **inten-** tionality and mastery. There are many speakers who have trained **just** as hard at giving presentations, but lack the degree of intentionality and mastery to make them runaway successes.

Among the factors that contribute to intentionality are willing- ness to:

◆ Work.
◆ Invest in your career.
◆ Give up on other interests to focus on professional speaking.
◆ Set SMART (specific, measurable, attainable, realistic, and time-limited) goals.
◆ Get to know your audience each and every time.
◆ Read and keep current in your area of expertise.
◆ Solicit salient feedback.
◆ Be outside of your comfort zone.
◆ Find the best coach to help you move to the next level.

The Power of Incremental Improvements

In major league baseball, a batter who gets two hits out of every 10 times at bat is called a .200 hitter. A .200 hitter [won't last long in the major leagues.] But a hitter who gets three hits out of every 10 times at bat is a .300 hitter and considered a great success. In the current market, .300 hitters are often paid with millions of dollars.[12]

—*Kenneth Wydro*

Small incremental improvements yield drastically better results because the power of incremental improvements is about growing inch-by-inch. Jan Carlzon, former president and CEO of Scandinavian Airlines Systems, recognized this when he said, "It is easier to do 1000 things 1-percent better than to try to do one thing 1000-percent better."

Master Presenters Develop Reciprocal Rapport

Most, if not all, of these skills are dependent on one's ability to develop a message and deliver that message effectively. Master Presenters do everything in their power to build a strong, powerful reciprocal rapport with their audience—and they do it within two minutes of beginning of their presentation. Master Presenters can do more in two minutes and have a stronger rapport with their audience than other presenters are able to achieve in an hour, two hours, a full day, or even a week. This begs the question as to how Master Presenters are able to achieve such a high degree of rapport.

Master Presenters achieve this by applying the following four methods, and/or combinations of methods:

1. Increase the audience's level of expectations/ aspirations and deliver over and above what the audience expects.
2. Continually demonstrate their level of expertise and mastery ofthe subject.
3. Demonstrate that their methods of delivery are at an "Oscar level" of performance.
4. Prove to the audience members, beyond a shadow of a doubt, how they will benefit from the presentation.

How Master Presenters do this will be examined in *The Seven Strategies of Master Presenters*. Each of the following seven strategies will be fully explored in the subsequent chapters of this book:

Strategy 1: Know Thy Audience

Strategy 2: Prepare Outstanding Content

Strategy 3: Use Superior Organization

Strategy 4: Develop Dynamic Delivery

Strategy 5: Make It Memorable, Actionable and Transferable

Strategy 6: Manage Yourself, Difficult Participants, and Difficult Situations

Strategy 7: Total Quality Improvement

Conclusion: The Power of Lifelong Learning

Interviews with Master Presenters from across North America will be used to illustrate each of the strategies and bring them to life. Lastly, exercises have been developed to help you identify your strengths and weaknesses, and to develop an individually tailored program to enhance your strengths and overcome areas of weakness.

How to Use This Book
and Put Your Good Intentions to Work

One Sunday as President Lincoln was leaving church, he was approached by an aide who asked him if he enjoyed the sermon. "It was well crafted and delivered." he replied.

His aide pursued the matter, asking, "So you liked the sermon?" Irritated, Lincoln replied, "No son, I did not!" "It was well crafted and delivered, but the preacher failed in one thing. He didn't challenge us to do anything great with what he shared—in that he failed."[13]

Just like the preacher in this story, we will have failed unless we challenge you to do something specific and concrete with what you learn. Therefore, at appropriate points in this book, you will be given exercises that are designed to make sure your good intentions are translated into concrete action steps, starting with the Presentation Skills Survey that follows. The survey was designed to help you think about yourself as a presenter.

Presentation Skills Survey

Completing this survey will help you to do a differential diagnosis of where your presentation skills are working for you and to better identify those skills you want to improve. You should also have a better appreciation of just how important these skills are, whether you are making a presentation to one person or a thousand.

1. Approximately how many presentations do you give in a year? ____
2. Approximately how many presentations do you attend in a year? ____
3. The best compliment you have ever received from one of your presentations was:

_____

4. How comfortable are you, in general, in giving presentations in front of a group?

Not at all   Very comfortable
comfortable

| 1 | 2 | 3 | 4 | 5 | 6 | 7 |

5. In terms of preparing for your presentations, how well prepared are you usually?

Not as well prepared   Very well
as I should be   prepared

| 1 | 2 | 3 | 4 | 5 | 6 | 7 |

6. In terms of delivery, how dynamic are you?

Not at all dynamic   Very dynamic

| 1 | 2 | 3 | 4 | 5 | 6 | 7 |

7. How effectively do you use a variety of presentation tools (props, flip charts, stories)?

Not at all effectively   Very effectively

| 1 | 2 | 3 | 4 | 5 | 6 | 7 |

8. How effective are you in obtaining direct and clear feedback from your presentations?

I receive very little feedback from my presentations				I systematically seek out feedback using a variety of assessment techniques		
1	2	3	4	5	6	7

9. How long lasting an impact do your presentations have on the audience?

Not at all memorable					Lasting memory 5 years or more	
1	2	3	4	5	6	7

10. How much of an impact do your presentations have on your audience?

Not at all impactful				Participants are absolutely committed to making improvements		
1	2	3	4	5	6	7

11. How important is the development of presentations skills and strategies for you and your career?

Not at all important				Becoming a better presenter is one of my top priorities		
1	2	3	4	5	6	7

12. The one thing you most need to change or improve to help you be a more effective presenter is:

_____

_____

◆ ◆ ◆

The ability to present with confidence and poise is critical to your career. Yet Master Presenters are not born, they are developed. In the next seven chapters, we will guide you step-by-step through the development process. Armed with this knowledge, a little time, and a lot of practice, you, too, can learn to speak like the masters.

STRATEGY

1

Know
Thy Audience

It was a great presentation. Unfortunately, it was the wrong audience!

—Brad McRae

We have all attended great presentations; the only problem was that they were for the wrong audience. There are two possible reasons for this. First, the presenter did not adequately research the audience and what it needed. Second, the speaker's presentation was not appropriately aligned with the audience's demographics and/or psychographics. The following example illustrates what can happen.

Jack Welch was chairman of General Electric for 20 years. During that time, GE grew from $26.8 billion in revenue to more than $130 billion. Welch also became one of the most celebrated business leaders in U.S. history. In his biography, *Jack: Straight from the Gut*,[1] Welch talks about one of his first speeches as chairman of GE to Wall Street analysts:

> I had been in the job for eight months when I went to New York City on December 8th, 1981, to deliver my big message on the "New GE." I had worked on the speech, rewriting it, rehearsing it, and desperately wanting it to be a smash hit.

It was, after all, my first public statement on where I wanted to take GE....

My first time in front of Wall Street's analysts as chairman was a bomb.

...the analysts arrived that day expecting to hear the financial results and the successes achieved by the company during the year. They expected a detailed breakdown of the financial numbers.... Over a 20-minute speech, I gave them little of what they wanted and quickly launched into a qualitative discussion around my vision for the company...

I pressed on, not letting their blank stares discourage me....

What happened to Jack Welch can happen to any presenter who does not take the time to truly know his or her audience. In the Introduction you learned that your presentations must be credible and relevant. The following eight techniques are designed to make your presentations as credible and relevant as possible.

8 Techniques to "Know Thy Audience"

We have all heard the maxim "know thyself." In order to give high-impact presentations, it is not only necessary to "know thyself," you also have to "know thy audience." And just because you have worked in the same organization for many years, don't make the unwarranted assumption that you know your audience. The following eight techniques are guaranteed to help you "know thy audience" whether speaking to your staff, peers, senior management, or giving a keynote address to the board of directors and shareholders at your organization's annual general meeting.

The eight techniques are:

1. Pre-session surveys.
2. Face-to-face interviews.
3. Telephone interviews.
4. Case studies.
5. Worksite visits.
6. Job shadowing.
7. Annual and/or other published reports.
8. Websites and Internet research.

Pre-Session Surveys

There are two main types of pre-session surveys. The first type is a generalized survey that is used to assess the demographics of the audience. This basic survey is designed to tell you how many people will attend, the ratio of male to female participants, the participants' educational levels, and how homogeneous or heterogeneous the audience is.

The second type of pre-presentation survey yields more detailed information, by asking specific questions to assess the participants' specific learning and/or developmental needs. An example of this type of survey (Figure 1-1) was developed by a pharmaceutical to help Brad identify the needs for a course on presentation skills to be given to representatives who call on physicians and hospitals. This survey would help Brad customize the presentation to be more relevant to the participants' specific needs. While the following example was designed as a pre-presentation survey for Brad and David's presentations seminars, with only minor adjustments you can adapt this example to work for any presentation.

FIGURE 1-1: PRE-SESSION SURVEY
The Seven Strategies of Master Presenters

Do you know: **(yes/no)**

The strategies used by Master Presenters?   _____

Your preferred presentation style and when to use it?   _____

Your audience's needs, expectations, and level of
knowledge of the subject matter?   _____

How to organize your presentations for impact?   _____

How to give a dynamic delivery that has in-depth content?   _____

How to create a presentation that is memorable,
actionable, and transferable?   _____

How to get genuine commitment by setting mutually
beneficial goals? In other words, how to increase the return
on investment from the presentation?   _____

(Please write in your answer)

Have you taken a presentation course before?   _____

If so, what did you learn?

_____

_____

What are your expectations for this course?

_____

_____

What would you like the facilitator to focus on?

_____

_____

Are you comfortable giving presentations to your customers or clients in both small and large groups?

_____

_____

What skills, knowledge, or strategies would make it easier for you to obtain a greater return on your investment?

_____

_____

What three challenges do you anticipate in the next three months where well-developed presentations skills would be an asset?

1._____

2._____

3._____

Please feel free to include any additional comments that will help in your learning process.

_____

_____

2. Face-to-Face Interviews

Face-to-face pre-seminar interviews can be incredibly insightful. If you ask the right type of questions, in the right way, and at the right time, you can achieve deeper levels of communication with the audience members with whom you will be speaking.

For example, if your audience consists mostly of IT specialists, you probably want to interview IT specialists to determine their profession-specific issues. Audiences appreciate speakers who show interest in, and knowledge of, their specific issues and concerns. If, however, your audience is very heterogeneous, you may find it desirable to interview a wide variety of individuals at different levels within that organization.

In summary, pre-seminar interviews will not only provide you with relevant information, they also cut down on preparation time, because you will have a much clearer focus on what you need to prepare for. Additionally, you will be much less likely to prepare information that your audience does not need to hear.

There are several advantages of having a written interview protocol: You will have had to think of the questions ahead of time, the questions can often be improved upon after a suitable time of reflection, and you are much less likely to forget to ask an important question during the interview. In addition, if there is an uncomfortable pause in the interview, you know exactly what question to ask next. Lastly, you have the opportunity to test the questionnaire in advance and incorporate any suggestions or corrections. At the same time, you should be flexible enough to add relevant information that the interviewee wants to tell you, and to modify the interview protocol accordingly where it makes sense to do so.

3. Telephone Interviews

Because face-to-face interviews can be time-consuming, the subject may be reluctant to consent to a sit-down interview. When this occurs, consider using telephone interviews. Telephone interviews offer two main advantages: convenience and a perception of anonymity. Of course the concept of anonymity is merely a perception, but the fact is, some people are more "open" in a telephone interview than in a face-to-face interview.

When using telephone interviews, you must concentrate on three things. First, you have to guarantee confidentiality when it is appropriate and/or when the interviewee requests it. This understanding must be considered sacrosanct. If you ever violate a source's trust, your source may never speak with you again. Second, you must be a superb interviewer. Third, you must have the ability to ask "high-yield questions." High-yield questions" result in high-yield answers. Several such high-yield questions are:

- What was the high point in your team and/or organization during the past year? What was the low point?
- What challenges is your organization facing this year that you didn't have to face last year?
- What are the issues or concerns regarding work that keep you up at night?
- If you could solve one issue, problem, or challenge at work within the next six months, what would it be?
- What is the biggest missed opportunity that is crying out for a creative solution in your team, department, and/or organization at the present time?
- What is one issue that no one in your organization is allowed to talk about that should be talked about?

Of course, you need to develop questions that work for you and are germane to the content area of your presentation. If you formulate and ask great questions, you will be amazed at the depth and quality of the information that you will receive. By doing even three or four telephone interviews, you can tailor your presentation so that it is much more likely to hit the mark.

Three is the absolute minimum number of people you should interview. However, by the time you talk to three people, you should have a much better idea of the issues people are facing in their organization. One interview is risky because that one person could either be the most contented or the most unhappy; the most knowledgeable or the least informed of all the employees within that organization. One word of caution: Don't let the attitudes or opinions of one person lead you to an inaccurate perception of the greater audience's needs.

We have found that on rare occasions when we have not taken the time to do this, our presentations can miss the mark. Although this has happened to Brad on only two occasions, those two occasions were two too many. One occasion involved an organization to which Brad frequently presents. Brad assumed that what worked well in two locations of the organization would work in the third, so he did not do any pre-interviews. Unfortunately, this was a false assumption and the presentation did not work very well. Remember, despite the similarities you may *think* two audiences have, each is composed of unique individuals with unique needs.

4. Case Studies

Case studies also work incredibly well for workshops, skills training sessions, or sessions where your goal is to help your audience solve problems more efficiently and creatively. For example, Brad recently gave a two-day workshop on the Seven Strategies of Master Negotiators for the IT department at the head office of a large international organization. Prior to doing the workshop, the participants were told by the head of the training department that submitting a case study was a requirement for attending the training session. The instructions to the participants appear in Figure 1-2.

Figure 1-2: Participant Instructions for the Development of Case Studies

Guidelines of Effective Case Development
(For *The Seven Strategies of Master Negotiators* Course)

Please write a one- or two-paragraph description about a challenging person and/or situation that you have had to deal with or are currently dealing with at work. The case studies can be anonymous and/or disguised as they will be used during the course to make the course more interesting and applicable to the type of work you and your colleagues do.

Effective cases are inherently interesting ones in which all parties stand to gain or lose depending on the outcome of the case. Effective cases are also ones in which the apparent solutions are not obvious but require collaboration and creative thinking so that optimal rather than suboptimal solutions are found.

If you have not found a suitable solution, please submit your case anyway. Previous participants have found that their colleagues have contributed many excellent ideas that have led to very good solutions. Other times, the group has decided that Mother Teresa or Gandhi could not have done a better job, and the person who submitted the case could rest easier knowing that some of life's problems do not have ready solutions.

Brad found that reviewing the participants' case studies gave him an in-depth sense of the type of problems that needed to be negotiated. Because the case studies were relevant to everyone in the room, he also gained a great deal of credibility. First, the case studies were real issues and problems that the participants had to face in their everyday work life. Second, the participants learned how to apply the course materials to actual real-life examples that they had to face, which thereby increased the transfer of training. Third, they could also determine if the problem in the case study was a problem in individual skill development or where or to what degree the problem was a systems problem, that is to say, how much of the problem had its origins in the organization's procedures, organizational structure, or climate and culture.

As a trainer, facilitator, or presenter, you can sense the energy level in the room increase when the participants' case studies are introduced. Having the case studies submitted in advance helps the trainer better determine which ones would be most appropriate to use and also where in the program or course would be the best place to use them in terms of the theory and/or course content that is being presented.

If you are not giving a workshop or a training session, you still might want to ask the participants to submit brief case studies (a paragraph or less) because they will still give you insight into the issues or dynamics of the organization, and this too will give you an opportunity to make sure that your speech or presentation hits the mark.

5. Worksite Visits

Worksite visits can also give you a feeling for the participants' work environment. Brad has gone 3,000 feet underground to prepare for an address to a group of miners. He also had the opportunity to speak to a group of participants who worked on an oil rig. Visiting the rig was very instructive and allowed Brad to tailor his presentation much more specifically to that particular audience.

Similarly, David has spoken for Volvo at its headquarters plant in Gothenburg, Sweden. Because it was in a country and a culture different from those he had experienced previously, he found that a tour of the facility proved helpful in relating his message to his audience. It provided him with a glimpse of the audience's work environment and he was able to include a few "local" references in his talk.

6. Job Shadowing

Job shadowing means that you go to the worksite to observe individuals as they work. As a result, the presenter can gain a good idea of what the employees do, and how they go about it. When securing permission to observe, you may also want to obtain permission to interview individuals as they do their work or as soon as possible after they have completed their work. For example, Brad prepared a presentation for the City of Halifax Police Department by getting permission to go on an evening patrol with one of the officers. Although he had seen many high-speed chases on TV, he wasn't prepared for what it felt like. Nor was he prepared for what it would be like to drive through one of the "worst" parts of the city being seen as a police officer. This experience helped prepare Brad for his presentation better than any face-to-face interview with even the most articulate police officer ever could have.

7. Annual and/or Other Published Reports

Annual and other published reports are another way to get valuable information about the company or organization you will be working with in advance of your presentation. There may be an issue that the company or organization has raised that you could contribute to through your presentation. Likewise, there may be something in the vision, mission statement, and strategic goals and challenges that could add a great deal of value to the presentation.

8. Websites and Internet Research

Having an accurate, informative, and up-to-date Website is a necessity in today's competitive business environment. Therefore, the prospective speaker can get some very good information, both directly and indirectly, about an organization. This information can also help in planning an organizational survey or face-to-face or telephone interview more precisely because you will have a better idea of what to ask. In other words, sometimes a combination of methods can bring about the best results.

If you do not have the internet skills to help you get the information you need, you can learn them easily by using various search engines such as Google. You could also consider paying someone (perhaps one of your children or a high school or university student) to do research on the internet. Lastly, don't overlook your local library—librarians are professionals trained in information retrieval and search strategies. We can't begin to tell you how helpful they have been to us and can be to you.

Knowing your audience is just the start. You will also need to align what you know about your audience with six critical variables that can affect how receptive that audience will be to your message.

Alignment

If you don't check your alignment, you may be in for a rough ride.

—*Brad McRae*

Most of us have had the experience of being in a car with tires badly out of alignment. As a result the ride was rough, unpleasant, and distracting. This analogy holds true for presentations as well. If the presenter is not aligned with the audience, the presenter will be in for a rough ride and the attendees will find the presentation unpleasant and will quickly become distracted. Therefore, *knowing* your audience is not enough; you also must make sure that your goals and the goals of the organization and of the audience are all in alignment.

Six critical factors can help align a presentation with the audience's and organization's needs and expectations. They are:

1. The fit between the topic you are presenting and the other presentations that will be offered.
2. The experience level of the audience.
3. The heterogeneous/homogeneous nature of the audience.
4. The fatigue level of the audience.
5. The mood of the audience.
6. The attendees' learning styles.

1. The Fit Between the Topic You Are Presenting and the Other Presentations That Will Be Offered

Find out all you can about the program, plus its theme and schedule before you agree to do your presentation. In the late 1980s, Brad was scheduled to do a presentation on stress management. He felt confident that he could do a good job. He had developed an excellent dynamic interactive presentation and had successfully given the presentation on numerous occasions. Brad was following the luncheon speaker who was Sharon Woods. Sharon is the first North American woman to have climbed Mt. Everest.

When Sharon first started her program, she didn't appear to be that dynamic. However, when she put the first slide on the overhead projector, it had the name of her expedition, "Everest Light" and Sharon became superwoman. She then played some videotape, which so graphically illustrated her climb that the audience could feel and hear the howling winds. It was as if Sharon took the audience on the climb with her up to the top of the world's highest mountain. Her presentation was magnificent. Unfortunately, after the break, Brad was slated to make his presentation on stress management. At this point, no one cared about stress management. As a friend of Brad's said, only half jokingly, "Sharon took us up the mountain, and you brought us back down!" Ouch.

Brad learned a lot about alignment from that disaster. If he could have done his presentation on "Peak Performers" it would have fit much better with the tone that Sharon had set. Since that day, he always asks to see a copy of the conference schedule before he agrees to present. If they don't have a complete schedule, he asks to see what they do have. If they don't have a schedule at all, he asks for as much clarification as he can get on the theme of that particular conference.

David learned a similar lesson at the end of a four-day conference.

David: I was the closing keynote speaker, set to go on at 10:30 a.m. as the final speaker of the day. After three solid days, the attendees were tired and ready to head home. All that stood between them and "freedom" was me. Unfortunately, there was a 30-minute break between the first speaker and me. If the first speaker had been dynamic or entertaining, his momentum could carry over through the long break. However, the speaker was neither dynamic nor entertaining, and in just 45 minutes, he proceeded to put the audience into a stupor. Break time came and the audience departed in droves. When it was my turn, less than half the audience remained. The frustrating part of it is that I could do absolutely nothing to prevent it. Thereafter, I always make a point of asking, "Who and what are scheduled on either side of my presentation?" so I can prepare accordingly.

2. The Experience Level of the Audience

Two unforgivable presentation sins are talking down to your audience and talking over their heads. Therefore, you must do everything in your power to find out the experience level of your potential audience. At times you will be given an audience that has inherently mixed levels of experience and you must develop materials that can be helpful to and enjoyed by participants at various levels. This means that the materials are so well prepared that participants at very junior levels and at very senior levels can benefit at the same time. Another strategy is to divide the group into subgroups and have them work on a project with people at the same level of experience. One of our favorite techniques is to have people at the same level in an organization work on a shared problem. For example, participants from engineering would work on the problem from an engineering perspective, while sales would work on it from a sales perspective, and manufacturing would work on it from a manufacturing perspective. They can then look at the problem and possible solutions based on each group's perspective.

3. The Heterogeneous/Homogeneous Nature of the Audience

The following example illustrates the importance of how heterogeneous or homogeneous your audience is.

Brad was once asked to give a presentation on time management at an exclusive resort. The group was the Young Presidents Organization and from the presentation description, Brad knew that this would be a difficult presentation to deliver. First, the audience consisted of children ages 9 and older plus their parents. He sensed that if he spoke to the parents, he would lose the children, or if he spoke to the children he would lose their parents.

The second factor that made the presentation difficult was that it was a murder mystery weekend. Now, if you were going to give a "serious" (or even "not so serious") presentation on time management, when would you least want the "murder" to occur: during the presentation or just before you present? As luck would have it, the "murder" took place just before Brad's presentation. It was very realistic. An ambulance came to take the body away and the Royal Canadian Mounted Police (RCMP) came to investigate the crime. Unfortunately, there were several 5-year-olds who thought it was a bit too realistic and promptly became hysterical. The presentation had to be post-poned until the 5-year-olds could be taken to a hotel room where they could see that the actress was indeed alive and the blood from the bullet wound was indeed ketchup. After the half-hour delay, they were ready to begin the presentation on time management.

At that point in time, how many people in the room were interested in a presentation on time management? We would venture to guess that no one was really interested. But Brad had a secret weapon. A humorous film titled *The Unorganized Manager* by John Cleese.[2] The film portrays a manager named Mr. Lewis who is completely unorganized at work and at home. About halfway through the film, Mr. Lewis has a heart attack, dies, and goes to heaven. At the pearly gates, Mr. Lewis rings the doorbell, which plays the "Halleluiah Chorus." St. Peter says that there is no Mr. Lewis due in heaven that day and he must be due at the other place. Mr. Lewis protests that he has always been a good man and has tried to do right. St. Peter shows Mr. Lewis that although he had good intentions, he was so disorganized and managed his time so poorly, both at work and at home, that he could not let Mr. Lewis in. Mr. Lewis begs for a second chance. St. Peter then coaches Mr. Lewis on how to better manage his time.

This well-made and humorous film got the audience's attention. The audience was thinking about time management and not, at least for the time being, about the murder mystery. Brad knew that he was now at a crucial point in his presentation. If he talked to the parents first, he would likely not get the children to participate. So he asked the children to rate from, A to F, Mr. Lewis's ability to manage time. There was a resounding chorus of Fs raising from their sweet voices. One of the boys seemed to be particularly vocal, so Brad asked him to rate his father on time management at home, thinking that he would say A, A-, or B+. Instead he said, "C-." You could have heard a pin drop in the room.

His father, like all the members in the Young Presidents Organization had to have started or become president of his or her own companies before the age of 39. Members also had to employ 50 employees and gross $5 million annually. In front of his peers, this young man had just called his father a 'C-' father. Brad learned an important lesson. Never ask a question in public that could potentially embarrass a member of your audience.

After the presentation, Brad walked up to the father to apologize and to state that it was not his intention to embarrass him. The father said that it was all right. He looked Brad in the eye and said that he had just received some very painful but important feedback. He said, "My son is 9 years old and he could easily leave our home by the time he is 18 or 19, and I did not want my son leaving home thinking that he had a 'C-' father."

This is an example of salient feedback. Salient feedback is feedback that is so personally meaningful that we actually change our behavior. We live in a feedback-rich world. Master Presenters systematically harvest that feedback, both at home and at work. Subsequent chapters cover techniques to get salient feedback on what we do well and on ways we can improve our ability to present to both homogeneous and heterogeneous audiences. It also points out the crucial importance of knowing how homogeneous or heterogeneous your audience will be and planning your presentation accordingly.

4. The Fatigue Level of the Audience

Always try to anticipate the fatigue level of your audience. Take this into account when you are planning your presentation. Brad had more than a couple of hurdles to leap when he was scheduled to speak in front of a potentially fatigued audience in a 4:30 p.m. time slot on a perfect summer day. Worse, he was up against an international buskers (street performers) festival being held in the same city at the same time. Not a pretty picture. Luckily, as one participant said, "The presentation was interactive, humorous, and dynamic. The topic was engaging enough that he won us over."

Suffice to say, you have to take the fatigue level of your audience into account when planning your presentation. Other instances when you are likely to have a fatigued audience is an after-dinner speech—especially if alcohol is served—and the first session in the morning after an evening's partying or banquet. Also, the first slot right after a large lunch can be tough.

5. The Mood of the Audience

The mood of the audience has a major effect on your presentation. Sometimes you will know that there are extenuating circumstances that are beyond your control and you will have to adapt your presentation accordingly. Other times, you will receive no warning as illustrated in the following example.

One of the presenters we interviewed reported having to face participants who were in one of the ugliest moods he had ever encountered in 20 years of training.

> I was asked to do a workshop on Resiliency and Change Management for a campus of a community college. It turned out that that particular campus was going to be closed and the news had been leaked to the participants the day before the workshop was to take place. Some of the programs were to move to another campus, some of the programs would be closed down because they were available at other community colleges in other parts of the state.
>
> The participants were furious not only with the decision, but how it was made. They had not been consulted and they felt strongly that the programs that were scheduled to be closed were both viable and vital for their community. And I can tell you categorically, they were in no mood for a workshop on Resiliency and Change Management.
>
> The only thing to do was to scrap the workshop. I might lose credibility with the college that hired me and I might not get paid, but I valued my life above both of these things. As the main issue was that they felt that they had not been consulted, I spent the morning working as a facilitator and they decided that the best thing to do was to write a letter to the president of the college expressing their wishes for a more participatory process and developing options on what they could do to prevent these programs from closing. I went from being a villain to a hero and I even got paid for the workshop, because we used resiliency and change management techniques to help the participants gain more control in a situation where they felt they had none.

From that experience and similar ones, we have learned to ask ahead of time whether there is anything going on in the organization that we should be aware of. Often people will clue you in, sometimes they won't, and sometimes there is a last-minute change in circumstances that takes place and you simply have to roll with the punches.

6. The Attendees' Learning Style

It is especially important to know the learning style of those who are attending your presentation. Knowing the predominant style of the group and how to communicate with attendees whose style is the same as and different from your own is one of the key characteristics of Master Presenters. One of the best ways to determine learning style is the TRAP model, which was developed by Peter Honey and Alan Mumford.[3] According to the TRAP model, there are four primary learning styles: theorists, reflectors, activists, and pragmatists. The authors summarize each of these styles:

> **Theorists.** Theorists adapt and integrate their observations into complex but logically sound theories. They think problems through in a vertical, step-by-step logical way. They assimilate disparate facts into coherent theories. They tend to be perfectionists who won't rest until things are tidy…They like to analyze and synthesize…
>
> [Theorists] are keen on basic assumptions, principles, theories, models and systems thinking. Questions they frequently ask are: "Does it make sense?" "How does this fit with that?" They tend to be detached, analytical and dedicated to rational objectivity rather than anything subjective or ambiguous…They prefer to maximize certainty and feel uncomfortable with the subjective…
>
> **Reflectors.** Reflectors like to stand back to ponder experience and observe it from many different perspectives. They collect data, both first hand and from others, and prefer to [consider] it thoroughly before coming to any conclusions…Their philosophy is to be cautious, to leave no stone unturned. [To] "look before they leap"…
>
> [Reflectors] prefer to take a back seat in meetings and discussions. They [observe and listen] to others [and]…get the drift of the discussion before making their own points. They tend to adopt a low profile and have a slightly distant, tolerant, unruffled air about them. When they act it is as part of a wide picture [that] includes the past, as well as the present and others' observations as well as their own.
>
> **Activists.** Activists involve themselves fully…They enjoy the here and now and are happy to be dominated by immediate experiences. They are open-minded… and enthusiastic…Their philosophy is "I'll try anything once…" Their days are filled with activity [and they love]…short-term crisis fire fighting.
>
> [Activists tend to] tackle problems by brainstorming. As soon as the excitement from one activity has died down they are looking for the next. They tend to thrive on challenge and new experiences

but are bored with implementation and longer-term consolidation... [They tend to be]...the life and soul of the party and seek
to be the center of attention.

Pragmatists. Pragmatists are keen on trying out ideas, theories,
and techniques to see if they work in practice... [They]...search
out new ideas and take the first opportunity to experiment with
applications. They...return from courses brimming with new ideas
that they want to try out in practice.

[Pragmatists] like to get on with things and act quickly and confidently on ideas that attract them. They don't like "beating around
the bush" and tend to be impatient with ruminating and open-
ended discussions. They are practical, down to earth people who
like making practical decisions and solving problems. They respond to problems [as opportunities]. Their philosophy is: "There
is always a better way" and "If it works, it's good."

How to use the TRAP model to improve the effectiveness of your
own training will be demonstrated in the following example.

Some groups will be made up almost entirely of action-oriented
pragmatists. If you do not know how to tailor your presentation to
this group you may encounter problems similar to Brad's experience
in the following situation.

Brad has taught *The Seven Strategies of Master Negotiators* course
to many groups of truck tire sales staff. If the information being presented was not directly related to how they could sell more tires, he
would lose his audience because they could make better use of their
time selling "in the real world." For the most part, they had little, if any
tolerance for theory, and did not like to reflect. They were action- and
results-oriented and if the workshop/seminar did not relate to their
needs, they communicated their dissatisfaction in no uncertain terms.

As a result, Brad reduced the theory to almost nil and focused on
action-oriented/results-oriented activities. The part of the workshop
that they appreciated the most was how to deal with killer clients—
those tough clients that you just can't seem to get very far with no
matter what you do—and Brad asked them to submit these as case
studies. The best case had to do with a potential client who was
totally uninterested in trying one workshop participant's truck tires.
The participant thought that this was because the potential client

was receiving a personal kickback from the competition's sales staff, although he had no direct proof.

The whole class brainstormed creative options for the workshop participant to try. Eventually they came up with two options that had a very good chance of working. Solution 1: One of the other workshop participants knew the owner and would put a bug in his ear. Solution 2: This participant's company bought their gasoline from the potential client's owner's gas stations, and they would make their continued purchase of gasoline dependent on reciprocal purchase of truck tires. In other words, working on real-life case studies appealed to this group's strong preference for an action-oriented practical learning style. It also perfectly illustrates the need to match one's presentation style to each particular group's learning style. When your presentation style is congruent with the group's learning style, you will have gone a long way toward becoming a Master Presenter.

EXERCISE
1-1

Please give a brief example of how you would modify an existing presentation to appeal to each of the four TRAP types:

1. Theorists.
2. Reflectors.
3. Activists.
4. Pragmatists.

An even bigger challenge is satisfying all four TRAP types in one presentation. If you conscientiously think about satisfying all four types, you will generally give a much better presentation unless you have a preponderance of one or two of the types in your audience. If that is the case, you will have to modify your presentation. Of course, it is much easier if you obtain this type of information beforehand. If not, you will have to modify on the spot as Brad did the first time he worked with the truck tire sales staff.

The best way to satisfy all four types is to have some generic template-type exercises that you know will work with each type. Keep the exercises short. That way, you will be more likely to have an exercise for each type. In Exercise 1-2, you'll learn how to use TRAP to plan for your next presentation or to redo an existing presentation.

EXERCISE 1-2

Make sure that your presentation covers all of the elements to satisfy all four of the TRAP types. A second useful technique is to ask a friend or colleague to "TRAP proof" or verify that your presentation relates to all four types. Solicit feedback from your participants to see if they are satisfied that you adequately cover all four of the TRAP learning styles: Theorists, Reflectors, Activists, and Pragmatists. Remember, most of us are much better at reaching some of the types than others. In addition, just because you are good at one or more of the types, ask for feedback on how you can improve your skills and abilities to reach the other types as well. Lastly, you can mindmap your presentation on a piece of paper or flip chart. Then using four different colors, color everything in red that would appeal to Theorists, blue that would appeal to Reflectors, green for Activists, and black for Pragmatists. This way, if any one group is over-represented or under-represented, it will stand out.

In this chapter we covered the importance of knowing your audience and then aligning your presentation to that audience's needs and expectations. Not knowing your audience and aligning your presentation to that audience's needs and expectation will not only waste your time and theirs, it can also lead to embarrassment at best and to career-limiting moves at worst, as the following example from a famous radio and television personality, who requested anonymity, illustrates:

> I was asked to emcee a charity event for the Muscular Dystrophy Association, and at the last minute they asked if I would also be the auctioneer. While I don't do that for a living, I occasionally serve in that capacity. When the auction started, I rushed up onto the stage. The first item was a package of dinner including a limo ride to and from an exclusive restaurant—for eight people. The bids were pushing a thousand bucks...and I blurt out: "Hey, this is the vintage restaurant, folks, not some Burger King!" A hush fell over the crowd. Who turned out to be sponsoring the event? Yep. Burger King.

Now that you know the importance of and how to know your audience and align your presentation to their expectations and needs, we turn our attention to how Master Presenters prepare outstanding content.

STRATEGY

Prepare
Outstanding Content

It usually takes me more than three weeks to prepare a good impromptu speech.
—*Mark Twain*

Some presenters are high in energy but low in content. Other presenters have excellent content but their style of delivery puts you to sleep. Twain's lesson is clear: Great speakers prepare great content. Great speeches are the result of great preparation. Our definition of a great presentation is one that has the *intellectual power* to move listeners to new ways of thinking and the *emotional power* to move them to new ways of behaving.

Preparation of content, organizational structure, and delivery often go hand in hand. When all goes well, it can be a rewarding and creatively stimulating process. However, when you get stuck, it can be like "hitting the wall" in a marathon. Although content, organization, and delivery must work together, we will look at them separately in this and the next two chapters. One advantage of looking at these facets separately is if you get stuck in one area, you can turn to another. However, to be a Master Presenter, all three processes must eventually be integrated into one seamless whole.

No delivery skills can save a presentation that has poor content. Therefore, Master Presenters develop masterful content. This chapter examines how you can develop masterful content:

- Speak from a strong point of view.
- Craft titles that the audience would crawl over glass to hear.
- Create impactful beginnings and endings.
- Find the perfect quote.
- Develop the perfect illustrative story.
- Use the Three "S" Advantage.
- Write "the zero draft."
- Create your content advisory board.

Speak From a Strong Point of View

Your content will be more powerful if you introduce it with a strong and unique point of view. Brad describes how this works with one of the best presentations he has ever seen.

Brad: Master Presenter, author, and past president of the American Psychological Association, Martin Seligman, started his presentation by saying that he was once interviewed by CNN about the current state of psychology in the world. Martin was only given one word to state his answer, to which he responded by saying, "Good." Because this was not much of a sound bite, the reporter said he could have two words, and Martin said, "Not good." The CNN reporter wasn't happy with this sound bite either, so he said he could have three words, and Martin answered, "Not good enough."

Martin then went on to state his point of view more explicitly by stating that psychology has done a good job in researching mental illness and is making strides in helping people get better. However, psychology has done a very poor job in researching happiness and helping people do a better job of attaining it.

Martin then went on to do a brilliant job of explaining the characteristics of people who lead *A Pleasant Life, A Good*

Life, and *A Meaningful Life. A Pleasant Life* consists of having pleasant experiences such as sharing an excellent meal with a good friend. *A Good Life* consists of using one's signature strengths. *A Meaningful Life* consists of using one's "signature strengths and virtues in the service of something much larger than you are."[1] He then told the participants, who were sitting on the edge of their seats, that we can have a *Full Life,* which consists of a pleasant, good and meaningful life.

I don't know if I have ever seen a presentation with more breadth and depth and at the same time content that was truly universal and deeply personal.

You can get a sense of Martin's ability to convey information from this strong and unique point of view, and take a test to determine and develop your own signature strengths, in his book *Authentic Happiness* or by visiting his Website *www.authentichappiness.org.*

You can also make your content powerful by asking a thought-provoking, rhetorical question that gets the participants thinking right at the outset of your presentation. For example David Ropeik, Director of Risk Communications at the Harvard Center for Risk Analysis, starts his presentation by asking the participants to make a series of choices about the perceived risk associated with various activities by taking the risk quiz in Figure 2-1.

A risk quiz....

+ Bioterrorism is a serious threat to public health.

+ Pesticides are a serious threat to public health.

+ Cell phones and driving are a serious threat to public health.

Figure 2-1

Most of the people who responded to the quiz thought that the chances of risk were higher from the external factors, when in fact they were higher from the respondents' own actions. In other words, the risk that any one person will have an accident or die while using his or her cell phone while driving is significantly higher than the risk associated with bioterrorism or pesticides. David used the quiz to get the audience thinking about how they assessed risk and benefits of activities more objectively and how to take appropriate corrective action.

Stephen Lewis has held the offices of the Canadian Ambassador to the United Nations, special adviser to the U.N. Secretary General of Africa, Assistant Secretary General with UNICEF, and is the Secretary General's Special Envoy for HIV/AIDS in Africa. Mr. Lewis is a world-renowned orator who presents using words of eloquence on behalf of making the world, especially Africa, a better place.

Mr. Lewis presented the closing keynote address to the Congress of Canadian Student Associations. This association is for university and college student leaders from across Canada. The speech took place on a Sunday evening; the keynote was scheduled to take place after the closing dinner at which point there would be an open bar and a dance. To make matters even more challenging, many of the student leaders had partied as only college and university students can on the Saturday night before. Yet when Stephen Lewis spoke, he captured their total attention for the entire length of his keynote address. His passion for his cause is nothing short of remarkable.

As a presenter, Stephen Lewis is also nothing short of a provocateur. After telling us of his first-hand experience in seeing the ravages of HIV/AIDS on the African continent, he pointed out that only a fraction of the money that was spent on arms or the 2003 Iraqi war could completely eradicate the HIV/AIDS pandemic in Africa.

He then stunned the audience by saying that gender inequality may be an even bigger worldwide problem than HIV/AIDS. Stephen spoke eloquently about women who are refused education just because they were born female; about baby girls killed in China just because they were born female; and women who, against their will, were raped and subsequently stoned because "they committed adultery" in Central America.

It is almost impossible to hear this impassioned, eloquent man speak and not want to help make the world a better place. Stephen always speaks from a strong point of view and earns the utmost respect of those who agree with him as well as those who don't.

In sum, Martin Seligman, David Ropeik, and Stephen Lewis all have mastered the craft of developing dynamic content by speaking from a strong and compelling point of view.

EXERCISE 2-1

Please write down three specific things you could do to develop your own strong and compelling point of view.

Craig Valentine, the 1999 World Champion of Public Speaking says:

> "You have to know your message and where it is going. Many speakers don't know their message strongly, clearly and concisely enough and that is the main reason why the audience can't follow it."

One sure-fire way to make sure you *do* know your message strongly, clearly, and concisely enough is to use the business card test. The business card test evaluates if you are able to write the central thesis of your presentation on the back of a business card. If you can do this, you'll go a long way towards developing a strong point of view, and you will be off to a great beginning.

My point of view is

Craft Titles That the Audience Would Crawl Over Glass to Hear

The title of your presentation is a hook. It sets up an expectation that the presentation will be worth the time and effort that the attendees have made to be there. Also, if competing presentations are offered at the same time, your compelling title will ensure that you have a full room. Therefore, you need to develop titles that an audience will find so compelling that they would sacrifice their last moment of free time to hear your presentation.

Examples of some of the best titles we have heard are as follows:

- *The Alfred Hitchcock Effect: How to Build Suspense into Every Presentation.*
- *Difficult People: How to Manage Them Without Becoming One of Them.*
- *The Internet Game Show: Maximizing the Internet's Potential in Your Organization.*
- *Danger! There Be Dragons: Implementing a Competency Based Succession System in Your Organization.*
- *What Color is Your Parachute?*
- *"No" Is a Complete Sentence* (for a seminar on sexual harassment).

All of these titles have four common characteristics. First, they are fresh and original. Even the order of the words is different from what we have come to expect. Second, they exude energy. The speed at which we read the title accelerates because we can't wait to see what it means. Third, they entice with bold promises and/or rewards that you will receive by attending the presentation. Fourth, they contain a hook that entices the potential participants to want to be there because the presentation promises to help the attendees develop a critical skill in order to accomplish more and/or to improve their lives in some significant way.

Try comparing the previous "live" titles with the following "lifeless" ones:

- *Internet Marketing for Beginners.*
- *How to Borrow Money, Make More Money, and Manage It.*

- *Time Management for Today's Manager.*
- *Getting Comfortable Outside Your Comfort Zone.*
- *Self-Directed Training: Is it Right for Your Organization?*

All of the "lifeless" titles have the following characteristics: We have heard the same title or something very similar to it many times before. The title is perfectly predictable, not at all unusual or surprising. The title has little or no energy—even in reading the title, our eye movements slow down to a crawl because it is so boring, or we skim over it as quickly as possible to avoid being bored.

What is the difference between the enticing titles and ones that sound like the presentation will bore the socks off you? There has to be an element of surprise, novelty, originality, magic, excitement, or enticement. A great title does not guarantee a great presentation, but it does prove to the audience that the presenter went to considerable trouble to develop it, and that is a good first sign.

EXERCISE 2-2

Please write down three of the best and three of the worst titles that you have heard.

Here are several suggestions for creating dynamic titles: Take a common phrase and bring it to life with a twist by doing something unusual or unexpected. Think of the title as a "teaser"—something to arouse your audience's curiosity and make them want to hear the rest of the story. Make it short enough and unique enough to be remembered. Do not be afraid to ask for help. Ask friends and colleagues to brainstorm creative suggestions. Get feedback from other people regarding the title's uniqueness and memorability. Think of your title as a billboard—it has to have stopping power even when passing it by at freeway speeds.

Powerful Beginnings and Endings

Memory research tells us that the material that is most easily remembered and has the most impact are the beginnings and endings. Therefore, Master Presenters pay particular attention to the development and the delivery of their introductions and conclusions.

Master Presenters may not know these "laws" by name, but they instinctively structure their messages to utilize the *law of primacy* and the *law of recency*. These "laws" prove the audience is most likely to remember what they hear first (primacy) and what they hear last (recency).[2] That's why so many Master Presenters insist: Open strong, close strong.

Twenty-five percent of the impact of any presentation is a powerful beginning and ending. We live in a world of instant messaging, fast food, microwave meals, and 30-second sound bites; your audience members are accustomed to a fast start. Therefore, you have no more than 90 seconds to get their attention. If you don't get it then, you can still get it, but it will take a great deal of work and effort on your part.

Some Master Presenters suggest listeners begin forming their opinions of the speaker even faster. Roger Ailes, author of *You Are the Message,* says, "Research shows that we start to make up our minds about other people within seven seconds of first meeting them."

This may seem like an unusually short time in which to form an opinion, so David puts it to the test. In his presentations, he asks participants to pair up, with one person serving as active observer. Then he tells them he wants them to merely look at the other person until David says to stop. At the end of seven seconds, he picks several observers and asks: "What opinions can you draw from what you saw?" It is amazing how much some people say they perceived. Comments range from, "He looks intense, knowledgeable, and scholarly," to, "She looks like a kind, thoughtful, caring person." All of these insights and opinions were formed in only seven short seconds. This exercise illustrates the power of the first impression.

Chris Clark-Epstein, Master Presenter and author, knows the importance of hooking your audience and demonstrating your competency as early as possible in the session. She says: "I am very, very cognizant of what I say first. I am a fairly extemporaneous speaker. However, I am very disciplined about my opening. The opening must be absolutely tailored to that group of people based on the research I have done on the audience. You could say that I am pathological about what that opening is about."

Brad: Memory expert Bob Gray is one of the most novel and unique presenters I have ever seen. Bob starts his presentation by demonstrating his ability to speak backwards and write upside down, backwards, and inverted with both his hands and feet while blindfolded. Bob then asks three volunteers from the audience to select the name of any country. Bob then lists the capital, population, and square miles of each country, which are then verified by another volunteer. Lastly, he asks for two volunteers to state the date, month, and year of their birthday, provided they know what day of the week on which were born. Bob then tells them the day of the week and they verify his answers. Bob then challenges the audience by telling them that he doesn't have a photographic memory, but rather a trained memory, and offers to teach them his memory techniques. Now, did his powerful beginning get the audience's full attention? You bet. You can see Bob perform these feats at *www.memoryedge.com.*

David: Mark Brown, the 1995 World Champion of Public Speaking says, "You must have your opening (one to four minutes) down cold. Have it so firmly rehearsed you could say it in your sleep." Why? Because as you take the stage you must take charge. And you can't take charge if you are unsure of your material.

Have you ever heard a speaker start slowly...and then stay slow? It is agonizing. On the other hand, have you ever heard a speaker open briskly and powerfully with a compelling statement that just makes you want to hear more? These are the speakers we perk up to hear. Here is an example of a compelling 30-second opening from a speech by Frank Morris:

"At this very minute around the world, parents are anticipating their child's second birthday...and with it comes the onset of the "terrible two's"...that special moment in which their precious little toddler becomes a diabolical demon of destruction. Now, you may laugh, but ladies and gentlemen, young and old, I suggest to you that the terrible two's are not restricted just to children..."

At this point, Frank has set the stage with his pace, rhythm, alliteration, and added an element of intrigue. The listener wants to know, "What does he mean by that?" That is a lot to accomplish in his first 61 words.

It is also true that 25 percent of the impact of any presentation is a powerful ending. Paradoxically, if you start with the end in mind, you will be much more focused when you start working on the body of your presentation or the beginning. Having a well-defined ending, focus, and a central theme for your presentation will make it easier to develop, easier to organize, and easier for the participants to follow and remember.

You may choose to end your presentation with a review of the materials covered, a terrific quotation, a story, or an anecdote. Because impactful beginnings and endings are so important, this topic will be explored further in Strategy 4 of this book.

Use the Perfect Quote

Master Presenters know that finding the perfect quote often jumpstarts their creativity. The quote illustrates exactly what you need to write about and/or talk about, or the quote gives you another way to organize the content. No wonder so many books, speeches, and presentations, or different sections within a presentation, start with just the right quote. The right quote sets just the right tone, evokes just the right feeling, and simplifies our understanding. This helps us grasp the deeper meaning and, at the same time, makes the presentation more memorable. The perfect quote can also be used as a unifying device to tie everything together at the right point within the presentation and at its conclusion.

Quotations are tremendous tools. They can help build your confidence in your presentation, boost your credibility, give you direction, and help you focus your presentation—but only if you remember where you saw it or heard it. Has the following ever happened to you: "I know of a great quote that would tie everything together perfectly, but I just can't quite remember the exact words"? Or, "I remember the words, but I forget who said it"? When this happens, you either scrap the quote or embark on a time-consuming search that often turns up empty handed.

In the past, Master Presenters had books and books of excellent quotes such as *Bartlett's Familiar Quotations.* While these books still serve us well, today's Master Presenters have computer programs that can help them find just the right quote by subject matter or by author, and allow them to enter their own favorite quotes so they can be easily retrieved.

For example, Brad developed a program on effective communication for the Association of Health Organizations. They had seven people who could deliver the program. They were very happy with the program and he was extremely pleased with the quality of the people who would be delivering it. When they were all satisfied that the program would meet their needs and the trainers were prepared, the director asked if there were a few good quotes that could help them better market their new training module.

Brad had been collecting quotes and had entered them in a folder, but this was very time consuming. As their numbers grew, it became increasingly difficult to identify and retrieve the ones he wanted, so he turned to computer software for help.[3] The result was a job that normally would have taken days to complete, took only minutes.

The computer program quickly found 127 quotes on communications. From those, Brad made the following seven selections:

> *Always keep your words soft and sweet, just in case you have to eat them.*
>
> —*Anonymous*

> *Watch your thoughts; they become words.*
> *Watch your words; they become actions.*
> *Watch your actions; they become habits.*
> *Watch your habits; they become your character.*
> *Watch your character; it becomes your destiny.*
>
> —*Frank Outlaw, author*

> *No one ever lost his job by listening too much.*
>
> —*Calvin Coolidge, 30th U.S. President*

We must never forget that the most powerful communication isn't what you say, it's what you do. What counts, in the final analysis, is not what people are told but what they accept. It is this concept of the role of communication in industry that characterizes effective leadership.

—Frank E. Fischer, American Management Association

The most important thing in communication is to hear what isn't being said.

—Peter F. Drucker, management professor

The two words "information" and "communication" are often used interchangeably, but they signify quite different things. Information is giving out; communication is getting through.

—Sydney J. Harris, journalist, author

Effective communication is 20 percent what you know and 80 percent how you feel about what you know.

—E. James (Jim) Rohn, speaker, trainer, author

These quotes were perfect for the training program because they emphasize the need for effective communication. Although this program isn't perfect, it sure beats trying to look up quotes or trying to locate that perfect quote when you just can't remember where you saw it. You can also enter your favorite new quote and you will know where to find it each and every time. Therefore, if you want to find the perfect quote, stimulate your thinking, and add focus and direction to your presentation, you may want to consider a computerized quotation program.

Other excellent sources for quotes are *www.Bartleby.com* and David's two favorite quotation books: *Simpson's Contemporary Quotations: The Most Notable Quotes Since 1950* by James B. Simpson and *Words of Wisdom: More Good Advice* by William Safire and Leonard Safir.

The Perfect Illustrative Story

Experience is the best teacher, and when learning the aims of an organization, it typically takes form of critical incidents. These are the stuff of stories and legends.

—Kouzes and Posner[4]

Long after the participants have forgotten the topic of the presentation, even after they have forgotten the name of the presenter, they will remember a story. Therefore, Master Presenters have mastered the art of story construction and delivery. The perfect story not only makes the material memorable, but also brings it alive for the audience. Like the perfect picture, the perfect story captures the essence of what needs to be learned.

In this section we are going to examine how stories can be used in the following six ways:

1. Introduction.
2. Icebreaker.
3. Example, explanation, or illustration.
4. Case Study.
5. Metaphor.
6. Conclusion.

1. The Story as Introduction

The perfect story can be a perfect introduction to your topic. For example, a university professor starts his ethics class with the following story:

> At Duke University, there were four sophomores taking Organic Chemistry. They did so well on all the quizzes, midterms, labs, etc., that each had an A so far for the semester. These four friends were so confident that the weekend before finals, they decided to go up to the University of Virginia and party with some friends there. They had a great time—however, after all the hard partying, they slept all day Sunday and didn't make it back to Duke until early Monday morning.
>
> Rather than taking the final then, they decided to find their professor after the final and explain to him why they missed it. They explained that they had gone to the University of Virginia for the weekend with the plan to come back in time to study, but, unfortunately, they had a flat tire on the way back, didn't have a spare, and couldn't get help for a long time. As a result, they missed the final. The professor thought it over and then agreed they could make up the final the following day. The guys were elated and relieved. They studied that night and went in the next day at the

time the professor had told them. He placed them in separate rooms and handed each of them a test booklet, and told them to begin. They looked at the first problem, worth five points. It was something simple about free radical formation. "Cool," they thought at the same time, each one in his separate room, "this is going to be easy." Each finished the problem and then turned the page. On the second page was written: "For 95 points, which tire?"

The professor then goes on to lead a discussion about under what circumstances should we tell the truth, tell a partial truth, and not tell the truth at all. Did the professor get the students' attention? Was the story absolutely appropriate for this audience? Was it relevant to the topic? Of course, the answer to all of these questions is a resounding *yes*.

Another example of using a story as an introduction comes from Brad's leadership course. The story is used to illustrate that almost everything a leader does or doesn't do is a potential act of leadership. Brad uses an article written by Norman Augustine, CEO of Lockheed Martin, which chronicles how the U.S. defense industry decreased procurement by more than 60 percent since 1989 as a result of the end of the Cold War. Consequently, 15 major companies were downsized and merged into four. In the article, the author describes 12 essential steps that led Lockheed through this difficult time and on to phenomenal success. The following illustrates one of the aspects of his leadership:

> Pay attention to symbols. For example, when we combined Lockheed's and Martin Marietta's headquarters in a building previously occupied by Martin Marietta, we moved everyone out and reassigned offices from scratch to avoid the impression that anyone had been bumped or that some people were more important than others. That action was critical from a social standpoint, and it is for that reason that we at Lockheed Martin try to treat acquisitions as mergers of equals. The attitude "we bought you" is a corporate cancer.[5]

The question Brad then asks the participants is, "Was it worth the expense to move everyone out and then to move all the successful candidates back in again?" After very little discussion, the answer is always yes. He then asks the class, "Why?" After a short discussion, they always say that not only was this action the fairest way to do things, it also was symbolic of Augustine's fair approach and set the expectation that he would be fair in dealing with staff in the future. This allows Brad to add that in two-thirds of the cases, mergers have been found not to be cost effective due to the culture wars between the two organizations that are merging into one. Most organizations and their leaders do not pay enough attention to the process by which the merger comes about. This is most shortsighted because the process is the foundation upon which the new organization rests. Note that the Norman Augustine story is made up of only 85 words. It is not the number of words that gives the story its impact. It is the story itself. Although these two stories are very different, what they have in common is that Master Presenters are master storytellers. They know that well-crafted and well-told stories are one of the best ways to begin a presentation, because they capture the audience's attention and establish credibility.

2. The Story as Icebreaker

Stories can also be used as icebreakers. The difference between an introduction to a presentation and an icebreaker is that an icebreaker is designed to help move the participant's attention from their thoughts outside of the session to what is going on inside the session. A story as an introduction, on the other hand, conveys the underlying message that the presenter intends to deliver. In this regard, the icebreaker is an invitation into the presentation. Icebreakers can be used at any time during a presentation, such as when the session begins, following lunch or a break, when the participants have their minds on a million other things. The icebreaker invites, beguiles, and entices the participants into the session. The message that an icebreaker gives is that this session will be either provocative; stimulating and fun; or insipid, dull, and boring.

For example, Master Presenter Terry Paulson uses the following story to illustrate the importance of treating people as you would like to be treated:[6]

> Not long ago I was flying to Los Angeles, where I was sched-uled to speak at a conference. I was at Kennedy Airport in New York, standing in line to check my bags, and the guy in front of me was giving the baggage checker a difficult time. He was being

terribly, obnoxiously abusive. I didn't say anything—the man was not only upset, he was big. After he moved away from the curb, I expressed my sympathy to the checker for the verbal bullying he had taken.

"Do people talk that way to you often?' I asked him.

"Oh, yeah. You get used to it..."

"Well, I don't think I'd get used to it."

"Don't worry...After all, the customer's always right."

"Well, I don't think he was right in this case," I said.

"Don't worry." The checker repeated. "I've already gotten even."

"What do you mean"...

"He's on his way to Chicago...but his bags are going to Japan."

The keys to a good story are that it must be yours and that it must be *mostly* true—by *mostly* true, we mean it can be embellished a bit, but must be based in fact.

Brad: I once heard a speaker who was obviously in trouble with his audience. The speech was flat and the audience members' faces reflected the flatness of the presentation. In truth they looked bored and I think were, like me, deciding if it would be too impolite to get up and leave. The speaker seemed to get the feedback from the audience but was not sure what to do with it. He then went through a litany of all of the bad things that had happened to him, finishing with his being kidnapped. The trouble was, the litany had nothing to do with his presentation, and his tale of being kidnapped rang patently untrue. Object lesson—be as genuine and congruent as you possibly can; the audience has built-in truth detectors.

David: There is a speakers' adage that says: "Don't let the truth get in the way of a good story." This does not mean it's okay to lie and represent it as truth. But all good writers and all good speakers know the value of "artistic interpretation." That is, telling the story in the most effective way for maximum impact. Think of your "real" story as an artist's canvas. If the artist wishes to depict the scene exactly as it appears before him, he could take a photograph instead of using his brush. Yet, most people will agree that an artist's interpretation of a scene is what makes it compelling. Good speakers do the same: They take the real event and interpret it, enhance it, or edit it for the greatest impact.

Remember, this is *not* a license to lie. The audience will not excuse a blatant attempt to deceive. But no one will ever fault a speaker for taking a real event and telling it in the most effective way possible. This may mean you have to leave out a few lines of unnecessary dialogue, leave out a character or two, or compress the time frame in which the event happened. This is creative storytelling, and Master Presenters do it well.

Don't forget the transition or tie in. If there isn't a natural transition between your story and your topic, you will have to develop one. Brad started with the following story in his "Emotional Intelligence" presentation to a group of project managers. Note how the tie-in at the end of the story is used as a transition from the story to the subject of emotional intelligence.

John invited his mother over for dinner. During the meal, his mother couldn't help noticing how beautiful John's roommate was. She had long been suspicious of a relationship between John and his roommate, and this only made her more curious. Over the course of the evening, while watching the two interact, she started to wonder if there was more between John and the roommate than met the eye. Reading his mom's thoughts, John volunteered, "I know what you must be thinking, but I assure you, Julie and I are just roommates." About a week later, Julie came to John and said, "Ever since your mother came to dinner, I've been unable to find the beautiful silver gravy ladle. You don't suppose she took it, do you?" John said, "Well, I doubt it, but I'll write her a letter just to be sure." So he sat down and wrote a letter: Dear Mother, I'm not saying you did take a gravy ladle from my house, and I'm not saying you did not take a gravy ladle from my house, but the fact remains that it has been missing ever since you were here for dinner.

Several days later, John received a letter from his mother that read: Dear Son, I'm not saying that you do sleep with Julie, and I'm not saying that you do not, but the fact remains that if she were sleeping in her own bed, she would have found the gravy ladle by now.

Just as John's mother knew the right technique to seek information about John and Julie's relationship, project managers use emotional intelligence to bring their projects to fruition—and it is the subject of how a better understanding and application of emotional intelligence can help that we now turn our attention.

Even though the audience may have heard the story before, the transition is uniquely yours. That takes it from being a stand-alone joke to being a valuable presentation device.

3. The Story as Example, Explanation, or Illustration

Master Presenter Bill Gove says, "Public speaking is simply this: Make a point, tell a story." That's the essence of public speaking: Make a point, tell a story. He said that years after he will have spoken somewhere, someone will come up to him and say, "Bill, I still remember the story you told about...." He said that proves the power of the story as example. Anchor every point with an example, and make your examples through your stories.

David: An example I use in a variety of ways is this: "I have a nine-year-old son named Matthew. When he was 4, he learned how to spell his name as a result of playing computer games. As you may know, kids' games almost always ask the child to log in. For a long time I logged in for him, but one day I said, 'No, it's time you do that for yourself, so if you want to play the game, you have to spell your name.' So he learned to spell his name by hunting and pecking on the keyboard. A few days later, he was away from the computer and I asked him to spell his name for me. He said, 'M-A-T-T-H-E-W-Enter.'"

Without fail, this story always gets a laugh. So if for no other reason than to lighten the moment, it has great use. But I use it to illustrate a variety of other points depending on my need. For example, if I'm talking about the pervasiveness of computers in our culture, I use it. Or if I'm making a point about how we learn, I use it. Or if I'm making a point about the way people depend on contextual learning, I use it. That's the beauty of a good story—it can serve many purposes.

You can use stories to illustrate your most important points. Darren LaCroix, the 2001 World Champion of Public Speaking, delivers a powerful message on the importance of failing. He opens with the question: "Have you ever fallen flat on your face?" Then, he literally falls face down on stage. Still down, he delivers the next several lines of his speech, while audience members strain to see him. He then gets up and brushes himself off and launches into a powerful, personal story of a very large personal failure. He tells the story of how, right out of college, he bought a Subway sandwich franchise, and how over the next few months, he proceeded to turn his Subway restaurant into a "non-profit operation." It takes courage to stand on stage and tell of a personal failure. But Darren's speech is effective precisely because of his story. Master Presenters know that we can never be persuasive when we tell someone else's story. But we can be remarkably effective when we tell our own. As Mark Brown says, "Nobody but you can tell your story, and nobody can tell your story the way you can."

4. The Story as a Case Study

Start with a story that is a puzzle, an exceedingly difficult problem, and/or a moral dilemma that will take all of the audience's wisdom and intelligence to solve. One of the best stories that fits this description is the story of river blindness from the book *The Leadership Moment*.[7] A synopsis of that story follows:

RESPONSIBLE TO WHOM

"The banks of the West African rivers…should provide ideal farmlands in an otherwise water-deprived region between the Sahara Desert to the north and the rain forests to the south. Instead, they are regions of human devastation. Entire communities have migrated to drier lands, abandoning their ancient villages and fertile valleys. River blindness is a scourge not only of human health but also of economic development."[8] Almost all of the people become completely blind by early adulthood. Thus it is common that children guide their blind parents.

You are president and CEO of Merck Pharmaceuticals. Your company has developed a cure for river blindness. The drug costs only three dollars per tablet. The only problem is that "The drug was needed only by people who couldn't afford it." Producing enough medication to eradicate the disease would cost $200 million, which does not include the cost of distributing the drug.

The Case for Donating the Drug to Western Africa. Your company has a history of being socially responsible. Your mission is both to help people and make a profit. No other company has developed a cure. This would certainly be a good public relations move. No other pharmaceutical company has ever made a donation of this size before. This action would also help all Merck employees develop pride in their company.

The Case for Not Donating the Drug to Western Africa. Firstly, $200 million is the amount of money required to bring a new drug, like Prozac or Viagra onto the market. It would be irresponsible to Merck's clients and shareholders not to develop a drug that would help both people and profits. Secondly, many organizations hold some of their retirement funds in Merck's stock. The company should not be donating a drug to eradicate river blindness at the expense of the company's shareholders' retirement, especially if the shareholders did not vote to spend their earnings in this manner. Thirdly, the task of distributing the drug is daunting. The World Health Organization has already declined taking on the task of helping to distribute the drug.

The participants have 15 minutes, first to work individually, and then to work in small groups to decide which course of action they are going to take (that is, to donate or not donate the drug to Western Africa) and to prepare a speech regarding their decision to stockholders at the annual meeting.

After the participants have given their presentations, we compare their solutions with how the real company president dealt with the situation in real life. The value of this type of case study is that it places the participants in a real leadership situation, asks them what they would do, and then lets them compare their answers with how the actual leader in the story led at that critical juncture. An additional benefit from this exercise is that the participants must present their solution in a manner that would be appropriate for the president of a large corporation, which underscores the relationship between leadership skills and presentations skills.

5. The Story as Metaphor

Mark Brown, the 1995 World Champion of Public Speaking, used a masterful metaphor in his World Championship speech. He used the Disney movie *Beauty and the Beast* as the framework for his message about ignorance, intolerance, and indifference. He first illustrated how these negative attributes were depicted in the animated movie. Then he smoothly shifted into a real-life parallel. He told a moving story of a beautiful television reporter who went undercover as an unkempt homeless person to illustrate how differently she was treated. He said, "This beauty took on a beastly appearance." Then as he described what the camera saw, he illustrated each of the negative attributes of ignorance, intolerance, and indifference in the reactions of those who passed by her. The story of the movie was played out in real life. And because of the power of his metaphor, the real-life story had so much more impact.

Metaphorical stories capture the theme of the presentation, making it real, concrete, and tangible. These stories reach out and grab your audience's attention. Harvard's John Kotter, one of the world's foremost experts on leadership and change, artfully uses metaphor in the following story:[9]

> *In 1983, a new CEO put the company through a major transformation process that was successful. By 1988, the old procedure manuals were no longer used, replaced by far fewer rules and a set of customer-first practices that made more sense in the 1980s. But the CEO realized that the old manuals, while not on people's desks, were still very much in the corporate culture. So here is what he did.*
>
> *When he took the stage for his keynote address at the annual management meeting, he had three of his officers stack the old manuals on a table next to the lectern. In his speech he said something like this:*

"These books served us well for many years. They codified wisdom and experience developed over decades and made that available to all of us. I'm sure that many thousands of our customers benefited enormously because of these procedures.

"In the past few decades, our industry has changed in some important ways. Where there once were only two major competitors, we now have six. Where a new generation of products used to be delivered once every two decades, the time has now been cut to nearly five years. Where once customers were delighted if they could receive help from us in 48 hours, they now expect service within the course of an eight-hour shift.

"In this new context, our wonderful old books began to show their age— they weren't serving customers as well. They didn't help us adapt well to changing conditions. They slowed us down...and it began to show up in our financials.

"...we decided that we had to do something about this—not only because the economic results were looking poor but even more so because we were no longer doing what we wanted to do and had done so well for so long: serve our customers' needs in a truly outstanding way. We reexamined their requirements and in the last three years have changed dozens of practices to meet those needs. And in the process, we set these [books] aside.

"...I'm taking time to tell you all this today for a number of reasons. I know that there are a few of you in this room, each new to the company in the last couple of years, who think the books over here are a joke, bureaucratic mindlessness in the extreme. Well, I want you to know that they served this company well for many years. I also know that there are people in this room who hate to see the books go. You might not admit it—the logical case for what we've done is far too compelling—but at some gut level, you feel that way. I want you to join with me today in saying good-bye. The books are like an old friend who's died after living a good life. We need to acknowledge his contribution to our lives and move on."

For many of the people who read this story, their first reaction is to burn the books. The wisdom in this story is that it acknowledges that past procedures worked, and that we should honor them. It helps us move away from thinking that today's technique is good, and yesterday's is bad. This becomes a problem because what is new today will be old and hence bad tomorrow, and this lessens or devalues the impact of anything that appears to be new. In fact, many employees then start to view the newest change as "the flavor of the month."

By eulogizing the books, the speaker in the story acknowledges both their usefulness at the time they were developed and also that it is time to lay a good friend to rest and move on. The metaphor of paying our respect to a good friend who deserves our respect and has passed on is a perfect way not only to acknowledge the respect that the employees had for their manuals, but also to acknowledge the manual's passing.

6. Stories as Conclusions

Stories can also be used as a powerful way to conclude your presentation. For example, Albert Mensah, a native of Ghana, delivers a powerful speech in which he speaks on the theme, "Underneath, we're all the same." He walks on stage wearing a denka, a ceremonial African robe. He tells his story of how, as an African immigrant, he was treated differently when he first arrived in the United States. He speaks of being treated as an outsider—a troublemaker—because he looked, spoke, and acted so differently. He proceeds to illustrate how damaging such thinking can be. Then, at the climax of his speech, he rips off the denka, reveals a beautifully tailored suit and tie and says with a knockout punch: "Because underneath, we're all the same." It's a powerful illustration—memorable and moving.

Another outstanding speaker, Sandra Zeigler, tells the story of Harriett Tubman, a woman who helped U.S. Civil War slaves escape to freedom. After telling Harriett's story, Sandra shifts the focus to the audience for a powerful conclusion. She says:

> This morning, if you are standing at a place in your life where two roads are diverging, you are standing where Harriett Tubman, a black, disabled, illiterate, penniless woman born in bondage, once stood. Take the less traveled road of freedom, instead of the well-worn path to surrender. And when you arrive at your destination, and you will arrive, go back. Go back to your cities and your neighborhoods and teach, train, and inspire others to achieve what you have accomplished. [She pauses.] Don't stop at personal success. [She pauses.] As a tribute to Harriett Tubman, become one of the great ones. The great ones go back.

Brad often ends his presentation on the Seven Strategies of Master Negotiators with the following story from the book *Getting to Yes:*[10]

> In 1964 an American father and his twelve-year-old son were enjoying a beautiful Saturday in Hyde Park, London, playing catch with a Frisbee. Few in England had seen a Frisbee at that time and a small group of strollers gathered to watch this strange sport. Finally, one Homburg-clad Britisher came over to the father: "Sorry to bother you. Been watching you a quarter of an hour. Who's winning?"

> In most instances to ask a negotiator, "Who's winning?" is as inappropriate as to ask who's winning a marriage. If you ask that question about your marriage, you have already lost the more important negotiation—the one about what kind of game to play, about the way you deal with each other and your shared and differing interests.

Brad then adds the following ending as a call to action:

> It is my hope that this presentation is a beginning for all of us, me included, to negotiate more effectively, in our personal lives, in our professional lives, in our states/provinces, nationally, and indeed, as the events of September 11, 2001, have so aptly pointed out, internationally. In those efforts, I wish you God's speed.

This is not only a great story to end the presentation on, it also emphasizes the fact that the participants will have ample opportunity to practice the skills that they have just learned in the days ahead, and it challenges them to do so both in their personal and professional lives.

How to Find the Best Stories

There are many ways to collect good stories. Books, magazines, movies, your local library, your organization's formal or informal archives, story clubs, book clubs, and stories about one's children, friends, and family life can all work well if they are not overdone or over used.

Many presenters use stories that they have found in issues of popular publications such as *Reader's Digest* and the *Chicken Soup for the*

Soul series of books. Although the stories are often cute, funny, and heart-warming, we must issue a word of warning: you can't use them because they are copyrighted. As well, as soon as you start to tell a story your audience has already heard, your credibility goes out the window. The listener thinks, "I've heard that from someone else. I wonder how much of the rest of this presentation is someone else's."

David: When I heard Master Presenter Bill Gove explain that public speaking was simply a matter of "Make a point, tell a story," I thought at the time, *That's good advice if you have a big story.* If you've climbed Everest, well, that's a story. Or if you've conquered cancer and then gone on to win the Tour de France, that's a story. But I had to admit that I had done nothing that significant enough to use as "my story." So, though I understood what Bill Gove said, for the next four years, I didn't do it. Then, one morning, I was reading the newspaper. I saw in a trivia column written by L. M. Boyd a small item that jumped off the page at me. It said: "Every human being alive experiences these six emotions: happiness, sadness, anger, surprise, disgust, and fear." I don't know why at that moment I thought of Bill Gove's "Make a point, tell a story," but the moment I brought those two thoughts together is the moment I changed the way I spoke. I thought, *If I have a little story, a little slice-of-life vignette that triggers at least one of those emotions, that story will connect with anyone.* What a revelation that was, because I stopped waiting for my big story and started using my little stories. And from that moment on, I stopped giving "speeches" and started speaking conversationally as I told my little stories. It has changed my approach, and it can do the same for you.

Other excellent sources of stories are our families, children, relatives, and friends. However, the story must be pertinent and under no circumstances should the presenter appear to be bragging, as this is very likely to alienate you from the audience. Often, a story where you show yourself to be far from perfect and where the story illustrates your point is the most intellectually powerful, fun, and entertaining. This is because the audience is more likely to identify with you as soon as they know you don't consider yourself superior. In other words, a humbling story is more likely to connect with the audience. For example, in one of Brad's negotiation presentations, he uses the following story to illustrate the concept that almost all negotiations must balance preparation and flexibility, and one way to improve this is to "Expect the Unexpected":[11]

A number of years ago, I was working as a regional manager for a national company. The work was very demanding so I booked Thursday evenings as private time. During this time I was taking ice-skating lessons and had an extremely capable coach. My friend and colleague, Harold Taylor, a nationally recognized expert on time management, taught me that firstly, if I wanted to protect my private time, I had to schedule it into my daily planner and secondly, that I had to treat it as equally important to other meetings that I had. He also warned me that I would be tested. However, I didn't expect to be tested so soon, so often, or so severely.

I started my lessons, was making progress in my skating and felt good about having a complete break from my work. In other words, I was feeling very good about taking care of myself. The following Thursday, the President and CEO of the national organization was visiting our region.

The president was well known for being able to work very long hours and a full day of meetings was scheduled in addition to a business dinner for that night. I asked if we could eat early because I had a meeting Thursday night (I did—although it was with my coach). The next week, the vice president was in town and once again we had a business dinner scheduled for Thursday night. Again, I asked if we could eat early because I had a meeting scheduled for later that evening—with my coach. I was beginning to feel like I had mastered one of the elements of time management and self-care.

The next Thursday night I was thoroughly tested. My children attended École Beaufort, a French immersion school in our neighborhood. Thursday night was the school's celebration of La Carnival, which recognizes the coming of spring. My son Andrew very much wanted the whole family to go to La Carnival. I thought that this was a teachable moment where I could help my son learn that parents deserved some private time as well. I carefully prepared for this negotiation. I was going to talk about the fact that I take my son to hockey and soccer on a regular basis, that we take a father and son trip once a year, played sports together, etc. However, before I made these points, as a good negotiator does, I asked my son, "Why is it so important to you that I go to La Carnival?" This gorgeous blue-eyed, blond haired 8-year-old looked up at me and said, "Dad, because I like you a lot."

I was wiped off the table. Speechless. I thought about it all the next day and came up with the following interest-based solution. My main interest was taking the lesson and for one night could easily miss the warm up and cool down. So I approached Andrew and asked him if it would be all right if we as a family went to La Carnival and were there for the start. I would miss the warm up, take my lesson, miss the cool down and be back at the school by eight o'clock. "Sure Dad." By taking an interest-based approach, both parties' interests were well satisfied.

Brad finds that audiences always relate well to this story and you, too, can find stories from your personal life that not only make the point, but also help to make you appear more human and approachable. At the same time, you must not overuse personal stories or you will appear to be egocentric, conceited, and unapproachable.

We recommend you start and maintain your own personal story file. From now on, any time you encounter any event or moment that triggers one of the six universal emotions (happiness, sadness, anger, surprise, disgust, or fear) write it down. You don't have to write the entire story, but you should jot down a reminder of the moment. Put it in your personal story file. Your "file" doesn't have to be anything elaborate, but you must find a place to store the golden stories that you discover. You can also start or join a story club. For example, you and several friends can form a group and every time one of you finds a good story, e-mail it to each other for feedback. Set up a special folder on your computer desktops. When you find a story that has potential, put it in this folder. You want to avoid finding and then losing the perfect story. You may think, "I don't need to write it down; but you'll be amazed at how many good stories you let slip away because you just forgot them.

Superb storytelling is one of the hallmarks used by Master Presenters. However, Master Presenters don't rely on storytelling alone. Storytelling is one of the three parts of the Three "S" Advantage. In the next section we will cover all three parts.

The Three "S" Advantage

The Three "S" Advantage is guaranteed to help you develop a more powerful, memorable, and impactful presentation. The three S's stand for stories, simulations, and a summary of the scientific evidence. For example, in Brad's Master Negotiator presentations, he begins with the concept that we can build our futures with creative or wasteful solutions. Step one is to illustrate the concept with a convincing story. Step two is to use a simulation that ensures that the audience experiences the concept by creating a teachable moment. Step three is to present a summary of scientific evidence that supports your point.

The reason you want to use the Three "S" Advantage is because of the incredible synergy that you can develop by combining these three elements. A mathematical analogy to illustrate synergy is $3 + 3 + 3 = 9$, however, $3 \times 3 \times 3 = 27$. If used correctly, the use of stories, simulations, and summaries of the scientific evidence can increase both the breadth and depth of your material as no other method can. The stories bring perspective and memorability, the simulations let the participant experience for himself or herself the point you are trying to make, and summaries of the scientific evidence add proof that reassures your audience that the material has withstood the test of time.

Stories

As noted, compelling stories draw the audience into your topic. They have humor, intrigue, suspense, or pathos. The audience is drawn into the topic, forgetting their everyday concerns. The audience lets out a gasp, or sits on the edge of their seats trying to figure something out that has become important to them. Good storytelling, like good joke telling, is an art. Master Presenters practice their stories over and over again, changing parts and studying how the audience responds, until they get the story just right. Long after the participants have forgotten everything else, they will remember a great story. All of the stories that Master Presenters use serve to make a point, and that point is so well crafted and so well told that it is etched indelibly into the participants' memory.

Simulations

> *The best piece of educational technology ever created was the flight simulator.*
> *Should we have simulators for all of our training? Yes. Why don't we? Too much*
> *money. But when you're sitting in your seat in a 747 and wondering about the*
> *skill level of the pilot, you don't say to yourself, "Gee, I hope he passed that paper*
> *test in flight school." You want to know that pilot [has] actually flown or has*
> *simulated flight in a number of the most challenging circumstances that he's*
> *"done it." Our training needs to be the same way.*
>
> —*Roger Schank*[12]

Simulations create three-dimensional models that allow the participants to experience the topic under discussion without the attendant risks that could occur in real life. Simulations allow people to get out of their comfort level; to experiment; to try out new behaviors; and see for themselves if they work, how they work, where they work, and, just as important, where they *do not* work.

For example, in Brad's negotiation presentations, the participants often simulate negotiating the sale of a house where the only remaining issue is the closing date. After the negotiation, they then analyze themselves and each other as to the negotiation style they used. Likewise, when David teaches writing programs for business, he explains that he was once hired to proofread a promotional piece for the launch of a new *Wall Street Journal* Interactive Edition. The PR person responsible for the launch said, "I've checked everything several times. I'm confident it's ready to go to press, but my boss said I have to get someone else to check off on it. It's mostly just a formality at this point, but he said if there are any mistakes, it's my neck." Then David passes out a copy of the piece and asks the participants to proofread it as if their careers depended on it. Why is this an effective presentation tool? Because it simulates a real situation with very real consequences.

Summary of Scientific Evidence

We have all attended presentations that were well organized and very well presented. But after all was said and done, they left a funny aftertaste. We had learned nothing new. They remind us of the famous Wendy's commercial in which a woman asked, "Where's the beef?" Presentations that use relevant scientific evidence add content and substance, which enables us to better understand the world and/ or see it in a new way. We are left feeling satisfied that the presenter took the time to create a meaningful presentation that has left us with content that we can use.

Step three of the Three "S" Advantage is to summarize the scientific evidence. For example, after a negotiation simulation that reveals the participants' negotiation style, Brad presents the Gerald Williams's research on negotiation style. Because the participants had just negotiated and experienced how well their style and the other participants' style worked or didn't work, the scientific evidence has 100 percent more meaning to the participants than if it were introduced on its own.

Note that the Three "S" Advantage is not to be used rigidly. You can present very effectively by using part of the model, or by using some elements of the model more than once. For example, Master Presenter and author William Bridges very successfully uses elements one and two, storytelling and simulations, in a presentation on transitions. During the presentation he would stop lecturing and/or storytelling, and at critical points he would ask the participants to form into groups of four to carry out an exercise or simulation. For example, he asks the participants to share a transition that they were in at a previous time in their lives and identify for themselves, and for each other, a skill or a strategy that helped them master that transition. Second, the participants were to state how that same skill or strategy could help them master a current transition or one that they would soon be facing.

Bridges could have lectured on this point until the cows came home and it would never have had the impact that "harvesting the past" had as an experiential exercise. The use of this exercise was much more powerful than a traditional lecture could have ever been.

Please note that the order of the three elements depends on which order works best for your particular presentation and your particular audience. After you become familiar with the method, you can vary the number of elements. For example, you may chose to start with a story, do a simulation, give a summary of the scientific evidence, and then end the section with another story. As you become more familiar with the Three "S" Advantage, you will be able to pick the precise element(s) to make your presentations as powerful as those of the Master Presenters you have met in the pages of this book.

The following exercise has been designed to help you master the Three "S" Advantage.

EXERCISE
2-3

Design an element of your next presentation or design an element of a current presentation using at least two of the elements of the Three "S" Advantage.

1. How will you use storytelling techniques to add impact to your presentation?

2. How will you use a simulation to add impact to your presentation?

3. How will you use a summary of scientific evidence to add impact to your presentation?

The Zero Draft

There is a wonderful book titled *Writing Your Dissertation in Fifteen Minutes a Day* by Joan Bolker. In the book, Bolker talks about writing "the zero draft." The zero draft is a private document designed for the writer to get his or her thoughts down on paper, which is also known as a "brain dump." Bolker's next stage is writing a private document for the writer's eyes only. In that stage, the writer is trying to figure something out, to arrive at the truth to the best of his or her ability, and the writer is his or her own audience. At this stage, don't be a perfectionist, and remember what John Maynard Keynes said, "It is better to be roughly right than precisely wrong." When you are writing everything but the final draft, give yourself permission to write notes in the margins about what you think, feel, have hunches about, and anything else that comes to mind about what you have written. In other words, you can produce a written dialogue and that dialogue will help you develop both your thinking and your writing. Even if 90 percent of these thoughts are later discarded, you will find that the remaining 10 percent will be rich and valuable. In stage three, the writer writes for his or her intended audience, and in stage four the writer has produced something of great value both for himself and for his intended audience.

The beauty of Bolker's stages is that they not only hold true for writing but also for developing a presentation. Think of the zero draft as a way to get your ideas down on paper. The first draft, outline, or mind-map can then be developed. At this stage, you are the audience and you can jot down in the margin any thoughts whatsoever about the presentation. Again, even if 90 percent of these thoughts are later discarded, you will find that the remaining 10 percent will be rich and valuable.

In truth you can begin the zero draft at any time before you do anything else or after you craft your title. Developing a presentation is really an iterative process. This means that you may develop a better title or story or draft at any stage in the preparation of your presentation, and although the elements are presented individually, they really work together synergistically. An improvement in any one of the elements can lead to an improvement in any of the other elements and an improvement to the presentation as a whole.

In stage three, you rework your presentation with a specific audience in mind, and in stage four you produce a presentation that has great value both for your intended audience and for yourself. But it doesn't end here; you must practice and get feedback on your presentation to fine tune both the content and the delivery.

Your Content Advisory Board

First, Master Presenter Ian Percy recommends that presenters of all levels and abilities use a Content Advisory Board (CAB). The purpose of the CAB is to give the presenter objective, pertinent, insightful, and crystal clear feedback on where that presenter's content is working and where it is not. Sometimes the material is not appropriate, sometimes the explanation is not clear enough, sometimes better or more timely examples are needed. Just as the milk you buy at the store has a "best before" date, so too does our material. No matter how much the presenter loves that particular piece of material, story, joke, or anecdote, it must be discarded because it is no longer fresh. Your Content Advisory Board must give you balanced feedback, both about what is working and what is not. Ideally, each member of the board will have different strengths, so select the people on your Content Advisory Board carefully. This just may be one of the most important decisions you ever make in your career.

EXERCISE
2-4

List up to eight people who might form your Content Advisory Board. List specifically what each of these people could contribute to your growth and development as a presenter.

Among the questions your Content Advisory Board should look at are:

1. Is the presentation content light, content heavy, or content right?

Content light is fluff, not enough new information, too much information the audience already knows, or an excellent five-minute point stretched and repeated to fill 45 minutes.

Content heavy is too much information and too many details to remember. Nothing stands out from anything else and there is an overwhelming amount of facts and figures.

Content right is just the right amount of content. It matches perfectly with the time period allotted, the expertise and technical level of the audience, and the context such as at the beginning of the day when people are fresh or at the end of the day when the audience members are tired and information-satiated.

Please rate the presentation on a scale of 1 to 7, with a 1 representing that the content is too light, 4 just right, and 7 too heavy.

Too light			Just right			Too heavy
1	2	3	4	5	6	7

2. Is the content meaningful, engaging, and does it resonate with the audience?

Are the audience members bored, listless, and mentally checked out or are they fully engaged, leaning forward, and watching the presenter with focused attention?

Not meaningful or engaging and does not resonate with audience				Meaningful, engaging, and resonates with audience		
1	2	3	4	5	6	7

3. Is the content new, thought-provoking, and inspiring?

In place of the same old content and same old clichés, Master Presenters give their audience new, thought provoking and inspiring information that once learned, allows the audience to view the world in ways that weren't possible before the presentation.

Not new, thought-provoking, and inspiring				New, thought-provoking, and inspiring		
1	2	3	4	5	6	7

4. Did you provide an incisive analysis along with the information you presented?

Today's audiences are bombarded with a plethora of information from many sources including the Internet. The best presenters also give their audiences the tools to analyze this information in ways that they could not have gleaned from any other source.

No incisive analysis					Incisive analysis	
1	2	3	4	5	6	7

◆ ◆ ◆

Preparing outstanding content is a result of a variety of elements. Putting together outstanding content involves speaking from a strong point of view and developing titles that will grab and hold the audience's imagination. Frame your beginnings and endings with content that has impact and then work on finding, creating, and developing the perfect illustrative stories. These stories, along with simulations and scientific backup will give you credibility and believability. Once you are ready for a trial run of your presentation, start with the zero draft and end with feedback. When you've succeeded in accumulating the perfect content balance, the next step is organizing it to make it as powerful and as memorable as possible. We'll address that next.

STRATEGY

3

Use
Superior Organization

A place for everything, and everything in its place.
—*Samuel Smiles, author*

No amount of outstanding content or effective delivery skills can save a poorly organized presentation. If the participants can't follow your presentation's organization or line of reasoning, they will assume that you don't know the material, haven't integrated it, are lazy, and don't deserve their attention. Therefore, Master Presenters spend a great deal of time not only developing the content and the delivery of their message; they also focus on developing superior organization. This chapter presents five techniques that will assure both you and your audience that your presentation is impeccably well organized. The five techniques are:

1. Developing advanced organizers.
2. Using the eight organizational structures.
3. Making sure it is cohesive.
4. Paying attention to your transitions.
5. Understanding the critical importance of timing.

1. Advanced Organizers

One of the exercises that we use in our course *The Seven Strategies of Master Presenters* is an exercise in one-way and two-way communication. The exercise works like this: We select a participant from the course to be the communicator. He or she is given a diagram of seven shapes (circles, rectangles, and squares) that are connected to each other. Using one-way communication, the communicator must describe—in as much detail as possible—the figures on the handout, while the listeners draw the diagram to the best of their ability based only upon the verbal description. The communication can only be one way and the communicator cannot use hand gestures—only his or her verbal skills—to describe the shapes in the diagram. The participants are not allowed to ask questions.

The exercise is then repeated with a different diagram that uses the same shapes but in an equally difficult arrangement. This time, however, the communicator and the listeners can engage in two-way communication. The quality of the diagram always improves when both the listeners and the communicator give each other feedback. The attendees ask for directions to be repeated, and both parties develop a richer way of communicating using angles, degrees, clock numbers, and analogies such as "it looks like a wagon" to make the communication richer, more thorough, and more precise.

Every once in a while, a superb communicator volunteers for the role of describer. What is different about this communicator is that the volunteer intuitively understands the concept of advanced organizers. By this we mean that the volunteer will start by saying, "I am going to describe a grouping of seven shapes, there is one square, two circles, and four rectangles," or he or she will say, "I will describe the shapes and their sizes in a minute, but before I do that, I want you to know that I will be describing the shapes in a clockwise direction."

Advanced organizers create a frame of reference for what follows. When advanced organizers are used, the people reproducing the diagram are told how the communicator will proceed, that is, in a clockwise direction, and that the diagram is made up of seven shapes. Because the participants know how many shapes there are and in what direction the shapes will be described, it makes the whole process of understanding their task that much easier.

Just as the superb communicator in the one-way/two-way communication exercise used an advanced organizer to help the participants reproduce the diagram, Master Presenters use advanced organizers to tell the participants how the presentation will proceed by giving them an overview of its structure. This structure also helps the participants organize the presentation in their own minds and, hence, remember it more effectively. Appropriate visual aids make the organizational structure more apparent to the listener. For example, how many times have you heard, "That was point number three," and you can't even recall that there was a point number two? That's why it is usually necessary to say at the outset how many points you will be making. Then, as each point is checked off, remind the listener: "That was point number two," while restating a key-word summation of the point.

Remember, it is not possible to be too clear. Research has proved that people both understand and remember information hierarchically. By using advanced organizers, Master Presenters help the attendees both understand and remember the presentation more effectively.

2. Eight Organizational Structures

It is impossible to give a strong presentation within a weak organizational structure. Therefore, Master Presenters have developed the art of organizing their presentations to the highest degree possible. Eight organizational structures that you can use are:

1. Chronological.
2. Geographical.
3. Analytical.
4. Functional.
5. Contrasts/comparisons.
6. Conflict.
7. Metaphorical.
8. Mixed.

Chronological Presentations

Chronological presentations are organized by time and progress from beginning to end. The unit of measurement can be seconds, minutes, hours, days, weeks, months, years, decades, centuries, and millennia. The movie *JKF,* most programs on the History Channel, and the acclaimed scientific series *Walking With Dinosaurs* are examples of masterful use of chronological events to tell the story in a logical or meaningful manner.

Chronological presentations are often used to tell a story. For example, the book *The Critical Path* tells the dramatic story of Chrysler's survival, and *Five Days in London* tells the story of how Winston Churchill persuaded the war cabinet not to capitulate to Hitler. In terms of an economic example, a speaker could open with a "now" perspective, such as, "Today, interest rates for home mortgages are the lowest they have been in 50 years. How did we get here? Let's go back to 1953 and examine what happened." Then, with a simple timeline, tick off key developments on watershed years. This gives a flow of continuity and brings cohesiveness to your message. As a side note, in this kind of presentation, it can become deadly dull if all you do is reel off years and statistics. For color and depth, mention an occasional "scene-setting" event. For example, "In 1959, the Russians shocked the world with the launch of Sputnik, the first man-made satellite to orbit the Earth. In that same year, interest rates shot up as well..."

Geographical Presentations

Geographical presentations use geographical places to help tell a story. One of the best examples is Pierre Burton's *The Last Spike*, which tells the story of the building of the Canadian Pacific Railroad. It is geographical because the story develops as the building of the railroad moves primarily from east to west. This story is also metaphorical in that it also tells the story of the building of a nation.

Speakers can use a similar device. Lance Armstrong, for example, could hold us spellbound if he merely took us on a stage-by-stage journey along the route of the Tour de France. It would have far more impact if listeners were invited to travel with him geographically through his story than if he skipped around.

Analytical Presentations

Analytical presentations analyze the topic, divide it into meaningful sub-topics, and demonstrate the relationship between them. For example, "High-performance teams have the following eight characteristics..." or, "The three disciplines of market leaders are..."

Each sub-topic is supported by empirical evidence—the better the evidence, the better the presentation. Excellent evidence is surprising or unexpected, and the listener is rewarded by hearing the depth of the evidence and the thoroughness of the research.

Functional Presentations

Functional explanations help to deepen one's understanding and appreciation of how things work or the benefits to be derived by using a particular product or procedure. Speakers like Susan Sweeney and Jim Carole help their audiences understand and appreciate various aspects of the Internet and E-commerce. Or just flip on your television in the wee hours of the morning and you will be bombarded with speakers using functional organization: There is one on every infomercial. This is their stock-in-trade. After 30 minutes, they have told you every possible use of their product (and then some). They hold nothing back. If there is a function, you've heard about it by the time they finish.

Contrasts and Comparisons

Contrasts and comparisons actually work well together. For example, Dr. Janet Lapp uses the power of contrasts and comparisons to help explain how Americans and Canadians are similar and different. She also uses humor when advising Canadians who speak in America and for Americans who speak in Canada. A subset of contrasts is doing a pro and con analysis. For example, suppose your company is equally divided over starting a marketing campaign now, because the competition is slowly taking market share away from your division's product, versus waiting six months to implement the plan, because a new innovative product is under development. We have found that when a topic spurs strongly held opposing points of view, it is desirable to first get agreement on common ground. Then acknowledge the arguments of the "opposite side" second, and advance your point of view last.

In terms of common ground in the previous example, the presenter may want to reiterate agreed upon principles of effective decision-making, the need to balance short-term and long-term goals, and the company's mission to be both innovative and profitable. The presenter would then consider the arguments for increasing advertising now: Market share lost now may never be made up, the company's board of directors and shareholders are becoming increasingly upset by decreasing market share, and the industry's yearly market share report will be published in six months. The presenter then presents the opposing point of view that the new product could become the new industry standard, but to be successful it will need every advertising dollar that the company can put behind it, including this year's entire advertising budget. Second, the company has a reputation of bringing innovate products to market and is overdue for a product that is a direct hit. Third, most companies fail because they overemphasize short-term profits for long-term growth.

Conflict

Using conflict to set up and organize your presentation is something that Craig Valentine, the 1999 World Champion of Public Speaking, recommends. He states that it seems to be human nature to like a good fight or a good conflict. He also points out that most movies introduce the audience to the conflict within the first 30 minutes. For example, it could be an intrapersonal conflict (conflict within oneself); an interpersonal conflict (conflict between two people); an intrateam conflict (a conflict within a team); interteam conflict (conflict between two or more teams); an intraorganizational conflict (conflict within an organization); and a conflict between two organizations, two states, or two countries. Many of the best stories a presenter can tell also revolve around the successful resolution of one or more of the different types of conflicts previously listed.

Metaphorical Presentations

The metaphorical presentation uses something that is well-known and understood to help the attendees understand something that is less well-known and understood. For example, Greg Levoy uses the concept of connecting the dots in his presentation *Callings*. The metaphor of connecting the dots means that we have life experiences that are exceptionally meaningful for us. When we "connect the dots," that is, discover the deeper significance that can be derived from figuring out the relationship among these various meaningful life experiences, we discover our calling. It is in connecting the dots that the picture, or in this case, our calling, emerges stronger and more clearly focused.

Alan Parisse[1] states that "the challenge of a presenter is to move from simplicity to complexity and then back to simplicity with depth." Metaphors are a good way to do this. Metaphors are also an excellent way to make your presentations truly universal, deeply personal, and imminently memorable.

Mixed Structures

Mixed structures use various combinations of the seven methods that were previously presented. For example, Master Presenter Terry Paulson uses the story of how air transportation has changed to anchor his topic of change management. He uses pictures and words (Figure 3-1 and Figure 3-2) to illustrate the changes the role of stewardess has undergone since the 1930s.

THE ORIGINAL EIGHT:
Ellen Church, Alva Johnson, Margaret Arnott, Inez Keller, Cornelia Peterman, Harriet Fry, Jessie Carter and Ellis Crawford

Figure 3-1

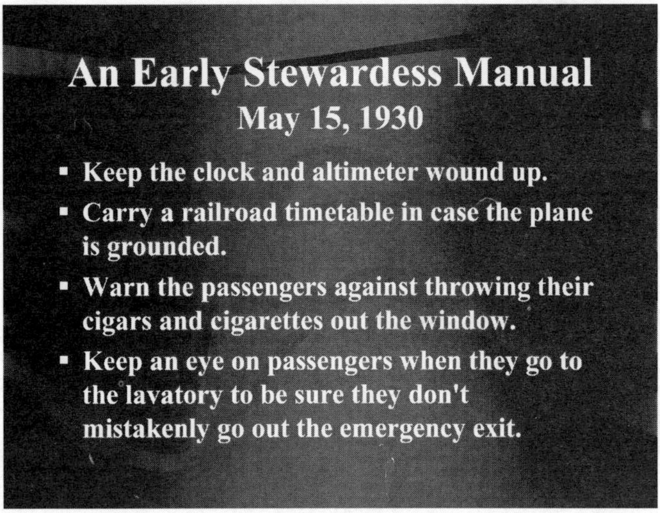

An Early Stewardess Manual
May 15, 1930

- Keep the clock and altimeter wound up.
- Carry a railroad timetable in case the plane is grounded.
- Warn the passengers against throwing their cigars and cigarettes out the window.
- Keep an eye on passengers when they go to the lavatory to be sure they don't mistakenly go out the emergency exit.

Figure 3-2

The slides that Terry uses demonstrate that progress entails change. We can look at the information Terry presents both chronologically and metaphorically. If we look at the information chronologically, we can clearly see that how flight attendants did their jobs in the early days of flying in very different from the way that job is carried out today. At a metaphorical level, these slides represent the changes we must all undergo in order to progress. Terry uses these slides to anchor the topic of change management both chronologically and metaphorically. In this case, the mixed structure works beautifully. It was fun and so unique that it is remembered as vividly today as when it was presented a number of years ago.

3. Make Sure It Is Cohesive

In the perfect symphony, the composer must make sure that every note that should be in the symphony is included and that every note that should not be included is excluded, as the following quotation from Leonard Bernstein[2] so artfully points out.

> We are going to try to perform for you today a curious and rather difficult experiment. We're going to take the first movement of Beethoven's Fifth Symphony and rewrite it. Now don't get scared; we're going to use only notes that Beethoven himself

wrote. We're going to take certain discarded sketches that Beethoven wrote, intending to use them in this symphony, and find out why he rejected them, by putting them back into the symphony and seeing how the symphony would have sounded with them. Then we can guess at the reason for rejecting these sketches, and, what is more important, perhaps we can get a glimpse into the composer's mind as it moves through this mysterious creative process we call composing.

We have here painted on the floor a reproduction of the first page of the conductor's score for Beethoven's Fifth Symphony. Every time I look at this orchestral score I am amazed all over again at its simplicity, strength and rightness. And how economical the music is! Why, almost every bar of this first movement is a direct development of these opening four notes: [...]

And what are these notes that they should be so pregnant and meaningful that whole symphonic movement can be born of them? Three G's and an E flat. Nothing more. Anyone could have thought of them—maybe...

Just as the perfect symphony has included all of the notes that should be included and has not included any notes that should in fact be excluded, Master Presenters do the same with their words. This is much easier said than done. How do Master Presenters make sure they have developed a cohesive presentation? The following seven steps will help guarantee that your presentation is as cohesive as possible:

Step 1: Write a Mission Statement

Write a mission statement for your presentation and decide if each bit of the content advances that mission or not. For example, David Ropeik's mission is to help people make smarter and safer decisions in regard to accurately assessing and acting on the risks that they encounter. Similarly, Jack Welch's mission while president and CEO at General Electric was that GE would be the first or second best in each market division where it sold products or GE would pull out of that division. The mission statement for your presentation will help you stay on target and focus your message. It also makes it easier to get feedback from others as to whether or not you are achieving your goals.

Step 2: Develop Goals and Objectives

Develop your goals and objectives for your presentation and decide whether each bit of the content is aligned with them. For example, "When you leave here today, you should be able to..." [enumerate the objectives]. You can also remind the listener of the value you are providing by having a visual trigger such as a flip chart checklist, and check off each objective as you address it.

Step 3: Formulate and Answer Central Questions

For example, in a presentation on time management, the presenter might use "How can we do more in less time?" or "Have you ever considered the power of the 'Not to do list'?" or, "Are there ways that we can increase market share without adding additional costs?"

Step 4: Diagrams as Aids to Clear Thinking

Even if you don't use them in your final presentation, creating diagrams, such as flow charts and storyboards, can help to make your presentation preparations clearer and better organized. An organizational technique David uses is a simple circle. He shows the central thesis—his reason for speaking—at the top of the circle, as if it were occupying the 12 o'clock position on a clock face. Each supporting point then falls in sequence around the circle in clockwise rotation. Thus, each point can be seen in a clear sequence, culminating back to the central thesis. You could use a straight line rather than a circle, but the connection between your opening and your closing would not be as clear—or might not exist at all.

Step 5: Test the Presentation

Test your presentation with friends, fellow presenters, and/or an audience and ask for feedback about what should be included and/or excluded. You can also ask about specific parts of the presentation.

When Mark Victor Hanson and Jack Canfield published their *Chicken Soup for the Soul* series, they collect a large number of stories. They then use a focus group to rate the stories on a scale of 1 to 100, and the highest-ranked stories were selected to appear in their books. Therefore, one way to test market the content of your presentation would be to ask a focus group of your friends and/or colleagues to help you select the content and structure of the presentation.

Warning: Give your focus group a specific task and keep a tight rein. If you open your presentation to scrutiny by too many free-thinking, free-wheeling people, you could end up with a committee rewriting your presentation, and that would not be good for anyone.

Step 6: Successive Approximations

Successive approximations means that although the presentation will never be 100-percent cohesive, each time you work on it and/or get some great feedback, it will get better and better and closer and closer to its ideal form.

Step 7: A Call to Action

What do you want your audience members to think, feel, and/or do as a result of attending your presentation? If you cannot specifically answer these three questions, you are categorically not ready to present. For example, in David's business writing presentations, he tells the participants, "As a result of today's program, you will be able to write a business letter more clearly, concisely, and confidently."

EXERCISE
3-1

In your next presentation, what do you want the participants to think, feel, and/or do differently as a direct result of attending your presentation?

1. I want my audience members to think...
2. I want my audience members to feel...
3. I want my audience member to do...

4. Transitions Are the Keys to Clarity

Transitions are the keys to separating your ideas and achieving clarity. Transitions signal to the audience that the presenter has finished one topic and is about to begin the next. Transitions also give the presenter time to integrate previous material to compare and contrast, cite trends, or have a short mental break before starting the next topic, or to signal to the audience that you are transitioning from the opening to the body or from the body to the conclusion. In other words, transitions are integral to the success of any presentation.

Transitions are as important as your content—even the world's best content is received poorly if you do not pay enough attention to the transitions. In fact, if you have ever lost your place when speaking, it was almost certainly a result of a poorly formed transition. Presenters usually can explain their key points, but it is in the process of getting from one point to the next that we tend to lose our way.

Transitions allow you to summarize what has just been said, to alert your audience that there will be a change in topic, and to give the audience a break, time to relax, and/or to digest the previous topic and get ready to actively participate in the next.

Transitions as Summaries

It has been said that we have to hear something seven times before we can remember it. Transitions provide an excellent opportunity to go over the content one last time. The transitional summary also allows the audience members an opportunity to see and appreciate the value of the content and what they have learned from attending the presentation. These summaries also afford the listener the opportunity to think about how the content can be linked together. The summary can also present the material in a slightly different way that may be clearer and more understandable for the participants.

Transitions as Signposts

Transitions can act as signposts telling the audience what material will be presented next. They act as an advanced organizer, which will help the participants organize the material hierarchically and hence remember the material better.

Transitions as Breaks

Brad: A number of years ago, I was swimming in a Masters Swim Program. The Masters Swim Program is for adults who want to stay in shape. We entered the pool at 6:30 a.m., two mornings a week. The coach was fantastic, and we were all making a great deal of progress. I swam more laps than I ever thought possible and between sets, that is, between different types of strokes or repetitions of the same stroke, we were allowed to rest—that is, the coach gave us 17 seconds to rest. Now 17 seconds is not a lot of time. However, I learned to relax more effectively than I ever thought possible during those 17 seconds. In fact, you could say that we learned to relax as effectively as we learned to swim.

Just as the 17-second break helped the swimmers recuperate, and therefore swim as effectively as they could, Master Presenters know when to give their audience a break, to catch up, integrate, and reflect on the material being presented. Amateur presenters just keep right on going.

David: When I first started presenting full-day seminars, I assumed that the audience paid for a six-hour program, so I planned on giving them six hours of information. What a mistake that was. I found that no matter how good the information was, or how well it was presented, at about the four-hour mark, people began to tune me out. I didn't realize I was oversaturating them. I had yet to learn the power of the mental break. Of course, we are always mindful of the need for physical breaks, but only Master Presenters are as thoughtful in providing mental breaks. A mental break can be as simple as a quick joke or a short, fun exercise. Does it have to relate specifically to the point you were making? Not necessarily. But it must be fun.

I found, to my surprise, that when I started adding in frequent fun moments, the listeners' comprehension and retention went way up. As a result, they learned and took with them more knowledge, even though I was presenting less information.

The necessity to allow for rest breaks, integration breaks, and reflection breaks is one of the techniques that presentation coach, Betty K. Cooper[3] teaches; only Betty calls it HUD. For Betty, HUD stands for Hear, Understand, and Digest. Therefore, in addition to acting as signposts that guide both the presenter and the audience through the presentation, transitions also play an important role in giving the audience a break so they can learn from the presentation or digest the information as effectively as possible.

6 Types of Transitions

Transitions are aids to clear thinking and effective presentations. Now that we have outlined the purpose of transitions, we will next discuss six proven transition techniques to separate your ideas. They are:

1. Delineation.
2. Words and phrases.
3. Pictures.
4. PowerPoint.
5. Voice.
6. Body language.

1. Delineation is the simplest way to make a transition. The presenter simply states that he or she will be covering three main points. For example, the speaker says, "The first area of interest is our competitor's new marketing strategy; the second point is how our firm will counter our competitor's new strategy; and the third point is how we will measure our effectiveness." It is also likely that each of the main points will have sub-points and each of the sub-points will have to be delineated from each other as well as from the main points.

2. Words and phrases can also be used to indicate a transition from one topic to the next. We are all familiar with words and phrases such as *next, the following example, point one, point two, point three*, or *phase one, phase two*, and *phase three*, and as you have seen in this book, *Strategy 1, Strategy 2,* etc.

3. Pictures can indicate to the audience that you are leaving the present topic and moving to a new topic. Two of the Master Presenters that we have seen who are superb at using pictures as transitions are Richard Bolles and Janet Lapp.

Richard Bolles is the most widely read author on finding a job. In fact, his best-selling book *What Color Is Your Parachute?* is a classic in the field. In both his book and in his presentations, Bolles uses old pictures that are no longer copyrighted to masterfully signal to his audience that a transition is taking place. Two examples of the pictures Bolles uses to signal a transition are as follows:

Figure 3-3

Figure 3-4

Brad: The one thing that Janet Lapp does that impresses me the most is that she is a master at transitions. For example, Janet uses slides of black and white pictures as transitions between topics. What I liked so much about Janet's use of these pictures was that they signaled a clear transition between one topic and the next, and at the same time let the audience have a very short relaxation break, and/or use the time to integrate and/or reflect on the material that had just been presented. This is Betty K. Cooper's HUD principle, which stands for "letting your audience Hear what was said, Understand what was said, and Digest what was said." This time it uses pictures in place of verbal pauses.

Figure 3-5

Figure 3-6

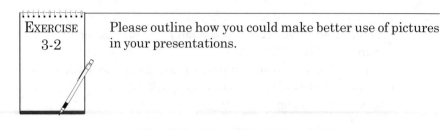

EXERCISE
3-2

Please outline how you could make better use of pictures in your presentations.

4. PowerPoint lets you use a specific type of slide or color scheme to indicate that you are making a transition in your thoughts and/or ideas, in addition to having a specific type of slide title that tells the audience that you are changing topics. Other useful techniques to indicate transitions in PowerPoint are to use a puzzle, headers and footers, and pictures within the PowerPoint slide. For example if you are going to use puzzles, the overview shows the completed puzzle (Figure 3-7). Then each piece of the puzzle represents a transition from one topic to the next.

Figure 3-7

One of the most unusual uses of pictures in transitions was a presentation Brad attended by Dr. Terry Paulson.[4] Terry presented at the 2001 annual meeting of the National Speakers Association in Dallas, Texas. Even for a seasoned professional speaker, this is one of the most nerve-racking presentations he or she will ever have to give because it is in front of peers, and because this is an extremely well- attended meeting, with more than 2,000 participants. If the speaker does well, it will be remembered for years, if not, it will be remembered for decades.

The picture Terry used was of a handmade quilt with different sections of the quilt representing the topics he was going to speak about, such as achievement, heroes, wisdom, purpose, change, and relationships. It was an exceedingly good choice for a couple of reasons. First, quilts remind us of the care and dedication that went into making them. They have a warm and cozy feel, and they take on a special meaning for us, for example, when a grandmother makes a quilt celebrating a special occasion such as a wedding or a birth. It is also no accident that a great deal of awareness and empathy was deservingly created for people who died of AIDS with the National Quilt Project. Terry used the quilt slide to organize his presentation, to make clear transitions, and to give the audience members time to reflect on the materials that had just been presented in the previous section.

Figure 3-8

What we liked so much about Terry's use of that picture was that it signaled a clear transition between one topic and the next, and at the same time let the audience have a very short relaxation break, and/or use the time to integrate and/or reflect on the material that he had just presented.

David Paradi uses footers at the bottom of his PowerPoint presentations.[5] This particular presentation had five sections: Overview, Research, Strategic, Programs, and Customer Service. Each word was highlighted with a box that appeared around words indicating to which section David was speaking. As well, the movement from section to section subtly reinforced the transitions. Also note that David used pictures in addition to the highlighted words to indicate a transition to a new topic within his presentation. Here is an example from one of David Paradi's presentations:

Figure 3-9

5. Voice allows you to use pauses, changes in tone, or different volumes to emphasize a change from one idea to the next. Most speakers underestimate the length of their pauses because they are uncomfortable with silence. Master Presenters on the other hand are comfortable with the four-second pause. In order to reach the desired length, at first you may have to count silently to yourself: "one locomotive, two locomotives, three locomotives, four locomotives." Perhaps an even more effective way to measure your pauses is one espoused by our colleague Dave McIlhenny. He said, "Don't count your pauses in seconds, count them in heartbeats." Thus, he taught presenters to "give it a full four-heartbeat pause." To become more comfortable with pausing, count the length of the pauses when observing Master Presenters. Also practice the same transition while speaking into a tape recorder, and experiment with different pauses. Listen to the results and solicit feedback from others. When we teach the Seven Strategies of Master Presenters or when we coach speakers individually, we help them learn to pause by silently counting. This is a relatively simple change, yet the results are astounding.

After you have mastered the pause, the next technique that Brad was taught by Betty K. Cooper, is the graduated pause. The graduated pause is used when you are introducing three or more main points of wisdom. After the first point, you use a one-beat pause; after the second point of wisdom, you pause for two counts; and after the third point, you pause for three counts. The net result is to build suspense, and the suspense builds impact.

Brad: Another vocal technique is to use different volume to emphasize movement from one topic to another. For example, in my Master Negotiators presentations, I illustrate building the world with creative or wasteful solutions by comparing two airports. The first airport was well planned and well used. The second was poorly planned and became a white elephant. I speak about the creative problem-solving that was behind the first airport in a loud and vibrant tone of voice. I then say, "You can contrast that with Mirabel [the white elephant]." However when I say, "You can contrast that with..." I say it with a much softer tone of voice to emphasize the contrast with my tone of voice as well as in the words themselves. In addition, you can also use different voices to mimic different people speaking about different ideas.

6. Body language, including the use of gestures and movement, can be an incredibly effective method to signal transitions. For example, you can use your fingers to reinforce the first, second, and third points. You can also use different parts of the stage. For example, you can move to the center of the stage, pause, and deliver your point of wisdom, conclusion, and so on. If you are talking about a difference of opinion between two experts in any given field, you can give expert A's point of view from center stage left, then give expert B's point of view from center stage right, and then move to center stage forward to give your point of view or to ask a profound question of the audience.

As you can see, these techniques can be combined to add even more emphasis. In the last example, when the presenter moved to center stage forward to deliver his or her conclusion, he or she could move to center stage forward, then pause, and add extra volume. All three of these techniques, moving to center stage forward, pausing, and increasing volume helped to differentiate the conclusion from the main body of the presentation.

EXERCISE 3-2

Part I: Look specifically at how Master Presenters use both single and multiple techniques to develop clear transitions from one idea to the next and from one topic to the next, and from one part of their presentation (for example, from beginning, to the middle, or to the end) of their presentation. Please list three specific techniques that made these transitions effective.

Part II: In the next section, please outline three specific techniques that you will use to make your transitions more effective.

5. The Critical Importance of Timing

If you are going to be a part of a conference or series of presentations, always ask to see the entire program. Brad was participating in a conference and the organizers only allowed for a 15-minute break in the afternoon. What they and all of the rest of the speakers didn't anticipate was that the ratio of female attendees to male attendees was about 10 to one. This meant that the washroom facilities were totally inadequate for the women who had attended. Breaks ended up being longer than scheduled. Add to that the fact that some presenters went over their time and Brad and the last speaker only had 30 minutes each to do their presentations. Among the lessons that Brad learned were to expect the unexpected, be prepared to be flexible, know what you can leave out, and audiences will forgive a number of things but going overtime is usually not one of them. In other words, you have to know and understand the structure of the presentation so well that you can change it on a dime so it will be just as seamless as the longer one would have been.

Ed Tate, the 2000 World Champion of Public Speaking, recommends preparing two versions of every presentation—a full-length version and a 10-minute version. This way, he says, if the time for the presentation is cut, you can go to the shorter version confident that you will still be able to make your most important point.

David: This is a lesson I learned the hard way. I was invited to deliver a 45-minute keynote address for a conference that was supposed to start at 8 a.m. on a Saturday. I arrived at the venue Friday night and met the conference organizer. I said, "I just want to verify that I will be speaking tomorrow from 8 to 8:45." She said, "Well, the opening *session* starts at 8." I said, "So what will take place before me?" She said, "There will be a flag processional, the pledge of allegiance, an invocation, a welcome from the district governor, a proclamation from the Mayor...." At this point, I said, "So what time will I start?" She said, "About 8:35." I added 45 minutes to 8:35 and said, "So you want me to stop at 9:20?" She said, "Oh, no! We have to be out of here by 8:45!" My 45-minute presentation had suddenly shrunk to a 10-minute presentation.

One of the participants in *The Seven Strategies of Master Presenters* course made a presentation, which incidentally is one of the finest presentations we have ever seen. The presentation was a perfect summary of the importance of superior organization and timing to illustrate his message. Even more interesting, it was not a presentation by a nationally known speaker.

The participant, Sandy, purposely misled the audience as to the topic, which he said was time management. Sandy placed a Styrofoam cup on a table at the front of the room. He then asked a rhetorical question: "How long would it take to smash a Styrofoam cup?" The estimates lasted from three to seven seconds. Sandy then smashed the cup on the table, which made a loud explosion. The noise and the subsequent startled response was enough to make sure that everyone in the audience was fully alert when he announced that the time it took to completely destroy the cup was 0.7 seconds.

Sandy then took us through the anatomy of a car accident where he graphically explained what would happen to the car and its occupants during the 0.7 seconds it took for a high-speed impact. The organization of the presentation was chronological. Sandy showed seven slides, depicting what would happen at 0.1 seconds, at 0.2 seconds, at 0.3 seconds, all the way to 0.7 seconds. Each slide had a picture of what was happening to the car and its driver at each one-tenth of a second. The pictures were somewhat blurry so as not to be so gruesome that the audience would not be able to process the cognitive message Sandy was trying to get across. The pictures were further muted as the text appeared and he explained what was happening during each tenth of a second. Sandy then ended his presentation with a call to action, that all vehicle drivers and passengers should wear seat belts at all times.

Why was this presentation so powerful? First, it had the element of surprise—the smashing of the cup. Then it had the perfect segue: seven-tenths of a second to smash the cup being perfectly analogous to the seven-tenths of a second it takes to smash a car. Lastly, the presentation was perfectly timed and organized using one-tenth of a second increments to explain what happened to the car and its occupants at each tenth of a second, and it ended with a clear call to action—wear your seat belts at all times.

As this chapter illustrates, a good presentation begins with good content, but good content without good organization is nothing but a jumble of competing ideas, examples, and images. Once your content and organization are top-notch, you can move on to the finer points of dynamic delivery—which is the topic of our next chapter.

STRATEGY

4

Develop
Dynamic Delivery

Speeches are like babies: Easy to conceive, hard to deliver.

—Pat O'Malley, author

The speech sounded very much like an economics lecture. It had no oratorical eloquence, and did not use many stories, jokes or illustrative references to give the speech human interests. You couldn't do much worse than that, could you? The speech was the first of a young orator named John F. Kennedy.

Many presenters overprepare on content and underprepare on delivery while others have little content but great delivery. Master Presenters find the ideal balance between the two. In this chapter, we will look at 13 techniques to help you develop a dynamic delivery:

1. Avoid hackneyed openings.
2. Use powerful language.
3. Make your presentation flow.
4. Add suspense to your storytelling.
5. Use props to add impact to your presentation.
6. Use drama to enhance your presentation.
7. Use the pause that brings applause.

8. Use humor appropriately.
9. Harness the power of experiential exercises.
10. Consider role-playing.
11. Use action learning.
12. Prepare for questions.
13. Develop endings with impact.

1. Avoid Hackneyed Openings

Hackneyed means "made commonplace by frequent use." There is no more common opening than the predictable and perfunctory "I am so happy to be here," or, "It is indeed a pleasure to be here." While that may be true, your listeners have heard hundreds, if not thousands, of presentations start the same way. The natural response for the audience is to tune out the presenter, and you lose the most valuable time you have to make a strong first impression.

In *The Sir Winston Method*, James C. Humes explains Winston Churchill's aversion to such phrases. Churchill once told an associate, "I never say, 'It gives me great pleasure,' to speak to any audience because there are only a few activities from which I derive intense pleasure and speaking is not one of them."[1]

You may think you need to open with an acknowledgement or praise of your hosts. Humes suggests your opening is not the best place for such comments: "If you really want to say something nice about the organization or if you have to single out a few in the audience for special mention, save it for the middle of the speech, when it is believed. Churchill believed that praise in the beginning of the speech comes off as flattery; the same praise in the middle of the speech comes off as sincerity."

EXERCISE 4-1	Listen to as many introductions as you can.
	Which were hackneyed, boring, and uninspiring? What effect did this have on your expectations for the rest of the presentation?
	Which were original, grabbed your interest from the first seconds, and were uplifting? What made them original? What effect did this have on your expectations for the rest of the presentation?

2. Use Powerful Language

Powerful language enhances your sense of presence and the belief that your message is incisive, important, and worth the participants' time and efforts to listen to it. Weak language lessens your sense of presence and engenders a belief that both you and your message are not worth listening to. Consider the following situation where a male university student wants to invite a female student on a date. Imagine him saying, "I wonder if you might possibly consider going to the movies with me on Saturday night, but I know you are very popular, so if you wanted to tell me at the last minute that would be all right too." Such weak language would probably produce a less-than-favorable outcome.

Likewise, using too many qualifiers in a presentation makes the speaker look unsure and uncertain. The audience will quickly assume that the speaker is neither worth listening to nor worthy of its attention.

For example, saying, "I guess what I'm trying to say is..." or, "I would like to share with you an opportunity I think we have..." puts the speaker in a position of weakness. On the other hand, if the presenter says to an audience of salespersons, "Would you like to learn a proven method that will help you close 10 percent more sales?" the presenter would have their full and undivided attention.

Another word that is often used in a weak context is the word *hopefully*. Being told that today's presenter is here to *hopefully* motivate the troops, sounds as though the speaker is speaking from a position of weakness. Imagine a cardiac heart surgeon about to do a double bypass on a patient saying, "Hopefully today's operation will go well." Most people would look for a new surgeon. If a presenter uses weak language, most audiences will soon look for a new presenter.

EXERCISE
4-2

Are there weak words or phrases that suck the life out of your presentations? Is there more powerful language you could use in its place?

3. Make Your Presentation FLOW

Expert presentation coach Max Dixon says you want your presentation to flow and that FLOW stands for what you say First, Last, Often, and Well.[2]

What You Say First

If you have ever attended or seen an exceptional concert, you may have noticed that both the beginning and the ending were exceptionally well done.

The primacy effect and the recency effect state that we are most likely to remember what we hear first and what we hear last. For example, view Barbara Streisand's *Timeless* concert, Fleetwood Mac's *The Dance* concert, or any other performer whom you especially admire and look carefully at how he or she constructed both the beginning and the ending to see the primacy and the recency effects in action. What you say first is critically important because many listeners have already formed an opinion of you as a speaker and are forming expectations of your presentation within the first seven to 90 seconds.

We recommend you spend a great deal of effort on getting your beginning and ending just right. Paradoxically, you are probably better off starting by preparing what you will say last. There are two principal reasons behind this assertion. First, the beginning is almost always the hardest to do. Second, deciding on your ending will help you focus your whole presentation. Craig Valentine, the 1999 Toastmasters World Champion of Public Speaking says, "One reason most speakers don't get their message across to an audience is because they don't know what their own message is. So before you speak or write a single word, you must determine exactly what you want the audience to think, feel, or do as a result of hearing you." Therefore, you need to ask yourself, "What do I want my audience to *think*, *feel*, or *do* as a result of attending my presentation?" This line of reasoning, starting with what you will say last, is summed up beautifully in one of the most famous lines from Stephen Covey's *The 7 Habits of Highly Effective People*[3]—"Start with the end in mind."

Your ending gives you a chance to summarize your main points; tell a short story; use a quote, poem, or metaphor to make sure that the meaning of what you are presenting is as three-dimensional and clear as possible; or to use a mnemonic to make it easy for your audience to remember your key points. The ending should also provide the final motivation to overcome the inertia that we all feel when we have to start a new task or do something differently than we have done before. Your ending should include something that can pass the "five-year test." That is, it should be so good that even though they may have forgotten you, they will remember your message five years into the future.

What You Say Often

In music, it is the refrain; in writing, it is the theme. A listener's mind will wander, no matter how dynamic the presenter or how compelling the message. Consequently, it is a mistake to think, "I said it; they heard it." Listening is greatly different than reading. When reading, you can always go back and reread. But when listening to a live performance, you can't go back and re-hear. Therefore, if it is important, say it more than once. In a similar vein, David talks about the three Rs of speaking: Repetition plus Restatement will help your message be Remembered.

With this repetition, you will give your audience a mantra they won't soon forget. It's just like in advertising where the best advertisements are so good they become part of our long-term memory. Think of some of the best advertisement slogans you have ever heard— slogans such as "Where's the beef?" and "Don't leave home without it." Master Presenters take full advantage of the same principle in their presentations. For example, in Brad's course on negotiating skills, he repeats, "You can't change somebody's mind, if you don't know where their mind is" seven times. We do the same in *The Seven Strategies of Master Presenters* course when we say that "most people overprepare on content and underprepare on delivery."

Caution: If what you say often is not meaningful, memorable, or sincere, it will have the opposite effect of what you intended. Instead of making your presentation soar, it will make your presentation bomb. So, if it's important, repeat it; if you repeat it, make sure it's important.

EXERCISE 4-3

Look at what you say often during your presentation. If it is important, do you say it frequently enough? Do you say it in a very memorable way? How could it be more like a mantra?

What You Say Well

Pay close attention to what you say well. Sometimes, when giving a presentation, the muse is with you and you are able to capture the essence of what you are saying—your word choice is perfect, and the phrase is highly memorable. One way to listen carefully and to improve at the same time is to record your presentations. Don't just record the big events. Record every presentation, including your practice sessions. Many speakers have had the experience of accidentally finding the perfect word or phrase, were absolutely certain that they would remember it, only to find that they quickly forgot it.

In addition to performing your own self-assessment of what you say well, ask others what *they* think you say well. At times, others will summarize what you say better than when you said it, so don't be afraid to modify even your best phrases to make them better.

Likewise, it is possible to use a quote as a refrain throughout the presentation. For example, in speaking to daycare workers on the importance of their jobs, Carla Angleheart repeated a line from Kahlil Gibran: "Love is work made visible," to electrify her point on the importance of their work. Sometimes what you say well and what you say often will merge as in Martin Luther King's "I Have a Dream" speech. Dr. King skillfully employed the vivid, memorable phrase "I have a dream" nine times in just over two minutes. He said it often. And he said it very, very well.

EXERCISE 4-4

Follow the next four steps to improve the FLOW of your next presentation.

Step 1: What are three specific things you could do to improve what you say First?

Step 2: What are three specific things you could do to improve what you say Last?

Step 3: What are three specific things you could do to improve what you say Often?

Step 4: What are three specific things you could do to improve what you say Well?

4. Add Suspense

Brad had a wonderful opportunity to hear Ann Bloch[4] present at the National Speakers Association (NSA) Annual Convention in August, 2000. Ann's presentation was titled *The Alfred Hitchcock Effect: Build Suspense into Every Story*. With such a great title, it was standing room only. Those who were fortunate enough to attend weren't disappointed because Ann's content was as good as her title.

She pointed out that more than 90 percent of all presenters use a chronological approach to organize and tell their stories, and that by adding flashbacks and foreshadowing, we can add suspense, novelty, and intrigue to our presentations. Ann stated: "Foreshadowing and flashback make ordinary stories spellbinding! [You can]...restructure your stories to captivate audiences from the first word. Like the legendary director [Alfred Hitchcock], you can reveal details deliberately, not chronologically, to sustain suspense. Master storytellers weave both techniques to mesmerize listeners."

Ann then artfully illustrated Hitchcock's three variations on a theme with three movies. The first movie was *Raiders of the Lost Ark*. In this movie, all of the action takes place chronologically. The film starts out with Indiana Jones lecturing on archeology in his classroom and then shifts quickly into the adventure.

To illustrate flashbacks, Ann chose the movie *Snow Falling on Cedars*. This beautifully told story is a courtroom drama, however, each time one of the characters takes the witness stand, the movie flashes back to explain that character's development as well as to move the story forward.

Ann then illustrated foreshadowing with the film *American Beauty*. Foreshadowing is a technique that tells you in advance what the outcome is or at least provides a clue as to how an event or action will play out. You then go back in time to figure out how the outcome occurred. For example, in many of Hitchcock's movies, the audience knows who the murderer is. Hitchcock then takes you back in time and you and the detectives have to figure out how that outcome was arrived at. In *American Beauty*, the film begins with foreshadowing when the male protagonist of the film says:

My name is Lester Bernham. This is my neighborhood, this is my street, this is my life. In less than a year, I'll be dead. Of course, I don't know that yet.

Then the rest of the film moves forward to that ending.

We can now look at how these three approaches can be used in telling a story that Brad uses in his presentation on negotiating skills.

Brad: When my daughter was 18 months old, she had a very bad eye accident. She tripped and fell head first into a store display and one of the pegboard hooks badly damaged her eye. We were incredibly lucky, and a year later Katie's eye had recovered perfectly. I use this story in my negotiation course to explain how I negotiated to have the hooks changed and the store made safer. Using the three variations, I can tell the story in chronological order, or I can tell it with flashbacks or foreshadowing.

Chronological:

My wife and son were negotiating the purchase of winter boots. He wanted the winter boots with the *Teenage Ninja Mutant Turtles* decal on them that were twice as expensive as the same boot without the decal. At the same time, my daughter, who was then 18 months old, spotted character slippers, which looked like stuffed animals and were suspended on pegboard hooks from three feet down to the floor. I let her out of her stroller, and she ran to play with the slippers. Unfortunately, as toddlers do, she tripped and fell head first into the display. To my horror, I couldn't get to her in time, and one of the display hooks caught her in the eye…. A year later, Katie's eye perfectly corrected itself and with a lot of persuasion, the store changed all 10 million of its display hooks at a cost of $2.9 million.

Flashback:

To this day, I still have nightmares of the day we went to have our family's Christmas picture taken. It all started out as an ordinary trip to the mall….

Foreshadowing:

My 18-month-old daughter cost several major department stores $2.9 million.

Each of these techniques works very well. I have tried all three methods in my presentations and the one that has the most impact for this particular story is foreshadowing. Experiment with all three and ask for listener feedback as to which one works the best.

EXERCISE 4-5

Part I: As they are being delivered, analyze the organizational structure of several of the stories from the best presentations you attend. Did the presenter use any combination of the methods presented here? Please note that this exercise is more difficult than it first appears, as Master Presenters often organize their presentations in a way that appears seamless.

Part II: Develop a story by using one of these three methods (chronological, foreshadowing, or flashbacks). Choose a technique that you have not used before or with which you have the least experience.

Doug Stevenson likens excellent story development and storytelling to making spaghetti sauce:

> You may start out with tomato sauce, but that's not enough by itself. Nobody would ever mistake plain old tomato sauce for tangy, savory spaghetti sauce. Tomato sauce is a good foundation, but you need to add oregano, basil, green peppers, garlic, (at least in our family!), and onions to make it fulfill its potential. Then it needs to simmer for a while. After all the ingredients mix and mingle, then you've got full-flavored spaghetti sauce.
>
> Your story is like that. It's a good place to start, but you need to add garlic and onions, which in story terms are the equivalent of a substantive point and a solid organizational structure. Then, you need to spice it up with acting techniques that help audience members SEE what you're SAYING. Then, the story needs to simmer over time, which is the creative process in which you write, re-write, rehearse, practice, and polish. Finally, you've cooked up a mentally and visually delicious story, which has the power to move people to laughter and tears, and which will be remembered long after you're gone.[5]

In summary, the power of stories depends on crafting superbly developed tales combined with a seamless delivery—just like Hitchcock.

5. Use Props for Impact

Props, if properly used, can add drama and impact to your presentation. In his best-selling book on presentation skills, *Do Not Go Naked into Your Next Presentation*, Ron Hoff says, "If there's a noun in your presentation, consider showing what the noun represents."[6] For example, in Brad's presentation on *The Seven Strategies of Master Negotiators*, he talks about how Master Negotiators know how to ask the right question, in the right way, at the right time, and that the answer to that question can be a key that helps the negotiator unlock the negotiation and resolve the issue to everyone's satisfaction. When Brad says the word *key,* he brings out a very large old antique key, allowing him to make the point visually and aurally, thus increasing the dramatic intent as well as helping the participants remember the point.

Props can make even dry and technical presentations come alive, as Brad illustrates:

Brad: I was coaching a group of senior managers at a local dairy on how to give "High Impact Presentations." Most of the material they had to present to their staff was of a rather dry and technical nature. One of the challenges that one of the presenters (Joe) had was to give a presentation on the cost of producing yogurt containers that subsequently became damaged and therefore could not be used. We developed the following prop in which he was able to get his presentation off to a strong start.

Joe started his presentation by dumping a handful of assorted coins into a wastepaper basket. Needless to say, this got his audience's attention. He then said, "Every time we damage a yogurt container, we throw money in the garbage, money that could help our company be more competitive through better research and development, money that could be used for better staff training, or money that could be spent on employee benefits such as an on-site gym or daycare facility."

Did Joe get and hold his audience's attention? Absolutely! He did it by the creative use of props to add significant impact to the beginning of his presentation and by showing his audience how it affected them (WIIFM—What's In It

For Me). In summary, props are an excellent way to make your message more creative, unique, and memorable.

Finding Props

To draw a parallel from the famous line from the movie *The Sixth Sense*: "I see dead people, I see dead people everywhere," Master Presenters see props, they see props everywhere. First of all, you have to train yourself to be vigilant, constantly on the lookout for props. For example, Brad was in a gift shop and saw the following picture that he found to be perfect for illustrating one of the five approaches to conflict management: Take It or Leave It.

Figure 4-1

Another excellent source to help you see the creative use of props are buskers or street performers. If the busker captivates his or her audience, he will make it in this extremely demanding business. If he is not captivating, he is soon looking for another job. Buskers must be relentless innovators because the job requires that they travel light. Therefore, they often make ingenious use of props, including the audience members. Watching buskers is also a great way to see how to increase audience involvement.

Plays are also excellent venues to see the innovative use of props in action. This is especially true if you have ever had the chance to see a one-person play. In a one-person play, an actor can play an entire cast of characters. The actor often changes characters by changing a hat while at the same time changing his or her voice and position on the stage. You can also ask your creative friends for their ideas on how to find and use props and look at how other presenters use props.

In the meantime, we wish you every success in discovering props to make your presentations more dramatic and impactful as the following example illustrates.[7]

> *In just a few words you have clarified [the] use of props. Recently I spoke to a sales team and referred to Client Objections as a can of worms best to be emptied. At which point I passed around a tin can filled with candy worms. Each participant took a worm or two!*
>
> *—Alice Wheaton, Canadian Association of Professional Speakers colleague*

Props as Trademarks

Brad: I felt that I was making a great deal of progress in the use of props when one day I walked into an advanced negotiation course wearing a neck brace after pulling a muscle. The participants had all taken the entry level negotiating course with me. I was surprised and delighted when one of them asked whether the neck brace was a new prop.

You can become so well-known for your use of props that they essentially become an unofficial trademark as they have for Master Presenter Harold Taylor. Harold is known for his dynamic and highly entertaining seminars on time management. In the center of the stage, Harold sets up a typical office desk representing the characteristically unorganized person. He has a table, which corresponds to the desktop, complete with a telephone, books, and papers piled on every available space. He then does a 15-minute hilarious routine that illustrates every time-management mistake in the book. This demonstration, combined with Harold's dry sense of humor, gets his audience going every time—even those who have seen it many times. As Harold is poking fun at himself, it is impossible for audience members not to see some of their own errors—especially as Harold is frantically going through all of the papers in search of an important piece of information he needs to close a deal on the phone.

The use of props will help you make your point, will help the audience remember your point, and will greatly contribute to developing your style and presence while presenting. If you are good enough, you may even develop props as part of your trademark as Harold Taylor has so successfully done.

6. Use Drama

In addition to the techniques that have already been discussed, drama can give life to just about any presentation.

David: One of the most stunning presentations I have ever seen was by J. A. Gamache, in a speech he delivered in the 2001 World Championship of Public Speaking. To achieve an extraordinary dramatic effect, he coupled creative staging with a prop. As he told a story of a poignant moment with his grandfather, he placed a simple wooden chair center stage. It was instantly apparent that as he spoke to the chair, that he was speaking to his grandfather. Technically, this was a monologue, but curiously, it was more like a dialogue as the chair brought his grandfather to life. But it became even more dramatic when, as he told of his grandfather's death, he lovingly tipped the chair, bringing it to rest on its back. No words were spoken; no words were necessary. The silence in the room at that moment was overwhelming.

EXERCISE
4-6

Describe a situation you have seen where a sense of drama greatly enhanced the presentation.

Describe how you will use drama to enhance an existing presentation or add value to a presentation you will give in the near future.

7. The Pause that Brings Applause

The right word may be effective, but no word was ever as effective as a rightly timed pause.

—*Mark Twain*

Darren LaCroix, the 2001 World Champion of Public Speaking, studied the videotapes of Toastmasters' World Champions from 1990–2000 and said, "One thing I found that every one of the winners had in common was that they all used pauses extremely effectively." In fact, Ed Tate, the 2000 World Champion of Public Speaking used one pause that was a full six seconds long. In stage time, six seconds of silence can seem like an eternity. Yet, in that powerful six seconds, he commanded the stage. He said more in silence than words ever could.

Brad: Twenty-five years ago I was a graduate student working on an advanced degree in psychology. I was extremely fortunate in securing an internship at the Family and Children's Centre. I found that all of the psychologists I got to work with were very knowledgeable and articulate. One psychologist, Chris Rainy, stood out as being the most articulate and I decided to use him as a model to help me become more articulate. Knowing about behavioral analysis, my first thought was that Chris sounded more articulate than I did because he had a larger vocabulary. However, when I observed him more carefully, Chris's vocabulary, with a very few technical exceptions, was not larger than mine. What I did notice, upon closer inspection, was that Chris sounded more articulate because he knew both when and how to pause. I decided to look more closely and found that Chris used four types of pauses: the articulation pause, the reflective pause, the dramatic pause, and the anticipatory pause.

The Articulation Pause

The articulation pause is a very short pause after almost every word. It allows the word to be pronounced clearly and distinctly. A good test of how articulate you sound is to record yourself speaking or reading. If your words flow too closely into one another, you will have to slow down and add a slight pause after each word until each is distinct. However, if the words are too distinct, you will sound too formal or stilted. One of the best things you can do is to record yourself speaking or ask others for specific feedback on how well you articulate your words.

EXERCISE
4-7

The purpose of this exercise is to help you learn to have a short articulation pause after each word. Please notice that although the following exercise is grammatically incorrect, it is incorrect for a reason: to allow almost every word to end in "s." If you don't use articulation pauses, then instead of each "s" and each word being distinct, you will find yourself hissing like a snake. Try repeating the following exercise three times. Ask friends or colleagues if you articulate each word. Also ask them if you have enough volume to reach the four corners of the room. An alternative is to recite Moses Supposes into a tape recorder and listen to how well you articulate each word and if your articulation pauses are long enough.

> Moses supposes his toes is roses,
> But Moses supposes erroneously.

The Reflective Pause

Why is a reflective pause so powerful? Because it emphasizes the last words the speaker said. In that moment of silence the listener is thinking, "The speaker is giving me time to think about what he just said, so it must have been important."

Sometimes we just need a little time to savor or reflect on an interesting point, conclusion, fact, statistic, or story. The reflective pause allows your audience to do this without feeling that it has to catch up as the speaker goes on to the next point.

As we discussed earlier, presentation coach Betty K. Cooper calls this the HUD principle (see Strategy 3). So many presenters are in love with so much of their material that they try to cram everything into one presentation. You can't cram wisdom, and wisdom is what excellent presentations are all about. Therefore, as presenters we need to give the participants time to Hear what we say, Understand our message, and Digest the wisdom.

The Dramatic Pause

With a word processor, we can add emphasis by boldfacing a word or phrase. When speaking, we can add emphasis by pausing both before and after the word or phrase that we want to emphasize.

David: When I tell the story of a time I experienced a very embarrassing speaking moment, I use a dramatic pause to emphasize one important word. The event I retell was of the moment in a timed speech contest that I discovered someone had switched my flip chart with someone else's. There was no time to correct the mistake, so I had to finish the rest of my speech without my critically important prop. I then explain that I immediately left the room and went out to walk the streets while wallowing in self pity. "I wanted to go back in there and tell everyone that it wasn't my fault. I wanted to tell everyone that it wasn't me who had screwed up, it was someone else. I wanted to go back in there and blame…[four-second pause, shake head]…but I knew I couldn't do that. Because I've learned that if I am to accept the credit for my successes, I must accept the responsibility for my failures."

In that four-second pause, the word "blame" resonates. It signals an abrupt shift of momentum and mood, all without words—and that pause creates more drama than words ever could.

The Anticipatory Pause

Anticipatory pauses build suspense. As in a well-told joke, you draw it out just enough to tantalize your audience. Jack Benny provided a memorable example of its use. With his well-honed reputation as a miserly tightwad, the classic moment played out like this: A robber points a gun at Benny with the demand, "Your money or your life." At least 10 seconds pass. The robber, puzzled at the delay, shouts, "Well?" Benny replies, "I'm thinking, I'm thinking!" The punch line was amusing, but it was in the anticipation that the real humor lay. Today's master of the anticipatory pause is Lou Heckler. You can hear Lou in action in a presentation titled *The Pause That Brings Applause*. By listening to tapes of Lou's presentations, you'll hear the anticipatory pause at its best.

8. Use Humor Appropriately

I am accused of telling a great many stories. They say it lowers the dignity of the Presidential office, but I find that people are more easily influenced by a broad, humorous illustration than in any other way.

—Abraham Lincoln

Humor can make or break your presentation, but it must be used appropriately. Everyone likes to laugh, but few people can tell jokes. No problem. Getting laughs when you speak is not a matter of telling jokes. The most effective humor comes through observation and attitude—real-world examples and illustrations. The real key to Master Presenter Jeanne Robertson's success throughout her career is, as *Toastmaster Magazine* states, "...her humor—specifically, her ability to laugh at the funny things that happen (or don't happen) to her; and to invite others to laugh along with her."[8]

> Telling funny stories doesn't give a person a sense of humor. A real sense of humor means being able to laugh at yourself, and being able to laugh at day-to-day situations that are often anything but funny when they happen...And therein lies the added challenge. Being a professional humorist entails far more than getting a laugh. Your goal is to inform, to motivate and to impart some bit of wisdom from your experience to your audience. Humorous treatment of a given topic or story is a means to that end. By using humor, your message will be both more enjoyable and more memorable.[9]

Jeanne developed a method called "Jeanne's Journal System." The system was developed to help presenters capture "life-experience humor."[10] But often, the story has to be worked and reworked so it can reach its full potential. The method she invented to find and develop funny stories is called LAWS where "L" stands for Look and Listen to daily life events that have the potential to develop into a funny story. "A" stands for Ask. Jeanne relentlessly asks her friends, colleagues, and total strangers to recount funny or amusing events that happened to them and if she wants to use them, she asks permission. She also relentlessly asks for feedback on stories as she is developing them because sometimes things that she thinks are hilarious, others don't find amusing, and sometimes material that Jeanne is ready to discard, others find hilarious. "W" stands for Write it up. Writing it up will help ensure that you don't lose it and will give you another chance to improve it. The "S" stands for Stretch. Sometimes, adding just a bit of exaggeration will turn a funny story into a hilarious one.

The following example illustrates how she uses this method:[11]

> *When our son Beaver was in junior high school, he and his friends wanted to wear only Izod shirts. If there was no little alligator sewn somewhere on the garment, that garment hung in the closet until it no longer fit. In addition, the Izod shirts had to be worn with Levi jeans. Period.*
>
> *[At the same age,] Beaver and his buddies were attending numerous basketball camps in the summer. Time and time again we mothers received the typical camp letter telling us to make sure to sew labels in the clothes our boys brought to camp. With all this information, however, it wasn't until I was reading an old joke book that I developed the following piece of material.*
>
> *...Before one camp, the coach had the nerve to write me a letter that instructed, "Mrs. Robertson, When you bring your son to our camp, please do not mark his name in his clothes with a black laundry marker. We prefer that you use sewn-in labels with his name."*
>
> *Sewn-in labels? Sure. I thought it was a joke letter. When I realized it wasn't, I put it on the floor and kicked it. Then I wrote them back.*
>
> *"My name is Jeanne Robertson. I will be at camp with my son on July 13. His name is Levi Izod."*

However, Jeanne didn't get the idea for this piece of material until she was reading an old joke book and came upon a joke with a similar theme. Therefore, Jeanne recommends studying joke books to help master the art of joke and story construction, and to stimulate your own creativity in finding and developing funny stories. Jeanne also says that she seldom uses standard jokes, but that she will use them occasionally if the joke is perfect for the occasion. As Jeanne states, "A good joke that is told well and illustrates a specific point is a work of art."

Jeanne has one more strategy that has stood her in good stead, and it will do the same for you if you use it. "If you don't jot things down when they happen, a lot of good ideas get away. If you don't write up your stories soon after, a lot of good stories never materialize." Then keep your stories in an easily accessible story/humor file.

Almost every Master Presenter we spoke to will tell you that they had a terrific story, joke, or humorous incident, but they had forgotten it. It was only through listening to a previously taped copy of a particular presentation that this treasured material was found. Keeping a story/humor journal will help you be aware of and collect and remember material that can make the difference between a good presentation and a great one. Therefore, we recommend you carry a notepad with you at all times. When something makes you laugh, write it down. With notepad at the ready, pay attention—you'll be amazed at the funny things you see or overhear.

Because humor can make or break your presentation, we will look at Canadian Association of Professional Speakers member Ross MacKay's five reasons for using humor and five rules on how to use it effectively.

Ross's five reasons to use humor are:

1. To connect with your audience.
2. To make a particular point.
3. To change the pace or tone.
4. To make your message more palatable.
5. To entertain.

Ross's five rules on how to use humor are:

1. Surprise your audience—that's what the punch line does.
2. Allow your audience time to enjoy the joke when it works—if it doesn't work, just pretend it wasn't a joke and keep going.
3. Use humor to advance to subject of the presentation. The biggest crime is to use humor to get a laugh but it has nothing to do with the subject.
4. Make sure that your humor is appropriate—appropriate to your audience and appropriate to the event. If you have any doubt, don't use it.
5. Personalize your material; even a standard joke or introduction can have meaning when it is personalized.

David: Ralph C. Smedley, founder of Toastmasters International said, "We learn during moments of pleasure." Therefore, there are times when humor is needed just because the audience is getting restless or fatigued. In such cases, the audience needs to laugh just to keep them focused on the serious topic at hand. On occasions when I see the audience's attention start to wane, I'll bring out a short, amusing anecdote. The audience laughs, is refreshed, and we move on.

Dr. Terry Paulson, CSP, is one of North America's top-rated professional speakers and is the author of the book *50 Tips for Speaking like a Pro.*

Brad: What's your secret for making your content so engaging?

Terry: Early on in my work I was a youth director for high school-age kids and if you weren't funny, couldn't tell stories, and weren't authentic and prepared, they'd kill you. It was an early lesson on how to engage an audience and at the same time make sure that the humor has content and is grounded.

I came out of a research background that was strongly analytical, and I had to learn how to deliver, out of complexity, simple messages that were engaging and fun. A lot of people talk about humor being great to start with and maybe important to end with; I use humor throughout to keep the attention level of an audience, especially with an audience that has a short attention span and starts to wander.

I make sure that my content stays current and is practical. And the humor is an added value. People expect to have quite a lot of material and then select what is relevant to them.

Brad: How did you develop your warmth and sense of humor?

Terry: A lot of people know the importance of research, stories, and inspiration and don't realize how valuable humor is until they start to collect humorous stories and anecdotes around your topic areas. It's a fun way to elicit information.

You have to work at finding things that make you laugh. Then add it into one of your stories. I develop timing by telling a story 70 times before I ever use it on the stage. As I adjust it or make it shorter my timing starts to improve. Always ask yourself, "Is it funny or does it move my content forward?" Find excellent examples and then sharpen your delivery.

Laughter lets them know they are not alone. Laughter makes one audience out of the sub-audiences. It creates warmth and it increases their attention level. One of the things that creates warmth is that I talk to individuals rather than groups. I have eye contact with one person for up to 15 seconds, picking different people in different areas of the audience, and it creates warmth because I am talking more conversationally.

9. The Power of Experiential Exercises

When people enter the room for your presentation you do not have everyone's attention. Paul is wondering if this presentation is going to be another colossal waste of his time; Tina is thinking that she will sit near the back so she can sneak out; Dan is wondering if he can get a date with Julie on the weekend; Sara is making her grocery list; Pauline is editing a memo she brought with her; Ed is feeling badly about the fight he had this morning with his wife; Sue and Katie are wondering if the vice president is really having an affair with his secretary; and Michele is mentally preparing for the presentation she will be giving after yours.

You have to earn your audience's attention and you have to earn it fast. You have 90 seconds or less to earn their attention. If, in this short period of time, they decide that you are not worth listening to—you may never be able to gain their interest.

One method to help you get your audience's attention is with experiential exercises. Experiential exercises actively involve the audience in an exercise whereby they experience the point or topic on which you are presenting.

For example, Stephen Covey gave a keynote address at the 1999 National Speakers Convention in Anaheim, California. More than

2,000 speakers were in attendance and the room was packed. Covey started the session with an experiential exercise called "Which way is north?"

Covey asked everyone in the room to point to the direction that they thought was north. In looking around the room, we could see that our fellow attendees were pointing to every direction imaginable. Dr. Covey then asked the people who were sure that they knew which direction north was to stand up, close their eyes, and point north. Only about a tenth of the people stood up and there was an immediate burst of laughter, because those of us who were not sure, could see that those who were sure were once again pointing in every direction. Dr. Covey then said that our pointing in all of the various directions was analogous to most organizations, that is, most of us assume that we know in what direction the organization is going, but in actuality, the people who work in that organization do not have either a clear idea or a strong commitment to the direction in which the organization is moving.

The second exercise Covey used had to do with negotiation and influencing skills. Party "A" was anyone who was wearing glasses; party "B" was anyone who was not wearing glasses. The goal of the exercise was that party "A" had to convince party "B" to try on his or her glasses.

Brad: As an expert who constantly lectures on negotiating and influencing skills and who has written a book about influencing skills, I was hooked. My party "B" was a very fashionably dressed young man. Apparently he did not like the idea of even trying on my conservative looking glasses. I tried everything I could think of to get him to try them on. For a minute, it seemed as if my entire self-esteem rested on his trying them on, while a great deal of his self-esteem equally rested on his not trying them on.

This was an important lesson for me More importantly, the magic started when Covey suggested that for all of us (who were in the influencing role), our glasses had a specific prescription that was made just right for us and not necessarily just right for the party that we were trying to influence. Then Covey hit us all—right between the eyes—by saying that each of us developed and was entitled to our own perspective, and how many times per day and upon whom do we try to force our own perspective. I immediately thought of the times that I tried to impose my perspective on my children. Even thinking about Covey's presentation, six years later, I can feel the power of that exercise. Not only do we often try to press our own perspective onto others, as presenters we try to force our learning style onto others.

To summarize, experiential exercises, if done correctly, are some of the most powerful tools a presenter can use to help the participants understand the point that is being made, integrate that point into his or her own experience, and remember that point, all at the same time.

EXERCISE 4-8

Briefly describe the most powerful experiential exercises you have seen in a presentation.

How can you use the power of experiential exercises in one of your next presentations?

10. Role-Playing

Role-playing is typically done in workshops rather than seminars, but we have seen Master Presenters use this technique in large groups as well. The advantage of role-playing is that the participants can actually see if they have mastered the material or not. In many cases, they find that although their intellectual understanding of the concepts are fine, it is another matter altogether to put them into practice.

There are two major ways in which role-playing can add depth and breadth to your presentation. First, role-playing can help participants determine their understanding of the material and get a sense of their skill at applying the key concepts. Role-playing can serve as a perfect demonstration of a case or a situation where everyone in the audience can observe the skills being taught applied to a real-life situation.

Role-playing can be one of the best ways to learn, but not everyone will want to participate. Therefore, we recommend that you remind your participants that this is a purely voluntary activity and that many people learn better by watching—this is especially true of the reflectors in the group.

In role reversal, the person with the problem takes on the roll of their own problem person. There are two main advantages to role reversal. The person with the problem will almost always gain insight into the person he or she is having difficulty with. Second, the person with the problem will be able to experience how different words, arguments and strategies come across from the point-of-view of the other party.

Sometimes in role-playing situations, the person presenting the problem may *be* the problem. For example, as soon as a strategy is developed, this person comes up with an argument as to why that the intervention will not work. In some cases the person may be right. The situation may be so hopeless that Gandhi, Mother Teresa, or Winston Churchill could not do a better job, and the only real alternative is to live with it.

There are other times, however, when the person who suggests the problem situation vetoes on the spot and has no genuine interest in trying to solve the problem. In fact, the person presenting the problem has a conscious or unconscious vested interest in not solving the problem. And although he complains vehemently about the problem, he does everything in his power to maintain the problem in its present state (homeostasis) similar to the person who is in a bad marriage, who spends all of his time in therapy complaining about the problem, but does nothing to resolve it.

If you, as presenter, find this is the case, you will find that both you and everyone else in the room are getting increasingly frustrated. There is a technique, called alternative endings that has been designed for situations just like this.

For example, Brad had a very lively group of salespersons in one of his negotiating courses. He asked the group to describe what a positive ending would look like and then instructed the participants in the role-playing to act out the positive ending. As you can see, this technique gets everyone out of a negative spiral by focusing on what a positive ending to the story might look like.

One of the problems with role-playing, role reversal, and alternative endings is that you can lose the attention of the participants in the room who are not directly involved with the role-playing. In order to keep everyone involved, to increase the number of ideas, and to enrich both the quality and the quantity of the feedback, Brad developed an enhanced role-play methodology that he calls The Virtual VCR.

The Virtual VCR

The Virtual VCR is a technique used to give the participants immediate corrective feedback as to how well they are communicating and negotiating, as well as a chance to implement that feedback in the immediacy of the situation.

Step 1: Imagine that in the room you are in contains a gigantic VCR and that the open space is where a case study will be performed and recorded on videotape. Each participant and the instructor have remote controls. The remote control has four buttons: Stop, Offer/ Ask for Strategic Advice, Rewind, and Play. What this means is that at any time during the role-playing, any person in the room can stop the tape, offer or ask for strategic advice, rewind the tape to the correct spot, and then replay the tape with the participants having been given a chance to try out the "corrective feedback."

Step 2: The second step is to decide on a case. It can be a case that the instructor has prepared, the students have prepared, a case that has been designed on the spot where all of the participants have input, or a case on film that can be stopped so that the participants can continue the role-playing.

Step 3: Assign roles in the case study to the participants. Start by asking for volunteers. If after a suitable period of time there are not enough volunteers, ask some of the participants whom you think would be favorably predisposed to volunteer, but first make it absolutely clear to the class that everyone has the right not to volunteer.

Step 4: Give the participants the "Positive Feedback" guidelines, copies of the 3 × 3 Feedback Form (see Strategy 7), and start the "The Virtual VCR."

Positive Feedback Guidelines:

- The feedback must be specific.
- The feedback must be balanced.
- The feedback must be positive and constructive.

The course instructor must be a strong facilitator for this exercise to work well. Too much corrective feedback and the participants will lose their feel of the flow of the case. Too little corrective feedback and the exercise becomes just another role-play.

11. Use Action Learning

Remember your high school biology teacher? The one who used lecture notes from when Charles Darwin was a student and showed outdated movies that were so bad that even she fell asleep? Contrast that with action learning. In action learning, the participants are working at solving real-life problems. And you can up the ante and the energy level by having the class compare their solutions with the real-life outcome. A colleague named Dave Buffett gave us the perfect example:

> I was in the midst of an Executive MBA program. The class was divided up into competing teams. Our goal was to plan for the acquisition of one company by another. The teams took their task very seriously and planned their strategies. All of the teams were to present their strategies at the beginning of the next class. Imagine our surprise, when in the next class, the instructor introduced a guest lecturer—the vice-president from one of the two companies. The students then had to present their strategies to the vice president and after their presentations, he would tell them how it actually turned out and comment on where their strategies were the same, where the students' strategies were better, and where his strategy was better.
>
> We were geared up to present our strategies and see how well we compared with the other teams in the room, when the instructor announced that the actual vice president who was in charge of his company's negotiation strategy would be in the room to debrief this case with us. It raised the ante 100 percent. We felt that we were actually negotiating a real-life acquisition. The atmosphere in the room was electric. Learning just doesn't get any better than that.

To find out more about action learning, we highly recommend the *Harvard Business Review* article "Driving Change" by Susy Wetlaufer.[12]

EXERCISE 4-9

Briefly describe an engaging presentation you attended in which you had to solve a real-life problem.

Did the presenter(s) debrief the case with a real-life outcome?

Next, briefly describe how you can use this technique.

Will you provide a real-life outcome?

Turn Your Failures Into Gold Mines

Brad: I am often amused that people who know that I teach negotiation skills assume that I am a Master Negotiator and, although I am getting better, I know that I will have at least one spectacular failure every year. One of the things that I have learned is that Mother Nature is a persistent teacher and we will be given the same lessons over and over again

One such lesson was when I was unable to negotiate the release of course handouts from the print shop, which I turned into a case study for my negotiation course. It is reproduced below:

Econo Copy Store

You are asked to give a talk on effective negotiating skills for the Association of Dispensing Opticians. The talk is to take place on Saturday, September 15, at the Algonquin Hotel in St. Andrew's-by-the-Sea. The Association has agreed to pay you your regular half-day fee, transportation expenses, and one night's accommodation at the luxury resort hotel.

You have to leave your home by 8 a.m. on September 15th in order to leave your 2-year-old son with his grandparents and catch the noon ferry, which will save hours of driving. You and your spouse are very much looking forward to this relaxing trip.

As a professional speaker, you have handout materials that you will use to help illustrate your talk. As you have been extremely busy, your spouse took the handout material to the Econo

Copy Store on September 11th. The 60 copies of the handouts were to be ready by 2 p.m. on September 14th.

You arrive home at 4 p.m. on September 14. Your spouse walks in the door a few minutes later and states that he/she just returned from the emergency room at the local hospital. He/she explains that as he/she was leaving to get your handouts, he/she experienced an excruciating pain in his/her lower left abdomen. Both your spouse and a colleague thought that it could have been a case of appendicitis. After several hours at the hospital, the blood tests indicated that it was a new version of the 24-hour flu that mimics appendicitis.

It is now 4:15 p.m. You have to pick up your son from daycare and pick up the handouts. You decide to get your son first. You arrive at Econo Copy at 4:45. To your horror, the door is locked, and you notice a sign that says "Office Hours 8:30 a.m.–4:30 p.m." To your immense relief, the store clerk is still there counting out the day's receipts. You now have to negotiate for the release of the handouts.

Brad: By turning this example into a case study, I have learned a lot from observing my participants' innovative approaches. We can also learn that sometimes things are not negotiable and we have to go with our best alternative.

EXERCISE
4-10

Have you ever had a failure that you could turn into a teachable moment or exercise? Take a few minutes to describe it.

How could you turn it into a teachable moment or exercise in a future presentation?

12. Preparing for Questions

If you have ever had the experience of being an expert witness, you know that it can be a very grueling experience. At its worst, the opposing lawyers will be out to destroy both your testimony and your credibility. The lawyers representing the side that called you as an expert witness will prepare you and conduct a mock trial. First, they will take you through giving your testimony. Second, they will play the opposing lawyers and cross examine you in a manner that is similar to the way that they think you will be cross-examined. In other words, it is a dress rehearsal, so you, the expert witness, will be as prepared as possible.

Master Presenters use the same method to prepare for the questions that they will be asked by anticipating those questions, by having someone else anticipate the questions, or by having a dress rehearsal—sometimes with different types of audiences—so they will be as well prepared as possible.

Communications consultant Roger Ailes says that you should prepare to answer the five toughest questions that the participants will ask you. You can think up the questions on your own, however, it is often a good idea to get others to think up the questions. You can then role-playing the answers to actually see and hear how well you answer. Don't be afraid to do this several times until you get the answers just right. Even if you aren't asked directly the same question that you have prepared for, you can often make an opportunity to get the question in. One of the most famous examples of being absolutely well-prepared was during the 1984 presidential debates between Walter Mondale and Ronald Reagan. At the time, President Reagan was the oldest serving American President and he knew the question of his age would come up in the debate.

Reagan's response was, "I will not make age an issue in this campaign. I am not going to exploit, for political purposes, my opponent's youth and inexperience." Not only did the studio and television audience break up, the camera got a close up shot of Walter Mondale's reaction and he was seen breaking up on national television.

As Roger Ailes said, "Reagan hit a home run." He hit a home run because he was prepared, and he was prepared because he and his campaign team had anticipated all of the difficult questions that Reagan might be asked.

EXERCISE 4-11

Set up a page in your notebook with the following and please list five of the most difficult questions you can think of for your next presentation.

Question 1:

Question 2:

Question 3:

Question 4:

Question 5:

Next, please list three people who could both ask difficult questions and give you direct and constructive feedback on how well you answered them.

Person 1:

Person 2:

Person 3:

Dealing With "Off-the-Wall" Questions

Opening the floor to questions can be a risky adventure. Occasionally, you will be confronted with questions that are unintelligible or inappropriate. If the question is unintelligible, first ask for clarification. See if you can answer by rephrasing the question. On follow-up, if the question still is not clear and you have a sense that the person asking the question needs more time to think about what he or she is asking, suggest that it is an interesting question, and say you would like to think about it or that you could answer it better at the break. On some occasions, you can also ask if anyone in the audience would like to answer. Be careful, though, that you keep the discussion under tight rein. Some in the audience can be more interested in impressing others than in moving the discussion forward.

When asked an inappropriate question, such as one that is intentionally confrontational or hostile, do not attempt to answer it. Instead say something like: "That is a question that will take some time to answer, please meet me at the break or after the presentation," or "I am not the person to answer that." Then to further emphasize your unwillingness to pursue an inappropriate line of questioning, quickly reposition yourself on the podium to face a different part of the audience. By doing so, you send a visual message: "That conversation has ended."

You can get a better sense of how professionals deal with difficult and/or off-the-wall questions by listening to professional interviewers on both radio and television. Listen closely to their ability to be polite, firm, to ask just the right question at just the right time, and to deal with difficult and off-the-wall remarks and questions.

13. Develop Impactful Endings

The ending of your presentation is your last chance to encapsulate everything you said in your presentation. It is also your last chance to bring all of the material together in one unified whole. There are many ways to end your presentation. You can use an electrifying quote or a thoughtful story. You can ask a reflective question or use a contemplative poem. For example, Brad read the following poem at the end of a keynote on self-esteem to an audience of physically challenged children and adults:

Don't Quit

When things go wrong, as they sometimes will,
When the road you're trudging seems all uphill,
When the funds are low and the debts are high,
And you want to smile, but you have to sigh,
When care is pressing you down a bit,
Rest if you must, but please don't quit.

Life is unpredictable with its twists and turns,
As every one of us sometimes learns,
And many a failure turns about
When he might have won had he stuck it out;
Don't give up though the pace seems slow—
You may succeed with another blow.

Success is failure turned inside out.
The silver tint of the clouds of doubt,
And you never can tell just how close you are,
It may be near when it seems so far;
So stick to the fight when you're hardest hit—
It's when things seem worst that you must not quit.

—Author Unknown

Not only is the poem in and of itself a very strong ending, at this particular meeting the poem was read as a pianist played the theme from *Chariots of Fire*.

Brad: When I started reading the poem, there was no music. By the time I got to the second stanza, the music was barely audible and was becoming increasing audible, but not so much that it interfered with the reading of the poem. When I finished reading the poem, the impact was electrifying. The poem was an exceptional choice, and the music was absolutely wonderful, however, the poem and the music together moved the audience significantly more than either could have done alone. They could see themselves as heroes and heroines, just like the runners in the movie, because just by showing up at the conference, they had proved that they had not given up. The audience could anchor this experience in both the poetry and the music.

An additional hint to make your ending powerful: Master Presenter Mark Sanborn cautions us not to put FEAR into your endings. FEAR stands for False Endings Appearing Real. This happens when the presenter is so in love with his or her material that he keeps presenting when it is well past the time to close. Instead, Brad and David recommend giving your audience HOPE: Helping Others Persevere Effectively.

EXERCISE 4-12	Please describe the most powerful closing you have ever heard. Why was it so powerful?
	How can you make the closing of your next presentation more powerful?

By this point in this book we have looked at the importance of knowing your audience and of aligning your content to your audience's wants, needs, expectations, and aspirations. We have looked at developing outstanding content and organization and at 13 methods that can make your presentation more dynamic. All of these efforts will have been for naught if your listeners don't remember your presentation and/or put it into action. We'll address this element of your presentation in the next chapter.

STRATEGY

5

Make It Memorable, Actionable, and Transferable

A common weakness of many presentations is that a month, a week, or even a day after the presentation, no one remembers what it was about. Or, if they do remember something about it, they are not doing anything differently than they were doing before the presentation. Therefore, for your presentation to be effective, you must actively work to make it memorable, actionable, and transferable. There is a great deal to consider in bringing this strategy to fruition, but it pays big dividends. Not all presenters will want to use all the techniques in this chapter. Keynote speakers, for example, typically use a minimum of the interactive learning techniques described here. But others, who present full-day or multiday seminars, will find these techniques invaluable.

Make It Memorable

Research has shown that 24 hours after hearing a presentation, the listener will forget at least 50 percent of all the information presented. In 24 more hours, *another* 50 percent will be forgotten. This means that in a mere 48 hours after hearing a presentation, no matter how attentive the listener is trying to be, no matter how good his notes are, he will forget about 75 percent of everything the speaker said.

In light of these statistics, this section examines the types of memory and presents 11 techniques that are guaranteed to enhance the memorability of your presentation. As an added bonus, you can use these memory techniques to help you organize your presentations.

There are two types of memory: short-term and long-term. Short-term memory allows us to remember a telephone number or someone's name right after we have heard it for up to two minutes. This is the type of memory we use when we don't see a need for the new information after its immediate use.

Long-term memory allows you to remember the person's name for the foreseeable future. Presenters who truly make an impact are the ones who can most effectively place their message in a listener's long-term memory. That is the first purpose of this chapter: how to make you and your presentation more memorable.

The following section examines 11 memory-retention techniques:

1. Repetition and restatement.
2. Active vs. passive learning.
3. Increasing audience attentiveness.
4. Memory aids and mnemonic devices.
5. Stories.
6. Defining moments.
7. Anchoring.
8. Metaphors.
9. Three-act plays.
10. Music.
11. Games.

Most presenters use some of these techniques quite well. But Master Presenters not only know how to use *all* of the techniques, they also know the perfect time and place to use them.

1. Repetition and Restatement

Repetition is the mother of learning.

—*Author Unknown*

If we repeat a fact seven times, we increase our likelihood of remembering that fact by 80 percent. This is why Master Presenters repeat, repeat, repeat. Then they restate, restate, restate. Master Presenters know that if they repeat or restate a key point seven times, the listener's retention will be significantly increased. A common weakness of some presenters is to assume: "I said it; they heard it. Move on." True, the audience may have heard your words, but it is possible, if not probable, that they didn't understand you. Even if they *did* understand you, they will promptly forget what you said. Master Presenters know that an oral presentation is greatly different than a written document. Why? Readers can always reread; listeners cannot re-listen. As a result, Master Presenters build in repetition and restatement as if they were imagining the listener is using a yellow marker to highlight the important points.

Master Presenters also vary their explanations and/or start with a relatively simple application of a principle and add complexity as warranted. If you have learned a second language, for example, you may recall how the instructor started with simple words, which led to simple phrases, which led to simple sentences. Master Presenters do the same.

A much less frequently used method of repetition is to ask the participants to summarize the material. In our courses, we stop periodically to ask the participants to state something that they have learned, or relearned up to that point in the presentation. If the group is large, you can't call on everyone. However, you can ask for volunteers, or you can call on people at random. A word of caution: When calling on people at random, we recommend you give them the right to decline the chance to participate. If you remember ever being embarrassed by a lack of preparedness when you were in school, you'll understand why this "free pass" is important.

When you have found a willing participant, ask him or her to repeat something that you or someone else has already said. To be more inclusive and less "selective," give everyone enough time to think of an answer, or have them write down the most important one, two, or three things that they have learned or relearned up to that point. After everyone has had a chance to think of an answer, then ask for volunteers to share their thoughts. You will usually find no shortage of willing participants as long as you have given them a moment to prepare.

This exercise makes learning active rather than passive. You will usually find the participants can summarize most, if not all of your teaching points. The beauty of this activity is that some of your points will be *repeated*, while others will be *restated*. And these two techniques are exactly what you are trying to accomplish.

Remember, though, it is still the job of the Master Presenter to fill in any missing points, to elaborate on any points that might need clarification, and to bring some sense of order to the comments that were randomly offered.

2. Active vs. Passive Learning

In passive learning, the participants are silent recipients of information that is all too often read to them. This is a technique that produces little, if any, long-term learning.

In active learning, the participants are more than silent partners. In active learning, the participants receive the same information, but are encouraged to transmit information back. Think back to the best teacher you ever had. Chances are, he or she involved you in the learning process on a much higher level than mere listening. Master Presenters depend on active learning techniques.

Which would you prefer: a presenter who explains a concept and gives one or two examples before moving on, or a presenter who gives a concept and then divides the participants into groups and asks each group to give an example of how they can apply the concept in real life? Most people prefer the active learning approach over the passive listening style.

In the active learning example just presented, there are four ways that the participants can be actively involved:

1. They can be asked to come up with a specific example of how the solution could be applied in real life.
2. They can be asked to listen carefully to the other examples in order to choose the one that they like best.
3. They can be asked to debate the merits of each proposed example in order to choose the one that the group will present.
4. They can be asked to listen carefully to see which group presents the best example(s) overall.

In Brad's two-day course *Dealing With Workplace Conflict*, he divides the participants into three groups and asks each group to read one of three different, short articles as homework. The first is "Thinking Outside of the Box,"[1] the second "Caught by Choice"[2] (a superbly crafted article on being caught emotionally in a conflict that we would be better off not being caught in), and the third is "Inter-Departmental

Conflict." On the morning of the second day, the participants are given 20 minutes to decide how they will present the material in their article to the class as a whole. They are instructed to make their presentations so interesting that when the other participants go home, they will want to read that particular article before doing anything else.

Brad: I have never been disappointed using this technique. The presentations are terrific, and the participants knew their material on a much deeper level and were much more likely to remember it than if the course facilitator had made the presentations. Just out of curiosity, I asked the participants how much more effectively they remembered the material from their presentations than if they had only read the articles— the average answer: 90 percent.

3. Increasing Audience Attentiveness

Two techniques that are guaranteed to raise the level of attentiveness in your audience are humor, novelty, and surprise. This is important because increasing attentiveness will help to move your material into the participants' long-term memory.

Humor. Humor is a sure-fire way to get an audience to pay attention. Why? Because everybody likes to laugh. So an audience will listen more attentively if they think the speaker is likely to say something funny. They will pay attention in anticipation of the next good laugh. That's how it works for the audience—they will listen more attentively just because they don't want to miss "any of the good stuff."

But Master Presenters know that humor has a greater purpose. They know that when we laugh, we relax; when we relax, we learn. In short, there is nothing more powerful than a message that entertains. That's why humor is considered an indispensable tool.

Of course, all speakers must be careful with their choice of jokes and/or stories because what is politically correct today can be totally unacceptable tomorrow. As times change, so do standards of acceptability. Also, what is acceptable in one place can be completely inappropriate in another. In the United States, for example, it is usually considered acceptable to joke about the President. That is permissible as a result of the constitutionally guaranteed right of free speech. In other countries, though, where individual rights and liberties are different, a speaker would be a fool to poke fun at that country's leaders. For example, David was honored to be invited to speak in Thailand a few years ago.

David: Before I spoke, one of my hosts politely asked if I intended to make any reference, humorous or otherwise, about the King or any member of the Royal Family. I told him I had no intention of doing so, to which he replied: "Good. You shouldn't do that here." It was a good reminder that what works in one country can be totally unacceptable in another.

Humor has both its risks and its rewards. When it works, it's wonderful. When it doesn't, it's deadly. So is it worth the risk? Our advice: Let common sense be your guide. It's better to err on the side of caution, so when in doubt, leave it out.

Another factor to consider is that jokes or humorous stories usually increase the attentiveness level of the individuals in your audience for a very short time. Unless you are naturally funny, and/or have developed a routine of jokes and stories that will raise the attentiveness level of your audience for sustained periods of time, there are other techniques that may serve you better, such as novelty and surprise.

Novelty and surprise. Brad attended the National Speakers Association conference in Los Angeles in 1997. The session he remembers most vividly was a session by Master Presenter and presentations coach Robert Pike.[3] Robert was able to raise the participants' level of attentiveness before the session even began by using the power of novelty and surprise. This is how he did it.

Brad: When I entered the room, I noticed that instead of reading their programs or talking with the person next to them, everyone in the room was split into small groups. They seemed to be working incredibly intensely on a project. The first thing I did was check my watch. Could I have been late? The answer was no. In fact, the session was not due to start for another five minutes. Boy, was I curious. Robert then instructed the people who had just come in to join a group. One of my group members informed me that our task was to list the top 10 languages in the world in order of how many people spoke each language. I was hooked, as was everyone who was in our group and all of the people who joined in after me. We hypothesized, debated, and "guesstimated." Time was announced, and we looked up at the overhead as Robert presented the correct list, in order, from the book *The Top Ten of Everything* by Russell Ash.[4]

The session's topic was on making one's presentations more interactive, and for me this exercise was the most memorable part of the whole conference. Robert was able to raise the attentiveness level of each individual and of his audience as a whole *before* his presentation even started.

Brad uses a similar technique in his course on *The Seven Strategies of Master Negotiators*.

Brad: Ninety-nine point nine percent of the workshops I have attended start out with introductions and expectations. I start my course with a negotiation. This is a two-person negotiation based on the buying and selling of a house. The instructions state that the buyer and seller have agreed on everything except the closing date. The buyer wants a closing date of June 1st, and the seller wants a closing date of June 30th. The participants have seven minutes to read their instructions and see if they can reach an agreement.

I have never seen this exercise fail to raise the attentiveness level of the participants and for the group as a whole. The participants are instantly engaged in the course, and the expectation is set that the course will be highly interactive and experiential.

EXERCISE 5-1	Briefly describe an example of how you have seen a Master Presenter raise the attentiveness level in his or her audience.

Next, describe a situation where you did your best at raising the attentiveness level of the participants in one of your presentations.

To complete this exercise, outline how you can do a better job of raising the attentiveness level in one of your future presentations.

4. Memory Aids and Mnemonic Devices

There are times in our lives when we hear a catchy slogan, motto, or tune and just can't seem to get it out of our heads. This is a technique that advertisers use all the time. Several examples are: "Nothing says lovin' like something from the oven, and Pillsbury does it best," "Where's the beef?" from Wendy's, or "Don't leave home without it" from American Express. Just as advertisers use memory aids and repetition, so do Master Presenters. For example, in Brad's *Seven Strategies of Master Negotiators* course, the participants hear the phrase, "Master Negotiators come to the table incredibly well prepared, while their less effective counterparts, come to the table overly optimistic and underprepared" at least seven times. Giving the participants a review sheet, a bookmark, or a business card with a slogan, motto, or "point of wisdom" also increases the likelihood that it will be transferred to the participants' long-term memories.

Another simple, yet effective memory aid is one David uses in his seminars in which he asks the participants to simply fill in the blanks with key words, points, or phrases. All who have ever taught in a classroom know the reason for this is twofold.

First, it is a focusing technique. Fill-in-the-blank activities keep the listener focused on the exact point David is making, and at the exact time he wants the listener to focus on that point. If you have ever been given a handout in which all the reference material is supplied verbatim, you have probably been tempted to either 1) read ahead, or 2) start to daydream, secure in the knowledge that you can always read the handout later. Either way, the presenter has lost the listener. For example, all of us have a handout somewhere in our files that we've been meaning to get back to but never have. The fact is, few, if any, of your audience members will refer to your handouts once they leave your program. That's why you have to make sure the important point sticks with your audience—at the moment the point is made.

The second reason why simple fill-in-the-blank activities are effective is that we are more likely to remember what we have written out in our own handwriting. There is something about the process of taking information in through the eyes and ears, processing it in our brains, and then recording it with our hands that gives us a sense of ownership of the material. It's as if you are telling yourself: "I wrote this down; it must have been important." Curiously, this works even if you were instructed to write it down. There is just an air of significance and permanence that comes through when we put words to paper.

Other types of memory aids include course summaries, tip sheets, and other mnemonic devices. A mnemonic is a clue designed to help us recall something more complex. Acronyms are common and effective mnemonic devices. For example, Roger Fisher, William Ury, and Bruce Patton, authors of the world's most widely read book on negotiating, *Getting to Yes*, use the term BATNA to represent Best Alternative To a Negotiated Agreement. If you remember the short acronym "BATNA," you can recreate the longer phrase it represents.

The main purpose of an acronym is to reduce complicated phrases or concepts to simple or memorable words and images. Many North American school children, for example, remember the five Great Lakes with the simple acronym HOMES: Huron, Ontario, Michigan, Erie, Superior. If you've ever heard that mnemonic before, you probably remembered it. And for those of you who never heard it before, there's an excellent chance you won't forget it, either.

If you are not sure if this really works, try this test. On a sheet of paper, write down the acronym we just discussed: HOMES. Set it aside. Come back to that page in 24 hours and test yourself. Odds are, you'll be able to remember what the acronym stands for and be able to recite the full version of what the acronym represents. Look at it again in a week, in a month, in a year. Again, odds are, you will still remember what it stands for. And when you consider that 48 hours after any presentation, most listeners forget 75 percent of everything they heard, any technique or device that helps move information into long-term memory is worth considering.

That's what memory aids do. They give the listener a hook on which to hang important information. If you remember the hook, no matter how silly it may sound, you are much more likely to remember the information paired with it. A word of caution on the use of acronyms: Many presenters use acronyms that are hard to remember. It should be obvious that if you can't remember the acronym, you certainly won't remember the information assigned it, but many presenters overlook this key point. Unfortunately, it is not uncommon to hear a presenter say, usually with great fanfare, "To help you follow along, today I will use...ta-daaah...an acronym!" (as if that is a revolutionary idea). Then they unveil some hopelessly bland, nondescript, or overused word such as ACHIEVE. Then they set out to assign meaning to each letter of the word. The problem is, the more common the acronym, the less likely it will be remembered. That is, if the acronym lacks uniqueness, it usually lacks memorability.

Just as a test, in 1993 David presented in Toronto a program on presentation skills to an international group of speakers during which he was to make 10 points. He looked for a 10-letter word or phrase that would allow him to make his 10 points, and also be so different that the listeners would not forget it. The acronym he came up with fit both requirements.

David: I introduced the acronym as follows. "Today I have 10 points to make, so to help you remember and follow along, I'm going to use a common speakers' device, an acronym. I looked for a word or phrase that would be appropriate for the occasion, but I couldn't find one that had the right combination of letters for the points I wanted to make. So in desperation, I put the first letter of each key point on an index card. Then I took my 10 cards, tossed them in the air and let them land where they may. Well, imagine my surprise when I found, with just minor rearranging, not one word, but two that would work." Then, as I directed their attention to a projection screen, I said, "So the two words I want you to remember today are ROACH MOTEL." As I expected, there was a momentary stunned silence. Then, about two seconds later, the place erupted in laughter. Why? I caught them by surprise. It was unlike any acronym they had seen, and totally contrary to the mundane acronyms they were accustomed to seeing. And it had two added bonuses. First, it introduced an expectation of fun. But more importantly, it was memorable. The truth is, I didn't know just how memorable it would be until last year, a full nine years after the program, I received a phone call. The caller said, "Is this David Brooks, from the ROACH MOTEL?" I was flattered, I think. Moreover, I was impressed, for sure. Because any time that a message is remembered for nine years, I know I've done my job.

EXERCISE 5-2	Please describe the best memory aid you have seen used in a presentation. How will you use memory aids more effectively in your next presentation?

5. The Power of Stories

Long after the audience has forgotten your name and the title of your presentation, they will remember your stories, which is why Master Presenters are such apt storytellers. One of the best storytellers in the business is Les Brown. Les spoke at the NSA National Meeting on August 8, 2000, in Washington, D.C. In the middle of his presentation, he stopped speaking and started snapping his fingers. Then he asked the audience to snap their fingers. As they were all snapping their fingers, Les started to tell a most awe-inspiring story about visiting a friend, Miss Francis, in the hospital. Les said, "I stopped at the nurses' station and asked directions to her room. The nurse said, 'You must mean Miss Positive,' and proceeded to give me directions to her room." Even though Miss Francis was frail and weak from the cancer and chemotherapy that had ravaged her body, when a favorite piece of music came on the radio, the frail woman started snapping her fingers to the tune. Les paused dramatically and said in his deepest, most resonating voice, *"Miss Francis did not let life take her snap away! And don't you let life take your snap away!"*

At that point, you could have heard a pin drop in the room. Professional speaking just doesn't get any better than that. However, Les Brown's story had an unexpected subsequent effect.

Brad: I left our house early one Saturday morning to give a keynote speech in Toronto that same afternoon. I was back home mid-morning the following day. As I drove up to the house, I noticed that one of our patio chairs was on the front porch. When I approached the front doors, I was surprised to find them open. Obviously, my children had forgotten something and had left the doors open. I then saw that they had left the back door open too. I was just thinking that I would have to give them a good talking to, when I noticed that the microwave was missing from its customary perch in the kitchen. Further investigation revealed that the stereo, VCR, video camera, and all of the CDs were gone. The kids didn't forget. We had been robbed!

The police came and went. As I waited for my children to arrive, I had half an hour to reflect. Boy, did I feel violated—especially thinking that the robbers had gone into all of our bedrooms.

I tried to be philosophical about it. No one was hurt. Others have had their whole homes destroyed. The robbers only took electronics. Everything could be replaced. I still felt violated and for the first time felt uneasy in my own home.

Then came the knock at the door. My children, Andrew and Katie, had arrived. I explained what had happened. My daughter was standing on the first landing of the stairs on the way up to her bedroom when she stopped. She turned toward me, looked me right in the eyes and said, "Daddy, don't let those robbers take your snap away." She had learned that lesson from listening to the audiotape of the Les Brown story—ironclad proof of the power of an excellent story, perfectly told, to be absolutely memorable—even to a 10-year-old.

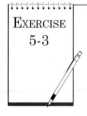

EXERCISE 5-3

Do you have a story or stories that a 10-year-old would remember? If you have one, try it out on a 10-year-old and see if it passes the memorability test. If you don't have one or if the one you have doesn't pass the 10-year-old test, get to work at developing one.

Test your stories often. Your audience will continually give you feedback both on the content and on the delivery. Experiment a bit. All of the Master Presenters we interviewed told us that story development is an experience in trial and error, and is a lifelong process.

6. Defining Moments

Defining moments are that part of the presentation where the audience not only gets it, but they also get that they get it. It is at this point that the goal or lesson of the presentation becomes crystal clear. It is also at this point that the audience understands precisely what the presenter intended to communicate and is given a choice to act, or not act, on what they have learned.

Peter Legge is business owner, author, presenter, and volunteer extraordinaire. He is recognized as a World Class Presenter by three speakers' organizations: Toastmasters International, the National Speakers Association, and the Canadian Association of Professional Speakers. What makes Peter such a Master Presenter that he is recognized by three organizations? First, Peter Legge is a keen observer; second, he is an accomplished storyteller; third, he is a relentless reader and student of history; fourth he is a master user of analogies; fifth, he is a gifted developer of transitions; sixth, he is an exceptional wordsmith; and seventh, he is a powerful asker of questions. This is illustrated with a segment of one of Peter's presentations: *You Never Know.*

> *His name was Fleming, and he was a poor Scottish farmer. One day, while trying to eke out a living for his family, he heard a cry for help coming from a nearby bog. He dropped his tools and ran. There, mired to his waist in mud, was a terrified boy, screaming and struggling to free himself. Farmer Fleming saved the lad from what could have been a slow and terrifying death.*
>
> *The next day, a fancy carriage pulled up to the Scotsman's farm, and an elegantly dressed nobleman stepped out and introduced himself as the father of the boy Farmer Fleming had saved.*
>
> *"I want to repay you," said the nobleman. "You saved my son's life."*
>
> *"No, I can't accept payment for what I did," the Scottish farmer said, and at that moment, the farmer's own son came to the door.*
>
> *"Is that your son?" the nobleman asked.*
>
> *"Yes," said the farmer.*
>
> *"I'll make you a deal. Let me take him and give him a good education. If the lad is anything like his father, he'll grow to be a man you can be proud of."*
>
> *And that he did. In time, Farmer Fleming's son graduated from St. Mary's Hospital Medical School in London, and went on to become Sir Alexander Fleming, the discoverer of penicillin.*

Years afterward, the nobleman's son was stricken with pneumonia, and penicillin saved his life. The name of the nobleman? Lord Randolph Churchill, His son? Winston Churchill.

Someone once said that what goes around comes around.

What we can learn from observing Peter Legge is that Master Presenters accomplish seven times more than less accomplished presenters because Master Presenters use multiple skills and teach on multiple levels, all at the same time. In the example above, we can see how Peter artfully used this intriguing story as an analogy to illustrate that what goes around, comes around. He then, both implicitly and explicitly, asks us to evaluate ourselves by asking the question, "Will we be happy with what we are doing today when it comes back to us tomorrow?"

EXERCISE
5-4

Part I: Think about three of the finest presentations you have ever seen or heard. Then identify the defining moment for each of these three presentations. That is, at what moment did you get it and "get that you got it"?

Part II: Identify a defining moment from one of your own presentations.

Part III: If you already have a defining moment, can you enhance it? Or if you don't have a defining moment, how could you craft one?

We end this section with Brad's Law. Brad's Law states that: "Master Presenters present their ideas more eloquently, more profoundly, and more powerfully than their less masterful counterparts—and in half the time." Peter Legge became one of North America's foremost presenters because he understands defining moments and knows how to use them eloquently, profoundly, powerfully, and succinctly.

7. Anchoring

Anchoring is the act of helping to anchor an idea, concept, and/or principle in another person's memory. This can be done visually, aurally, and kinesthetically.

Visually. Master Presenter Janet Lapp demonstrates anchoring visually with the following memorable visual metaphor:

> I try to create useful, deeply connecting programs with humor and stories that are hard for audience members to erase from their minds. I do that in the framework similar to music composition—say a symphony from the Romantic Period—with highs and lows, different speeds, all built toward a climax. I find that works well. Then of course I use visual effects. For example, sometimes I physically carry someone on my back across the stage; usually a fairly robust man, and the audience connects that with carrying around too much, doing too much. Then I follow with a quote by Peter Drucker: "Businesses don't fail because they don't know what to do; they fail because they don't know what to give up."

The fact is, some people "listen" with their eyes. That is, visual learners can learn more by seeing one physical illustration or demonstration than any printed or spoken explanation will ever accomplish.

Aurally. Another way to anchor your material in your audience's long-term memory is to anchor it aurally. For example, Brad was in London in 1986 and decided to visit the underground war rooms where Winston Churchill lived and held some of his war cabinet meetings, which had recently been reopened as a museum. Remarkably, they were untouched since they had been closed in 1945 at the end of the war. The underground command center made quite an impression. However, the most memorable part of the visit was hearing Churchill's voice saying, "We will never, never, ever surrender..." Brad says that he can still hear Churchill speaking in his mind today, as if he just visited the museum. The memory was anchored aurally.

Master Presenter Marcia Steele provides another example.[5] In Marcia's presentation she speaks eloquently of her experience emigrating from Jamaica to New York. Then she stops and sits down in a chair on stage next to a writing table. Instantly, the audience is transported back into time, as it hears the recorded voice of Walter Cronkite announce the tragic news that Martin Luther King, Jr., has been assassinated. Marcia uses nothing but sound to illustrate a transition in her life and in the life of her country. It is a powerful moment, anchored aurally.

Kinesthetically. Kinesthetic learners are those who learn best by touching or doing. They are "hands-on" learners. One of the principles that Brad teaches with determination in *The Seven Strategies of Master Negotiators* course is, "You can't change someone's mind if you don't know where their mind is." He used four methods to make sure that the participants remember this phrase. The first is repetition. He says it at least seven times. The second is to anchor it kinesthetically in a handshake with one's partner. The third is to start the phrase and ask the class to finish it. The fourth is by using the phrase as one of the answers in a quiz at the beginning of the second day.

Brad: I anchor a key point kinesthetically by asking the participants to find a partner. I then demonstrate the Master Negotiators mantra, "You can't change someone's mind if you don't know where their mind is" with a volunteer from the audience. We repeat the mantra while we are shaking hands as if we had just been introduced. Please note that the rhythm of the handshake is matched to the rhythm at which the words are being spoken—which is modeled at a slow tempo. The purpose of this exercise is to anchor the words through hearing, but also kinesthetically in the feel of the handshake. The principle is further reinforced because handshaking is symbolic of agreement. By the time this exercise is repeated three or four times with the audience members, the phrase, "You can't change someone's mind if you don't know where his or her mind is" is anchored both aurally and kinesthetically, which helps to transfer it to one's long-term memory.

One way to think about what we are tying to accomplish when we say that we want to anchor it kinesthetically is to think about a song, jingle, or advertisement that starts to drive you crazy because it keeps playing itself over and over again in your mind. What we want to accomplish here is the same thing, only we want to do it on purpose. Therefore, the participants are instructed that every time they shake someone's hand, the phrase, "You can't change someone's mind if you don't know where their mind is" is to be repeated silently to themselves. In other words, we are using the psychological principle of pairing, that is, taking something that naturally occurs at a high rate, and pairing it with something that would naturally occur at a low rate, thereby increasing the frequency of the activity that naturally occurs at a low rate, and hence the likelihood that it will be remembered.

Another technique to anchor it kinesthetically is through the use of one-minute neck massages.

Brad: I use this technique to help people remember one of William Ury's five-part model for breakthrough negotiations. Once again, the participants are asked to select partners. I make sure that no one is left out, so if there is an extra participant, that participant can work with the seminar leader. Each participant is instructed to give his or her partner a 30-second neck massage. They are to massage their partner's neck while saying: "Going to the balcony means keeping your eye on the prize, not getting emotionally hooked, and looking at the situation as an incredibly wise third-party." The masseuse is to massage gently all the while saying the above phrase at a slow rate. The instructor repeats the phrase two times, and the masseuse is instructed to say the words out loud along with the instructor. The masseuse and person being massaged then switch roles and the process is repeated.

The exercise will only work if the instructor and the participants feel comfortable using it. You need to point out at the beginning of the exercise that if anyone is not comfortable doing the exercise, they can simply repeat the phrase to themselves. In addition, this is also a good exercise to bring about a change of pace when people have been sitting for a long period of time. It took me a while to get up enough nerve to use it and the feedback that I have received from the participants has been overwhelmingly positive.[6]

EXERCISE
5-5

Think of the best examples where you saw a Master Presenter anchor his or her point visually, aurally, and kinesthetically.

Think of two or three places where you can anchor a learning point visually, aurally, or kinesthetically in one of your upcoming presentations.

8. The Power of Metaphors

A metaphor is a figure of speech in which a word or phrase denoting one kind of object or idea is used in place of another to suggest a likeness between them. For example, Toastmaster Hans Lillejord says, "Some words are diamonds; some words are stones," which is a metaphor. Conversely, you could say, "Some words are valuable; some are worthless"—but the diamonds and stones metaphor evokes a much stronger imagery. For visual and auditory learners, vivid images are more likely to connect and to stick.

A captivating metaphor that catches the participants' imaginations is often one of Master Presenters' most powerful tools. For example, in successful change management, an appropriate metaphor can help the organization better understand what is necessary to move not only from one organizational structure to another but also from one organizational culture to another.

The amalgamation of five fiercely proud and independent hospitals into a combined Health Sciences Centre illustrates the difficulties involved in this type of transition. During this time Brad developed a course on managing change and uncertainty and then trained all of the trainers in staff training and development on how to facilitate the course. One of his favorite techniques is to divide the participants into subgroups of five or six, and then ask them to draw pictures to identify metaphors that represent the current state of the organization and a picture of what the ideal state of the organization would look like.

Although at the outset the groups tend to be resistive, once they start on the task and get into it, the energy and creativity in the room becomes readily apparent. For example, one group of participants at the new Health Sciences Centre used the metaphor of Rubik's Cube to represent the complexity of amalgamating five hospitals, four distinct cultures, and 14 unions.

The idea of using Rubik's Cube as a metaphor for the transition was perfect. The amalgamation was so complex that trying to solve one problem often created another problem somewhere else, just as in trying to solve the Rubik's Cube—that is, getting all of one color on one side of the cube—most often created a patchwork of color on another side of the cube. However, the power of this metaphor is that the Rubik's Cube does have a solution—a very difficult and time-consuming solution, but a solution nonetheless. In this case, the metaphor helped the participants easily grasp and remember three important lessons: the difficulty of the task of solving all of the problems; the hard work, effort and time necessary to solve the problems; and the understanding that the cube (and the amalgamation of the five hospitals) is ultimately solvable.

Another group had a very different but equally powerful metaphor. This group chose the metaphor "follow the yellow brick road" from *The Wizard of Oz*. As in the metaphor of the Rubik's Cube, the journey was long and difficult, but the final destination could be reached safely in the end. The major focus in this group's metaphor, however, was on the qualities that the participants and the organization as a whole would have to possess in order to successfully complete their journey. These qualities were the qualities that the Lion, the Tin Man, and the Scarecrow were valiantly searching for: courage, wisdom, and caring or compassion.

When we looked at these two drawings together and the metaphors they contained, we had a very powerful way to conceptualize the challenges facing the new hospital. The Rubik's Cube perfectly exemplified the complexity of the merger and the need to patiently work on solutions. The metaphor from *The Wizard of Oz* perfectly represented the human qualities necessary for a successful transition. Metaphors provide an excellent tool to speak about some of the unspoken conversations that can hold the organization back and help transform the difficult coversation into skillful dialogue that can help move the organization forward. It is also true that the participants will remember particularly meaningful metaphors long after they have forgotten your name or the title of your presentation.

9. The Power of Three-Act Plays

Brad was asked to do a workshop on managing change and uncertainty for a local high school. By interviewing a representative sample of the staff before the workshop, he was able to determine their main concerns: new education legislation that was before the legislature; the number of school boards in the province was being decreased from 26 to five through consolidation; the new legislation would mean the teachers would have less control over their day-to-day activities; workloads were increasing while preparation time was decreasing; and their administration was offered early retirement, which could result in an entirely new and unknown administration for the school.

Brad: My experience in reading about and conducting workshops on managing change and uncertainty has taught me a great deal about this subject. One of the most important lessons that I have learned is that during times of change and uncertainty most of us feel adrift. We tend to feel less anchored to the past because the old ways are no longer working. We feel less anchored to the present because by their very nature, change and uncertainty tell us that the present will no longer be viable, either. We also tend to feel less anchored to the future during times of change and uncertainty because, by its very nature, the future is less clear. In other words, we are less anchored, period.

The purpose of this workshop was to help the teachers examine their present situation in relation to their past, present, and future anchors. We examined our past transitions and looked at the skills, strategies, and supports that anchored us through those changes. We examined our present situation and looked at the skills, strategies, and supports that exist in our current world that will help us work through our current transitions more effectively. Lastly, we looked at a number of techniques that could help to anchor the future. When the future is sufficiently clear, it acts as a magnet drawing us toward it.

In using this technique, the participants are invited, either individually or in groups, to write a short three-act play. It is helpful to think about three components for each act: a description of the setting in which the act will take place, a storyline for the act, and music for the act. Let me give a description of how this was done by one of my client groups.

The first play was in the form of an allegory. I observed this group preparing their play. An English teacher in the group had written a number of plays and under his guidance, this group wrote their play in vivid detail, where Act One presented the story of a young teacher who had just arrived at the school after completing his degree and teacher's training. He was idealistic, enthusiastic, and full of passion for his chosen career.

In Act Two, we find the young teacher totally disillusioned with the teaching profession in general and this school in particular.

In Act Three, the young teacher is taken under the wing of a wise, older teacher, and he becomes realistically grounded in expectations of what he can and cannot accomplish.

10. The Power of Music

In this same workshop, another group of creative teachers used music to anchor their points in a way that the audience will never forget.

Brad: The second play was in the form of a musical review. The group carefully chose the songs for each of the three acts and sang the words to each song, loudly and clearly. The song for Act One was "Bridge Over Troubled Water." Given the fears about what could happen to their school under the new education legislation, this choice was very appropriate. The song for the Act Two, where things get worse was "Help" by the Beatles. And the song for Act Three, where things get better, was the ballad, "We'll Rise Again" by the Rankin Family, with the words about seeing "the future in the faces of our children" being exceptionally appropriate.

The singing of "We'll Rise Again" was a moving experience for all of us. It captured in music the teachers' and administration's vision of what they liked best about their school and how they wanted to anchor that vision in the future. When I tell this story in seminars and keynotes and accompany the story with this inspiring piece of music, often there is not a dry eye in the room.

Each of these plays and songs expressed important elements about the way the staff saw the school, about their fears, and most importantly, about their vision of the future and what they wanted for their school.

Another technique is to ask the participants to write lyrics to a song. The participants must use course material in their song. Composing and singing a song will help move the material from the participants' short-term memory to their long-term memory. Reviewing, choosing, and prioritizing the course material means that the course participants will be more likely to remember the material. Secondly, the material that the course participants choose to go into the song becomes highlighted with extra meaning.

Brad: The participants in one of my *Seven Strategies of Master Presenters* course composed the following song. The song was based on a Newfoundland ballad.

> Chorus
> It's the bye that writes the speech and it's thy bye that gives her.
> It's the bye that avoids the TRAPS by knowing all my listeners.
> Tell them what's in it for me. Remember HUD and A.B.C.
> Open with a dandy hook and don't forget to close her.
>
> Use good evidence, simulations, and stories that surprise ya.
> And don't forget to start it off with an advanced organizer.
>
> Chorus
> Practice, practice, practice it's not too big a chore, and when you think you've done enough, it's time to do some more.

After the participants compose and sing the course theme song, they teach their song to the other course participants, thereby increasing the involvement of all and increasing the memorability of the course material and increasing the fun and entertaining value of the presentation all at the same time. In summary, plays and songs are a unique way to add memorability, fun, and creativity to your presentations.

11. The Power of Games

Learning is directly proportional to the amount of fun you have.

—*Robert Pike* [7]

Twenty-five percent of the impact of your presentation comes from a powerful beginning. Another 25 percent comes from a powerful ending. Thus, it pays to have terrific endings. One way to do this is with games.

There are three things that a great ending should include: a review or summary of what was learned, a call for action, and a mnemonic device (memory aid) to help the participants capture the essence of what was learned.

Games can help you do all three. They can review and summarize your material, add fun and creativity to your presentations, and increase the level of attentiveness of your audience and therefore make your presentations more memorable.

Negotiation Jeopardy. Brad uses a game he calls "Negotiation Jeopardy" where questions are derived from the course summary.

Brad: The contestants are divided into two or three groups depending on the number of participants in the course. Up to 14, I usually divide the participants into two groups; with 15 or more, I use three groups. It is a closed-book and closed-notes exercise. The participants quickly become involved trying to remember all of the course materials. All of this helps move the concepts from the participants' short-term memory to their long-term memory.

One very interesting thing about this review is that the participants usually don't even see it as a review. They see it as a game, and it doesn't take long for the contestants to become very competitive with each other. This raises their level of attentiveness, and that increased level of attentiveness also increases the likelihood that the material will transfer to the participants' long-term memory.

Who Wants to Be a Millionaire? The groups that work on this game always have an incredibly good time. They carefully prepare the questions in ascending order of difficulty. One of their members plays the role of emcee and carefully asks the contestant if he or she would like to move up to the next level, realizing of course, that if he or she misses, all of their "previous winnings" will be for naught.

The group that organizes the "Who Wants to Be a Millionaire?" contest picks the contestant from among the remaining course members. In my experience, they always pick one of the most extroverted and fun-loving members of the class, and this also adds to the excitement and fun of the game. As in "Negotiation Jeopardy," the participants are having so much fun that it raises their level of attentiveness, and this again contributes to anchoring the course materials in their long-term memory.

Newspaper Personals. Newspaper personals are a great way to have fun, raise everyone's level of attentiveness, and increase memorability. All you have to do is to ask the participants to do a skit modeled on the personals in newspapers. For example, the five components most often used to describe Master Presenters are: credible, competent, dynamic, compatible, and caring. Five participants are selected and given signs for each component. Each participant then has to introduce him- or herself and their characteristic in the style of a personal want ad. For example, "I am a single, caring 33-year-old male. I demonstrate credibility by thoroughly researching both my subject and my audience. I take full responsibility for things I don't know and will get back to the participant or the group as soon as I can find the answer." Or "I am a dynamic five-foot-eight female. I bring energy, enthusiasm, and passion to all of my presentations. I am looking for audiences who share similar characteristics." In sum, this is a great way to make your presentations more interesting. You never know what the participants are going to come up with and this element of surprise adds greatly to both the learning and the memorability of the experience. Some of the skits are so hilarious that the person doing the skit will have earned a nickname based on his or her skit that will last for at least the remainder of the presentation.

Bumper Stickers. The purpose of this exercise is to distill the wisdom learned in the presentation into the form of a bumper sticker. The bumper sticker should be a catchy phrase or acronym. The bumper sticker should also be easy to remember.

Brad: One group that I worked with was dealing with a lot of uncertainty related to the fact that their business would be significantly downsized. I was asked to give a presentation on managing change and uncertainty.[8] As part of the presentation, I presented a psychological study that helps people better understand the effects of uncertainty. The study looked at the increasing levels of stress that women who were married to men in Vietnam experienced and how their stress increased markedly with increasing levels of uncertainty. The three levels of uncertainty were women who were married to men who were killed in action (KIA), prisoners of war (POW), and missing in action (MIA). The study demonstrated that the women who were married to men who were MIAs experienced the greatest uncertainty and, hence, the greatest degree of stress. At the end of the presentation, I divided the participants into groups and asked them to make a bumper sticker to help summarize what they had learned.

The group that impressed me the most was a group that turned the letters POW into "Positive Opportunity Waiting." Other groups have turned the letters of their organization into a powerful motto: for example, "ATV" as standing for "Attitude, Teamwork, and Vision." After explaining the exercise, divide the participants into groups of four. Give each group 15 minutes to develop their bumper sticker and debrief.

Pantomime. Pantomime is a great way to make the end of your presentation fun, creative, and memorable. It is perfect for the end of the day when the participants are tired; you want to raise the energy and fun level.

Brad: In my Advanced Negotiation Course, the participants work very hard, so at the end of a long day I often divide the participants into small groups. Each group is asked to develop a pantomime to represent the most essential element of the day's learning. One of the most effective was where two of the men took off and exchanged their shoes to represent looking at the issue from their counterpart's perspective.

Acronyms. Acronyms are somewhat similar to bumper stickers, only in this case the participants have to take a word, such as "presenter" and match each letter to an element of the presentation process to help the participants remember the course material. One that the Harvard Program on Negotiation uses is BATNA to help the participants in their negotiation courses remember "Best Alternative to a Negotiated Agreement" and I used the acronym TRAP to remember that one's audience is composed of theorists, reflectors, activists, and pragmatic learners.

You can try this technique out in the space below to help you remember some of the principles from this book with the word PRESENTER.

P

R

E

S

E

N

T

E

R

We have just examined 11 techniques to help your audiences remember the material you present. These techniques included repetition and restatement; active vs. passive learning; increasing audience attentiveness; the use of memory aids, stories, defining moments, anchoring, metaphors, three-act plays, music, and games. Before you do anything else, make sure that you understand and know how to implement as many of these as possible. You can then go onto the next step, which is to make it actionable.

Make It Actionable

I hear, I forget; I see, I remember; I do, I understand.

—*Confucius*

Confucius said this in 970 B.C. and it is just as true today. This is why Master Presenters involve their audience to the fullest extent possible. To help you turn your audience's good intentions into concrete, tangible, and actionable steps, use the five proven techniques presented below:

1. Developing an action plan.
2. Setting SMART goals.
3. Developing a specific follow-through form.
4. Scheduling a follow-up class.
5. Using the Three-by-Three Form.

Note that elements from these various techniques can be combined in order to develop an actionable presentation that increases return on investment by maximizing transfer of training.

1. Developing an Action Plan

Master Presenters encourage and inspire their participants to take action. For example, a critical part of Brad's leadership development program is for the participants to carry out a project that will improve their leadership ability, overcome obstacles, and improve their ability to influence others. The participants design their project in the first class meeting and report back several months later on the progress that they made.

The nature of the projects has been very broad in scope from getting career counseling to getting a new job; from getting neighbors to clean up after their dogs to pressuring the city to make streets safer; from getting into better physical shape to upgrading one's standing as a coach and building a world-class swimming team and the facilities to go with it. One participant worked on safety at work and was so successful that he received a raise, while another, who was faced with laying off several long-time employees, found a way to make the organization more profitable resulting in no layoffs. Each one of their projects called for a demonstrated effort on the participants' part. It was a powerful lesson in leadership. Is there another way that they could have better learned about leadership? We think not! The Center for Creative Leadership[9] completed some seminal research that documented that 50 percent of what we learn is learned though experience. Peter Senge, author of *The Fifth Discipline*, states that the foundation of team and organizational effectiveness is personal mastery. This assignment makes the participants' learning both memorable and actionable. Part of developing an action plan is to turn that plan into SMART goals to ensure that that plan will come to fruition.

2. Set SMART Goals

SMART goals are goals that are Specific, Measurable, Attainable, Realistic and have a Time deadline. Far too often, at the end of a presentation, people set goals that are vague and are difficult to meet.

Brad: To counteract this tendency, I ask the participants in my negotiation workshops to set SMART goals at the end of the session. I then ask the participants to share their goals. I also give people the right to pass if they have set a private goal that they would rather not share. The sharing of goals gives me the opportunity to make sure that each person has, in fact, set a SMART goal. Also, hearing each other's goals gives some participants the opportunity to modify their goals if someone else has done a better job of making their particular goal specific.

For example, the "S" and the "M" stand for specific and measurable; for a goal to be both specific and measurable, it must pass the "Yes-No" test. The "Yes-No" test states that the goal must be so specific and measurable that we can count whether the specific behavior that the goal intends took place or not. For example, if a participant said, "I am going to use active listening with my associates for the next month," it is not specific or measurable. If, on the other hand, she said, "I will use intermediate summaries three times with my associate Claire over the next three weeks," it is measurable and specific.

"A" stands for attainable and "R" stands for realistic. Take long-distance running for example. If you were not currently training, it would be foolish to try to run a marathon. Therefore, we have to be careful that the participants do not set goals that cannot be met. In my course on the Seven Strategies of Master Negotiators, a realistic and attainable goal would be to use the "Master Negotiator's Preparation Form"[10] three times within the next month. Setting a goal to use the form for every negotiation during the next month would be both unrealistic and unattainable.

Lastly, the "T" stands for setting a time deadline. This is based on the principle that a commitment is not a commitment unless there is a deadline attached to it. Having a definite end point makes it much more likely that the participant will evaluate his or her progress. Having participants write a letter to themselves, which will be mailed, and/or having them work with a peer, using the buddy system, will also increase the likelihood of reaching their goal.

EXERCISE 5-6

Please take one of your own goals and make it into a SMART actionable goal.

Next, outline the steps you will take to help your participants/audience develop SMART goals.

---

3. Develop a Specific Follow-Through Form

Another way to make sure that the participants set SMART goals is by developing a specific and detailed follow-through form.

Brad: The Master Negotiator's Preparation Form (see Appendix C) is the most detailed of the forms that I use to help the participants transform their good intentions into tangible action. This form covers every aspect of preparing for a negotiation. The form also helps remind the participants of each of the steps that are necessary to come to the table impeccably well prepared.

EXERCISE 5-7

Develop a form (using the one in Appendix C as a guide) that makes it easy for your participants/audience to turn the material you presented into concrete and actionable steps.

4. Schedule a Follow-Up Class

A follow-up class is an excellent way to review the participants' progress and refine and develop the skills that were taught in the first course.

Brad: In my advanced negotiating course, I start by asking the participants to form pairs and interview each other as if they were one of the world's best media interviewers. The interviewer asks questions about a negotiation the interviewee was in and felt good about. The example can come from work or outside of work. The interviewer is instructed to be as supportive as possible and to allow for the fact that it may take some time to think of an example. The interviewer is also instructed to help identify specific skills that were used in the negotiation. After five minutes, the interviewer and the interviewee are instructed to switch roles. We then start the class with each person briefly introducing his or her partner, giving a very brief summary of the negotiation, and listing the specific skill or skills that were used. This exercise serves as an excellent transition into the course, and is also a thorough review of all of the material that was covered in the first course. I then divide the participants into three groups. Each person in each group shares a current negotiation issue with which he or she would like some help. The groups are then given an hour to help each other as much as possible using the Three-by-Three Form to evaluate three things that are done well and three targets for improvement.

5. Use the Three-by-Three Form

You can use the Three-by-Three Form by asking the participants to list three strengths of the person doing the exercise and to make three suggestions for improvement. Our preference is to ask other people in the class to summarize the feedback on the form for the person who has just presented. This technique has a number of advantages. For example, in *The Seven Strategies of Masters Presenters* course, by the time four or five people say that the presenter has a great opening statement, the person is much more likely to listen to and accept the feedback. Likewise, if four or five people tell the participant who presented that he needs to slow down and add pauses to let the other person participate more, the person presenting the case is much more likely to believe it and take corrective action. The completed Three-by-Three Form, which now serves as an excellent summary, is then given to the person who presented. An example of how this form was filled out for *The Seven Strategies of Master Presenters* course follows.

FIGURE 5-1: SAMPLE THREE-BY-THREE FORM

Name: <u>Joe/Jane Participant</u>

Please list three things I do well as a presenter:

1. Great storyteller.
2. Excellent examples.
3. Creative use of pictures.

Please list three specific targets for improvement:

1. Speaks too quickly.
2. Needs to pause so the audience can hear, understand, and digets.
3. Needs more variety in transitions.

The Three-by-Three Form can easily be modified to best suit the purpose of any presentation. For example, when the course is on presentation skills, the word *negotiator* is substituted for the word *presenter* and the feedback is on how the participant presented, or if the course is on sales, the feedback is on the participant's ability and targets for improvement in sales.

Making it actionable requires using the five techniques discussed to help your audiences remember, understand, and use the materials you present. Help make sure your presentation's goals are actually implemented by developing action plans, setting SMART goals, developing follow-up forms, scheduling follow-up classes, and using a three-by-three form. Then you are ready for the last step in this chapter, which is to make it transferable.

Make It Transferable

There is a growing recognition of a "transfer problem" in organizational training...It is estimated that while American industries annually spend up to $100 billion on training and development, not more than 10 percent of these expenditures actually result in transfer to the job.

—Timothy Baldwin and Kevin Ford [11]

One of the biggest complaints about presentations is that, although they may be interesting and even entertaining, they have nothing to do with the real life. In other words, little or nothing is transferable. This means that much of the billions of dollars that is spent each year on training in North America is wasted. A notable exception to this way of thinking is taken into consideration at the Ford Motor Company.

Jacques Nasser, Ford's past president and CEO, used teaching, mentoring, and "action learning" to drive change at Ford. Action learning is learning by doing and setting goals or targets, with senior managers acting as the teachers/facilitators/mentors. The participants have 100 days to turn the goals of their projects into concrete results. Nassar states:

> Ford's change program is based on teaching, but it eschews the traditional classroom setting. Teaching at Ford is achieved through a multi-faceted initiative, including small group discussions of strategy and competition, stints of community service, and 360-degree feedback. At the initiative's center is a hands-on, three-day workshop that culminates in an assignment designed to let "students" demonstrate that they understand Ford's new mindset: [whereby] they must deliver a significant new cost saving or revenue source to Ford's bottom line.[12]

One of the key elements of transferability is making the participants accountable for utilizing the course materials. In the above example, the employees at Ford were given assignments that would help the whole company "work better, smarter, and faster."

Methods to Increase Transfer of Training

There are 10 proven methods that you can use to increase transfer of training:

1. The buddy system.
2. Role-playing.
3. The Virtual VCR.
4. Telephone and/or e-mail follow-up.
5. E-dialogues.
6. Continuous-learning or mastermind groups.
7. Writing a letter to your boss, manager, or supervisor.
8. Learning contracts with the learner's boss, manager, or supervisor.

9. Making the learning part of an employee development plan or succession plan.
10. Making training part of the organizational culture.

The buddy system is an excellent way to help ensure transfer of training. Just as we floss our teeth more frequently just before going to the dentist, using a buddy helps to ensure that the learner is compliant in putting his or her learning into practice. Participants can be paired up in groups of two. The buddies draw up a contract, exchange written goals, contact information, agree to meet at least once a week, and develop a schedule as to who will initiate contact on alternating weeks.

Part of the buddy system contract should focus on how you will support each other when you implement a new skill, how you will help each other overcome obstacles to implementing the new skills, and how you will help each other maintain the desired change. As Mark Twain said, "Anyone can quit smoking. I've done it a thousand times." Making the change is the easy part; maintaining the change is an altogether different problem. Knowing that the participants will be responsible for teaching and coaching each other makes them more accountable to each other and to themselves. A good working relationship with your buddy can make all the difference between carrying out your good intentions and not carrying them out.

People often learn the most when they teach others.[13]

—*Broad and Newstrom*

Role-playing can also help in the transferability of skills, just as role-playing can help you make your presentation more dynamic. The advantage of role-playing is that the participants can actually see if they have mastered the materials or not. In many cases, they find that although their intellectual understanding of the concepts are fine, it is another matter altogether to put them into practice. Role-playing, role reversal, alternative endings, and the Virtual VCR were explored in detail in Strategy 4.

Brad: I always emphasize that role-playing is one of the best ways to learn. However, I also emphasize that this is a purely voluntary activity and that many people learn better by vicariously watching—this is especially true of the reflectors in the group.

Telephone and e-mail follow-up work in the same way as the buddy system does in holding each other accountable, but it takes place over the telephone or through e-mail. Typically, the participants are encouraged to set up debriefing/coaching sessions once a week for a minimum of three weeks. Participants can also stay in touch through a combination of e-mail, telephone, or follow-up meetings.

E-dialogues allow participants to set up and participate in their own private and/or public chat room where each participant can pose a problem, dilemma, or challenge, while previous course participants and/or the course instructor offer their advice. Don't underestimate the power of this technique.

Brad: I had a client who was a very successful programmer. He was thinking that he wanted to change careers and become a pilot. Given that he was in his mid-40s, he wondered if he would ever recoup his investment if he made the change. He received an incredible response to his question when he posted it on a chat room for pilots. Some of the responses were three pages long, single-spaced. We were impressed by both the quality and the quantity of the responses he received.

Continuous learning or mastermind groups are groups of like-minded individuals who collectively help each other develop their skills and strategies through peer mentoring. They also hold each other responsible for developing specific goals in specific time frames. To be effective, the group should meet at least once a month. For example, the members in our continuous learning group all decided to attend a conference on Authentic Leadership together. After the conference, one of our group members agreed to type up all of his notes and share them with everyone else in the group. Another participant agreed to look up the references that were given on the course and make those materials available to the rest of us. A third member agreed to schedule monthly conference calls so we could hold each other accountable for the goals that we made.

Have participants **write a letter** to their boss, manager, or supervisor stating what they learned in the course and how they will apply it. The advantage of this technique is that it makes the action plan from the course a legitimate document. It also actively brings a participant's boss, manager, or supervisor into the loop, which increases accountability.

A learning contract with one's boss, manager, or supervisor is much the same as writing a letter. It may be more substantial and be in place over a longer period of time. Lastly, the learning contract, by its very nature, tends to hold all of the parties who are signatories to the contract to a higher level of accountability.

Make the learning part of a plan. Brad had the pleasure of working on an employees' succession plan at a large cooperative. A number of upper-management positions would be opening up due to retirement three years later. Thirty-two middle managers applied for each of the eight senior management positions. If the process were perceived to be anything less than thorough or fair, it would damage both the organization and employee morale. The assessment involved three parts. The first part was a very thorough 360-degree feedback in which candidates are assessed by their manager, boss, or superior. They are also assessed by their subordinates and peers and the candidates also assessed their own ability on nine key factors and 39 subscales. Second, the candidates also took a number of psychological tests. Third, the candidates attended an assessment center where they were assessed on their ability to present ideas, think on their feet, organize a speech, and negotiate. A written evaluation based on a SWOT analysis (Strengths, Weakness, Opportunities, and Threats) for their current division within their organization was also completed. All of this data was synthesized and each candidate received a rating from 1 to 100 as to their suitability for advancement, their strengths, and targets for improvement. Each candidate was thoroughly debriefed and given specific recommendations for improvement. A detailed action plan was developed comprising of relevant readings, courses, and mentoring assignments within the organization. The candidates were deeply motivated and perceived the process to be thorough, fair, and relevant. Did the process increase transfer of training? Absolutely!

Make the training part of the organizational culture. To be truly effective, it is a not enough to give presentations. The training has to become part of the organizational culture. To do this, it is not enough to just give all of the employees training; they have to *hear* stories of how the training can help make a better company and better employees. Also, if one of the employees forgets how to use the skills and strategies, other employees can coach that person on how to use the appropriate skills, strategies, and techniques. In other words, in transformational training, the role of the presenter is to help transform the participants from trainees into trainers.

Brad: I taught *The Seven Strategies of Master Negotiators* course at a two-day staff-training event for an employee assistance organization. At the time, I was in private practice as a trainer half-time, and worked for this particular company half-time as their regional manager for the Maritimes. About a year and a half later, I was discussing a sensitive employee issue with the president and CEO of the company. As we were discussing strategy, he asked me what my BATNA was. And although I frequently taught this concept, in this particular case, I had forgotten. This was terrific evidence that there had been excellent transfer of training. The story of how the "pupil" in this case taught the "teacher" served to reinforce the value of using this particular strategy in that corporate culture.

You know that you have been successful in presenting your material when you see it used. Encouraging your participants to teach the material to others, review the material with their managers and supervisors, using the buddy system, and developing action plans are essential if transfer of training is to take place. Perhaps the best indication that it has done so is when it becomes part of the organization's culture.

To summarize, no matter how good or well-presented the material, it will lose most of its value if we do not make it memorable, actionable, and transferable. Master Presenters put as much work into this part of presenting as they do into the development, delivery, and organization of their material. To become more like a Master Presenter, we suggest that you reread and apply the strategies and skills that are presented in this chapter until you are using them effectively in each and every presentation. If your message is worth saying, make it worth remembering. You and your audience will benefit.

STRATEGY

6

Manage Yourself, Difficult Participants, and Difficult Situations

There are two kinds of speakers: those that are nervous and those that are liars.
—Mark Twain

Managing Yourself

This chapter deals with how to manage yourself, difficult participants and difficult situations. It is also about how Master Presenters get into the zone of peak performance,[1] and once they are in it, how they stay there. In explaining the peak performance curve, the authors state:

> As job pressure increases, performance increases up to a certain point and then declines thereafter. The rustout lacks enough pressure in his job to bring forth his best performance. The burnout has too much pressure, has passed the peak, and has slipped down the performance curve. [Master Presenters have learned to perform]...at the top part of the curve—not too much pressure, not too little.

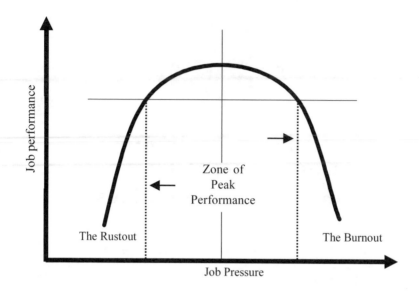

Figure 6-1: Peak Performance Curve

The zone of peak performance is where we do our best work. It is analogous to running a marathon. Some people just don't have the motivation or the energy to train enough. They may start the race, but they are too rusted out to finish. At the opposite extreme is the burnout. Burnouts have overtrained and overtaxed their bodies, so that when it is time to start the race, they are sidelined. A better place to be is the zone of peak performance.

The first method to get into the zone of peak performance is to focus on ways to make sure you are working effectively with yourself. Among the topics covered in this section are:

- Make appropriate attributions.
- Monitor/change your self-talk.
- Perfect perfectionism.

- Increase your sense of control.
- Six methods to control anxiety.
- Change nervous energy into focused presentation power.

For example, it is important for you to ensure you are making attributions related to effort and/or the need to develop skills rather than ability. For example, if John is having difficulty organizing his topic and he tells himself that he just doesn't have the ability to present, then he has told himself that there is really nothing that he can do about his problem. The probable consequence of this type of attribution is that he will feel badly about himself because of his perceived deficit. On the other hand, if he tells himself that his presentation difficulty can be overcome by more effort, more time, more practice, or by developing better delivery skills or finding a good presentations coach, then there is something that he can do about his problem. The trick is not to be helpless and reactive. We have a choice: be helpless and reactive or be empowered and proactive. Our choice lies in learning how to monitor and change our self-attributions.

Make Appropriate Attributions

Attribution theory deals with how we react to difficulty or obstacles. In this section we are specifically interested in the attributions you make or the things you say to yourself about yourself when you encounter a difficulty or an obstacle. There are two main categories of attributions: those dealing with effort and those dealing with ability. Each of these attributions will result in markedly different types of behaviors as illustrated in Figure 6-2.

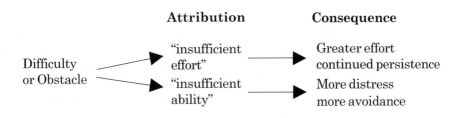

Figure 6-2

Master Presenters continually instruct themselves to take control and become active no matter what obstacle they are facing. In the following example, there were unforeseen circumstances that were impossible to ignore.

David: It was February 1, 2003 and I was to be the opening speaker at a conference set to begin 9 a.m. in Arlington, Texas. At about 8:40, I overheard someone who had just arrived discussing the space shuttle Columbia. News of its tragic explosion and disintegration directly overhead was unfolding and spreading by word of mouth. Yet, by 9 a.m., as the program began, the majority of the 200 people in the room had not heard anything about it. The conference chairperson opened with this: "I just heard from my husband that we are being instructed to stay inside because potentially hazardous debris is falling all around us." "What?" someone shouted. She replied, "Debris from the space shuttle!" "What are you talking about?" "The space shuttle—it just exploded above us!" At this point, the situation was chaotic. No one was sure what had happened yet, and everyone felt devastated. And I was up next.

I knew the audience was not likely to hear my presentation and I thought about discarding it. I then thought it better to ask the audience what they preferred. So I opened with an acknowledgement of what we knew. I explained that what I had to say that day was not as important as what was happening. I asked for a moment of silence in recognition of the astronauts who had just lost their lives. And then I asked if they wanted me to proceed. Unanimously, they said yes, proceed as planned. The program went on by audience request, though more subdued than normal. Afterward, I received many wonderful comments from participants thanking me for the manner in which I handled a difficult situation.

In this case, David made the right decision by listening to his self-talk. One way to help you take a better look at the attributions you make and how they subsequently affect your behavior is to examine your self-talk.

Monitoring/Changing Your Self-Talk

Your self-talk, also known as self-statements, inner speech, or internal dialogue, plays an important part in determining your behavior. As a child, one's self-talk is completely external. For example, a little boy learning to talk would say to himself, "Johnny, put ball in box." As the child grows older this self-talk becomes more rapid, fragmented, and subconscious. Unless close attention is paid, most adults do not fully realize what they are saying to themselves or the way in which their self-talk influences their behavior.

Self-talk can be negative or positive. The three types of negative self-talk are:

1. **Talk-irrelevant.** This includes talking to yourself about anything other than the target behavior or task at hand. For example, "I should have gone into another career where I wouldn't have to make presentations."

2. **Self-depreciating.** This includes any statements where you put yourself down, such as, "I never could present," or, "I don't even like to talk in small groups, how can I present to a formal audience?"

3. **Task-depreciating.** This includes statements where you denigrate the importance of the task, such as, "There are no opportunities for advancement in this organization anyway, so what's the use of knocking myself out over a presentation?"

Examples of negative self-statements that participants in our *Seven Strategies of Master Presenters* courses have made to themselves include:

- *Because I haven't started working on my presentation now, it's already too late.*
- *What's the use of "another" look at this topic?*
- *No matter how hard I try, I just can't come up with a creative title.*
- *I find organizing this presentation very difficult and frustrating.*
- *Whatever I put together will not be good enough.*
- *I am frustrated with not being as articulate, creative, or polished as other presenters I know.*

- *I take too much time formulating ideas and sentences.*
- *I'm just not smart enough.*

There are also three types of positive self-talk, they include:

1. **Task-relevant.** This type of positive self-talk occurs when you coach yourself to stay focused, for example, "I have one hour to work. What do I want to accomplish?"

2. **Self-appreciating** talk sounds like: "I worked well this morning," or, "This paragraph is well organized."

3. **Task-appreciating** talk sounds like: "Being able to make excellent presentations gives me more choice in the kind of work I do."

Examples of positive self-statements that participants in our *Seven Strategies of Master Presenters* course have made include:

- *My job prospects will be improved as my ability to give presentations improves.*
- *With consistent planning and good work habits I can write and complete my presentation by the scheduled date.*
- *My colleagues or friends will be very helpful and they will give me excellent feedback on what works and what needs to be improved.*
- *Starting to work on a presentation is always difficult, but it works out in the end, so worrying is not productive.*
- *My presentations have improved, my thinking is more sophisticated, and the ideas are good; the language just needs some polishing.*

The best way to find out what kind of self-statements you make is to use a sampling procedure to help you analyze your self-talk. Writing down your positive and negative self-statements as you work or think about working on your presentation can help you do this. But instead of keeping track of your self-talk all of the time you are working on your presentation, which would be very distracting, select several time periods during which you will collect this data. For example, you may want to monitor your self-talk when you start working on your presentation, when you stop working on your presentation, or when you think about working on your presentation and decide not to.

Exercise 6-1 has been designed to help you record this data and should be recorded for a period of one week.

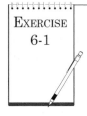

EXERCISE
6-1

Using the template that follows as a guide, keep a record of your presentation-related self-talk for one week. In the left-hand column, record all task-irrelevant, self-depreciating, and task-depreciating self-talk. In the right-hand column, keep a list of your task-relevant, self-appreciating, and task-appreciating self-talk. You may wish to develop a code for frequently occurring self-talk, for example, HP for "I hate presenting," NGP for "I've never been any good at presenting," or BTIT for "That's better than I thought," NGEx for "The point is excellent, now all I need is a great example."

SELF-TALK RECORDING SHEET

Negative Talk: task-irrelevant, self-depreciating, and task-depreciating	**Positive Talk:** task-relevant, self-appreciating, and task-appreciating

Research on self-fulfilling prophecies. Some remarkable research on the effect of changing negative self-talk to positive self-talk is worth noting. In a series of studies on creativity, students were divided into two groups: those who had previously been identified as "creative" and those who had previously been identified as "uncreative." These students were then given various creativity tests and were asked to solve the problems while thinking out loud. The results showed that the uncreative students emitted significantly more task-irrelevant statements, and significantly more self-depreciating and task-depreciating statements while the creative students emitted significantly more task-relevant, self-appreciating, and task-appreciating statements.

When the uncreative students were trained to change their negative self-talk to positive self-talk, the results indicated that these students made significant increases in originality, flexibility, and divergent thinking. In addition, there were positive changes in these students' self-concepts.[2]

Because developing a presentation is a creative activity, changing your self-talk from negative to positive will improve the originality and creativity of your presentation as well as improve your self-concept as a presenter. To test this, make a concerted effort to change your negative self-talk.

After recording your self-talk for one week (in Exercise 6-1), use some of the techniques that follow when you encounter negative self-talk.

1. Use the Stop Technique. For example, say Stop silently to yourself when you first notice that you are becoming distracted, then refocus on the task at hand.

2. Use a current negative world event to keep things in perspective. For example, when you think, *I'll never get this presentation finished by the deadline*, say to yourself, *Compared to the war in _____ or current famine in _____, how important is this?* Then take three deep breaths and continue working.

3. Use thought reversal. For example, *I hate presenting. Well, I didn't like tomatoes, spinach, oysters, or _____ either at first, but I like them now.* Or change, *I don't want to work this evening,* to, *I will reward myself with a walk in the park, hot bath, or _____ when I put in this evening's allotted time.*

Try this for a week and do Exercise 6-2. When you have finished, compare your self-talk recording sheet from Exercise 6-1 with the one from Exercise 6-2, when you actively intervened to change your self-talk.

EXERCISE 6-2

Keep a record of your presentation-related self-talk for week two. You should actively intervene when you realize you are engaging in negative self-talk. In the left-hand column record task-irrelevant, self-depreciating, and task-depreciating self-talk. In the right-hand column, keep a list of your task-relevant, self-appreciating, and task-appreciating self-talk. Remember, you can develop a code for frequently occurring self-talk. You may wish to develop a code for frequently occurring self-talk, for example, HP for "I hate presenting," NGP for "I've never been any good at presenting," or BTIT for "That's better than I thought," NGEx for "The point is excellent, now all I need is a great example."

SELF-TALK RECORDING SHEET

Negative Talk: task-irrelevant, self-depreciating, and task-depreciating	**Positive Talk:** task-relevant, self-appreciating, and task-appreciating

Perfect Perfectionism

Many presenters suffer from perfectionistic tendencies. These tendencies usually increase during times of high anxiety, and you will need to identify the point at which your need for perfection becomes dysfunctional. One way to do this is with a cost/benefit analysis.

For example, you can ask yourself what is the cost of developing a 99-percent perfect presentation compared to the cost of developing a 95-percent perfect presentation. The cost of that extra perfectionism may not be worth it. For example, one of our clients, Linda, found that she was so focused on developing a perfect presentation that she wasn't getting anything done. Once she realized the cost of her perfectionism and allowed herself to develop a less-than-perfect first draft of her presentation, she began to be productive. Not only did she get the work done, but it was at a less personal cost to herself. In addition, the quality of her work was as good as, if not better than, before.

Besides dealing with your own expectations, many presenters often project their perfectionistic tendencies onto their potential audiences and allow these expectations to inhibit their work. One of the things that helped Brad with this problem was to say to himself that it is his audiences' job to assess the quality of his work and it wasn't up to him to do their work for them.

David: When I started as a speaker, I thought my goal was to be perfect. What a mistake that was. First, I learned that perfection is not possible. Next, I learned that it is not even desirable. I also learned that an occasional fumble or stumble can actually help you connect with an audience. It shows you are human and thus, more approachable. The audience reads that as "The speaker is real, fallible, and just like me." It is important to note, however, that I said "an occasional fumble." A few are acceptable; too many are intolerable. A colleague, E. J. Burgay, said, "Perfection is not possible. Mere excellence will be good enough."

Similarly, I learned that if we hold on to a project until it is "perfect," it will never be done. I admit, I fought this tendency all the time. I continually fussed over a project until it was "perfect." The problem was, I could always find a way to make the project better, so my work was never done. Finally, Stephen Kerndt, a colleague, told me of the best advice he received. He said, "Done is better than perfect, every time." When I finally accepted that wisdom, I was able to take a project to completion, comforted by the knowledge that I could always go back and make it better. But if I waited until it was perfect, I would be waiting forever. In sum, Master Presenters don't waste time and effort striving for perfection, but they do strive for excellence.

Locus of Control

Psychologist Julian Rotter did research on locus of control. According to Rotter, people are located along a normally distributed continuum (see Figure 6-3), where one end point is characterized by people who are external and the other is characterized by people who are internal. People who are at the external end of the continuum believe that what happens to them is a result of fate, chance, luck, or external circumstances. In other words, they tend to view themselves as being acted upon rather than as actors. People who are at the internal end of the continuum believe that what happens to them is a result of their own behavior. Master Presenters take an internal stance regarding themselves in the development of their presentations.

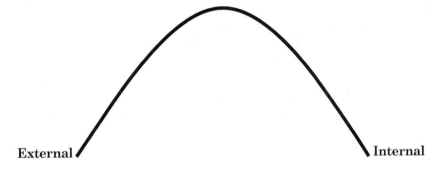

External **Internal**

Figure 6-3: External/Internal Locus of Control

Five factors related to your locus of control in regard to developing, rehearsing, and delivering your presentations are:

1. Your level of commitment to finishing your presentation.
2. How you handle the roadblocks and obstacles that get in your way.
3. The amount of persistence you bring to the task.
4. The ability to forgive yourself and start over again when you make a mistake.
5. How you control excess anxiety.

1. Commitment. It has been said that the two hardest things in developing a presentation are starting it and finishing it. Starting and finishing a presentation takes a high degree of commitment. One technique that is helpful is to ask yourself how committed you are to finishing your presentation. There are three levels of commitment:

intellectual, irregular, and true commitment. At the intellectual level of commitment, you say you are committed, but your behavior doesn't match. In other words, you are not doing anything tangible and little, if any, progress is being made. At the level of irregular commitment, you work on the presentation one day, but not the next. Progress is painfully slow and when you do get back into it, you waste a lot of time trying to figure out what you are doing or where you are heading.

If you are operating at the level of true commitment, you follow Stephen Covey's advice by "putting first things first." You know that you are at the level of true commitment by looking at your behavior. You have set up a work schedule and you are sticking to it. You are taking advantage of working at prime times (the time of the day when you are most alert and work and concentrate the best). You have also made sure that you will not be interrupted unless there is an emergency.

One way to increase your commitment is to plan a reward for when you have achieved a milestone in completing your presentation or even a section therein. The reward could be anything from a dinner out, going to see a much-anticipated movie, a walk in the park, or a game of golf.

2. Handling roadblocks. There will be times when you are working well, there will be times when you are working adequately, and there will be times when you are not working well at all. This is to be expected. It is important to note how you handle the times when things are not going well. Let's look at how two presenters handle the same situation. Tom was working extremely well and was very pleased with himself. The following week he had to do some unexpected traveling, which threw off his whole work schedule. Tom became very discouraged, stopped working completely, abdicated control, and ended up depressed. Sue was in a similar situation, but had scheduled some extra time into her plan, just to accommodate unexpected delays. Therefore, the extra travel time did not completely upset her work schedule. Her strategy was to ask herself if there was anything she could learn from this situation, in order to prevent or minimize this type of interference in the future. In other words, she reestablished control by being solution-oriented rather than problem-oriented. Sue knew that there would be some days when she would work better than others and she did not criticize herself for the things that went wrong.

You have enough to do in developing your presentation without wasting time and energy by being your own worst enemy.

3. Persistence. To run a marathon requires a great deal of training and a lot of persistence. In fact, completing a marathon has as much to do with persistence as it does with ability. A presentation is like a marathon. Developing a presentation becomes a question of putting the time in whether you feel like it or not, and it is up to you to structure your life in order to get the job done. You can do this by using techniques such as having a set time and place to work, setting manageable time-limited goals, monitoring the use of your time, or eliminating or postponing other activities. These techniques will help you to program your presentation into your daily schedule. Eventually the natural rewards of completing the presentation will make working on it easier and easier and as you build up momentum, the issue of persistence will largely take care of itself.

4. Forgiving yourself. Even with the best of intentions, we all make mistakes. One of the factors that separates Master Presenters from their less masterful counterparts is the ability to limit the damage from the mistake and to learn from it so that it doesn't happen again.

> *If you don't fail now and then, it means you aren't reaching far enough,*
> *and you aren't growing.*
>
> —*John Paul Getty*

Master Presenter Richard Bolles says everyone is entitled to an off day:

> An unknown genius once said, "To forgive oneself is to give up all hope of ever having a better past." In other words, you look back only briefly, to see what you can learn from that mistake, and then you resolutely turn your face toward the future. Those who cannot forgive themselves are those who keep dwelling on their past mistake or mistakes, in their mind and in their meditative moments, as though this could create a better past. I never do this. I expect to fail sometimes so, when I do, I simply say, "Ah well, that's part of being human." Part of being human is also learning to improve.

I once gave a talk where the listener evaluation of "excellent or good" was only 66 percent. The next time I gave a talk (to that same group, as it turned out) I got an evaluation of "excellent or good" from 97 percent of the listeners. That never would have happened had I obsessed over what went wrong the year before. That is the secret for all of us. We are human. We will fail sometimes. But every moment you or I spend dwelling on that failure only saps us of the energy we need to deliver better talks in the future. We only have so much energy in us; what energy we have should always be employed in the service of the future, not of the past.

It is interesting to note how forgiving our audiences and our society can be, if the person admits the mistake. For example, every day we hear of someone who makes a mistake, whether personally or professionally, and as soon as they admit the mistake people rush to support them. In fact, there are many times when the person who admitted it fares better in the public eye than someone who didn't err in the first place. Conversely, when you err and try to deny it, it can be much more harmful than a frank admission of the facts would have been. Richard Nixon and Bill Clinton can attest to this. Similarly, audiences forgive a presenter's blunders if the presenter acknowledges or addresses them; audiences will not be as tolerant if the presenter ignores or denies blunders.

One of our colleagues, Pat Lazaruk, told us that one of the best things someone said to her at a train-the-trainer program was: "You are going to make mistakes and do things you wish you hadn't when you are presenting. This is referred to as 'laying an egg.' Turn around admire your egg, hatch it for the wisdom it contains, and then move on."

In other words, acknowledge your mistakes, apologize if appropriate, and proceed smarter. This is a natural part of the learning process.

5. Controlling excess anxiety. Almost all speakers, including Master Presenters, have or have had anxiety before and during a particular presentation. In fact, a certain amount of stress, tension, and anxiety are necessary in order to be a peak performer as the peak performance curve demonstrated in Figure 6-1. The trick is to control the excess anxiety, not let it control you. In the section below, we will examine six methods Master Presenters use to control excess anxiety.

Differentiating Between Normal and Excess Anxiety

Just differentiating between normal and excess anxiety will help you. Some anxiety, stress, and tension are necessary. Your job is not to *eliminate* anxiety; that would be counterproductive. Your job is to *control* your excess anxiety. For example, normal anxiety is when you are totally prepared for your presentation. You may still be nervous about presenting, but you are confident that as soon as you get going, you will settle down. Excess anxiety is when you worry that you will forget some important points or that you will get them in the wrong order or that you don't know the transitions from one part of the presentation to the next. You start the presentation with a great deal of fear and foreboding and it never gets any better. Techniques to control excess anxiety follow.

Make a checklist. Almost nothing makes presenters more anxious than arriving to give the presentation only to find that some key material or a critical piece of equipment is missing. One of the reasons that flying is one of the safest ways to travel is that the pilot and co-pilot must go through extensive checklists before taking off. Master Presenters not only have a checklist, they have a Plan B for those times when something happens that is beyond their control, such as the computer or projector dying in the middle of a presentation, a general power outage, or other such calamities. In other words, if you plan for the unexpected, then you won't be thrown off if it occurs. And make no mistake, at some time, some type of disaster will occur.

David: I recommend three checklists: one for packing before you leave home, another for setting up onsite, and a third for packing up at the end of the presentation. Copies of my checklists are shown in Appendix D. Whenever I discover— always too late—that I left something behind, it's the result of not using one of these checklists.

Physical activity. Exercise is the natural antidote to stress. Therefore, getting into good shape and staying in good shape is a natural stress reducer. Go for a run or a brisk walk before your presentation. If it is raining or too cold, go up and down the stairs, jog in place, or do a few push-ups. Presentations author David Peoples suggests you can release tension by pulling at the rungs of the chair you are sitting in or pushing up under the table at which you are seated to alternately increase and release the tension. Please note that this needs to be done as unobtrusively as possible. And don't overdo it; you don't want to look as if you are in the middle of a workout.

Deep breathing. Rapid, shallow breathing increases stress, but slow, measured, deep breathing is nature's tranquilizer. Try it the next time you feel nervous prior to taking the platform. Take 10 deep breaths over the course of one minute—three seconds to breathe in and three seconds to breathe out. By concentrating on the rhythm and timing of the breaths you take, your focus will become sharper—partly because you will not be dwelling on all the typically negative "what if's," and partly because you will increase the oxygen level in your blood. Just make sure you don't overdo it and hyperventilate.

Use lip gloss or lip balm. Often when you become nervous your mouth dries out, especially your lips. We then mentally make the attribution that our dry mouth proves how anxious we are and this reinforces our thought that we are nervous. It's a vicious circle. There are two ways to intervene: We can change our attributions and we can treat the symptoms of anxiety such as dry mouth. A simple application of lip gloss, lip balm, or Vaseline will keep your lips moist and increase your comfort level.

Talk with participants before presenting. Talking with participants before the presentation starts can be a great way to relax. The reason is that after you've shared a few pleasantries or shared a few laughs, the ice is broken. When you take the stage, you are no longer speaking to a group of strangers. As a bonus, you may get some valuable clues on how to better align your presentation with that particular audience's needs and expectations. As an added bonus, by focusing on the participants, you will be less likely to focus on yourself and your own nervousness.

Know your opening and closing cold. Know your opening and closing so well that you could present them in your sleep. Almost all presenters we interviewed reported that once they get through the opening and it goes well, there is a big sense of relief. On the other hand, when the opening doesn't go well, there is a marked increase in distress.

David: I have a standard four- to five-minute humorous opening specifically designed to read the audience. It's some of my sure-fire material that I have high confidence in. I know that when I get my usual response, I'm going to have a good presentation. On the other hand, when the response is subdued, I know I will have a tougher go of it. When my best material doesn't work, I know I will have to make adjustments to my presentation and/or brace for a less-than-satisfying presentation. If I constantly changed my opening, I wouldn't know if the problem was with the material, with the audience, or with me.

Similarly, knowing your closing as well as your opening will give you added confidence at a critical point in which many presentations are made memorable or forgettable. Remember the laws of primacy and recency—we remember best that which we hear first and last. Therefore, your conclusion should be as perfect as possible. If you close as strongly as you open, you will be well on your way to becoming a Master Presenter.

Make eye contact with friendly participants. In any audience there will be friendly faces—find them, they will give you reassurance when you need it most. Start by making eye contact with a friendly face in one part of the room, and then do the same thing with someone else in another part of the room. Search out the participants who are nodding in agreement as you speak. There may be a sparkle in their eyes or an encouraging smile. Come back to these people when you start to feel uncomfortable or ill at ease. Soon you will be feeling more comfortable with most, if not all, of the participants.

Increasing Your Sense of Control

To help you increase your sense of control in developing and delivering your presentation, ask yourself the following questions: "To gain more control over the development and delivery of my presentation, how should I behave differently?" or, "How can I structure my personal environment/situation/life so I have more control?" If possible, check your conclusions with an objective colleague and then design a plan to act on your recommendations. You may want to pay particular attention to how you could increase and demonstrate a higher level of commitment to finishing your presentation, how you deal with and overcome roadblocks, the level of persistence you apply to your work, the types of attributions you make when you encounter an obstacle or make a mistake, and how you could better control excess anxiety. Answer these questions as specifically and in as much detail as you can in Exercise 6-3.

EXERCISE
6-3

Please write down the steps you could take to increase your control over developing and completing your presentation in a reasonable amount of time.

In summary, you always have more control and more options than you think. Sometimes it just takes a little help to see that you do. Even though it may be difficult to admit to yourself that you need help, it is a statement of strength rather than of weakness. You owe it to yourself to explore all of your options. Getting good help is one option that should not be overlooked.

Dealing with Difficult Participants

The worst kind of children are grown-ups.

—*Loesje International Poster, Holland*

Now that you are managing yourself more effectively by monitoring and changing negative attributions and negative self-talk into positive attributions and positive self-talk, and you have increased your internal locus of control, strengthened your commitment, and overcome perfectionism and other internal roadblocks, it is time to face the issue of difficult participants. Difficult participants can knock us out of the zone of peak performance and they are likely to appear when we least expect them.

There are two types of difficult participants: situationally difficult and chronically difficult. Master Presenters do not get discouraged by these individuals, rather, they learn from them. All of us can be situationally difficult. For whatever reason, some days are just more difficult than others. Chronically difficult people are difficult most if not all of the time. These are the kind of people who can't have a good day until they've ruined someone else's. Master Presenters have learned the Law of Non-Resistance. The Law of Non-Resistance states, "Everyone who comes across our paths, comes across our path for a reason, to teach us something about our own skills and talents."[3]

When it comes to dealing with difficult participants we have three choices: We can become a victim, a survivor, or a thriver. In this section we will learn to thrive—or at least survive—difficult participants by learning the power of a correct diagnosis, the power of the change first principle, the power of appropriately increasing one's muscle level, and the power of asking the audience how they would like to deal with the situation.

For example, one of our training associates, Pat Lazaruk, says, "You can change your reaction to people's reactions to the material by asking 'What do the participants need?' In other words, being more focused on being a vehicle to their learning/development than worrying about yourself. As a presenter you need to get over yourself!"

This is easier said than done, yet all Master Presenters have done it. Cavett Robert, the founder of the National Speakers Association, said all good speakers go through three phases of development. The first phase, where *every* speaker starts, is concern about oneself. In this phase, the speaker is consumed by such thoughts as, "How do *I* look and how do *I* sound?" Presenters who never get past this "I-focused" phase let their personal insecurities and anxieties keep them from connecting with their audience.

Presenters who learn through practice and perseverance to get over themselves then move to the second developmental phase: concern about your message. That is, the now-confident presenter is most concerned about the value of the information being presented. When this phase is mastered, Robert says, you move into the third and final phase of maturity: concern about your audience. This is where good presenters become great and Master Presenters are made.

The Necessity of an Accurate Diagnosis

At least half of any medical cure is a correct diagnosis. As a presenter, you have to determine if you are dealing with a difficult person.

We all have bad days or troubling issues that can make us difficult in certain situations. Other people are consistently and persistently cantankerous and for no particular reason. Therefore, we have to learn how not to take it personally. It may be that the man in the second row is not paying attention because he has just had an argument with his wife.

Brad: I remember doing a presentation where one of the participants seemed totally disinterested. In fact, she refused to even make eye contact with me. I fretted about trying to reach her during the whole presentation and I am sure that the presentation was less effective because of it. I also must admit that I felt very relieved once it was over. After everyone left, I commented to the presentation organizer that I was sure I would get at least one poor evaluation. The organizer immediately knew who I was speaking about even though I didn't mention her name. The organizer then said, "Oh, I talked to her on the way out and she loved your presentation. In fact, she said it was one of the best she had ever attended." I was dumbfounded—my diagnosis could not have been further from the truth.

David: I have had similar experiences in which I misread the listener's response. I was presenting a full-day program to a roomful of lively and responsive people. That is, everyone was lively and responsive except one. Three rows back and on the center aisle was a woman who was clearly not having a good time. She didn't take notes, she didn't answer questions posed to the group, she didn't participate in any activity, and when the audience laughed, she frowned. For the first hour or so, I obsessed over this. I was confident that I could "bring her around." Yet, every attempt to draw her into the fun and excitement failed. After about 90 minutes, I gave up and wrote her off. At the end of the day as I packed up my materials, she walked toward me. I thought "Uh-oh. I'm about to find out just what she didn't like." Imagine my surprise when she said, "I just want you to know that I learned more in this program than from any I've ever attended." Wow, did I ever misread her. What I took as disinterest was instead intensity. She was so focused on learning that she wouldn't allow herself to be distracted by all the other "lively and fun" activities. What I learned from this is that some people's outward appearance belies their true feelings.

As these examples illustrate, sometimes the difficult person turns out to be ourselves. We know the topic and the materials so well that we don't set up the presentation properly. In any presentation it is helpful to highlight that the tone/opening you use goes a long way to clarifying expectations and setting the tone with the participants. Clear agendas and guidelines for how the presentation will be structured are important to most people. On the other hand, there are difficult people in the world and their difficulty comes in varying degrees.

The Change-First Principle states that if you want to change the behavior of another person or your relationship with that person, you first have to change your own behavior. In a similar vein, the literature on Brief Solution-Focused Therapy states: "If it is working, do more of the same; if it isn't working, do something different."

Doing the unexpected, the Change-First Principle, and "if it isn't working do something different," all have a common element. That element is changing a behavior pattern. When the old pattern no longer works, try a new pattern that does. In order to do this more frequently, we have to be aware of when we are at a "choice point"—those critical points in a situation when, if we choose to do something different, the situation will move forward toward a resolution. On the other hand, if we choose to do more of the same behavior, we will continue the old pattern, reach an impasse, or escalate into a conflict.

As presenters, we are constantly negotiating, as the following example illustrates.

Brad: My workshops are highly interactive, and the participants spend a lot of time doing simulations and role-playing in the workshop. Just before the beginning of one workshop, one of the participants, Bob, came up to me and said, "I don't believe in role-playing. It is a complete waste of time. I have been to lots of workshops. I have never learned anything from role-playing and I refuse to do it in this workshop."

This worried me because my workshop is highly experiential and I have three to four negotiation role-play simulations planned over the next two days.

I replied, "There are some things that are difficult to learn any other way."

Bob replied, "That's just a motherhood statement."

Obviously I wasn't getting anywhere with this approach, so I changed strategies. My response to this statement was, "I am willing to be wrong."

To my surprise, Bob replied, "I am willing to be wrong, too."

Bob went on to participate in all role-playing in the course and even volunteered to participate in the most difficult role-play in front of the whole class. Hence, changing my behavior changed Bob's behavior.

In summary, we would all do well to follow the advice of Master Presenter Janet Lapp: "If you seek out difficult people, you will find them, or you will create them. Do your homework, align with your audience's needs, expectations, and aspirations, go to where they are without forcing yourself in."

When negotiating, the muscle level is the amount of power or force you bring to the table. There are two common mistakes when it comes to using power: too much too soon, and too little too late. Let's see how we can apply the concept of muscle level to dealing with difficult participants and how to apply different levels of muscle depending on the level of difficulty we are dealing with.

As stated previously, at least half of any medical cure is a correct diagnosis. Similarly, dealing with difficult participants requires a correct diagnosis of the problem and of the amount of power or force necessary to rectify it.

We will now look at how to match the amount of power or force we bring to the situation at various muscle levels.

Consider a situation in which a particular participant seems to have it in for you and the topic of your presentation.

Muscle Level One: Get more information. See the person in private during a break and engage him or her in light conversation. Try to find out as much as you can because some of this information may shed light on that person's behavior.

Brad: At one of my presentations, one of the participants seemed not to be paying any attention whatsoever. This surprised me because I have given this presentation numerous times before and had always been successful. Secondly, all of the other participants in the room seemed to be fully engaged. Half way through our conversation at the break, Rob told me that he had just been informed that he was losing his job through downsizing, that he had always had excellent performance appraisals, and that he had gladly moved his family several times to meet his employers' needs. He went on to apologize for finding it hard to concentrate because he felt so betrayed and poorly treated.

I told him that I understood, that he was welcome to stay or leave, and that I had some excellent materials on resume writing that I would be glad to send him. Rob decided to stay in the training because he felt that the skills would help him in future positions. After our discussion, Rob concentrated extremely well considering the circumstances.

Muscle Level Two: The person continues to be disruptive both to your teaching and to other members of the audience. At this point, you can ask the other participants for their input. Describe the problem as a process problem, not as a person problem. In other words, don't ask the group to help you label Bill's behavior as disruptive, boorish, immature, and destructive (even though you may really want to do so). Instead, ask a process question. Ask the participants if they would rather proceed in the direction and manner you have proposed or if they would like to move in the direction, and/or manner that the participant proposed, or if there is a third alternative. Being open to suggestions, and being assertive enough to bring the issue forward will increase your credibility. Most of the time the participants will make it clear that they want to follow your direction and this will effectively silence your critic/distracter. In a very few cases, the participants will suggest an alternative that will work more effectively for all concerned parties, and in even fewer cases they will agree with the direction that your critic has proposed. Your job now is to act on the wishes of the participants. Don't be afraid to ask for their help in formulating the new agenda. After the agenda has been agreed to, don't be afraid to ask for a break so you can regroup and plan the next segment of the presentation.

Muscle Level Three: At this level, the difficult person starts disagreeing with everything you say and tries to take over the presentation by monopolizing all of the air time, and so on. You have met with the person individually and tried to negotiate a settlement to no avail. What this person is counting on is that you will not say anything publicly in front of the group, even though he or she is disruptive in front of the group.

Now is the time to call the difficult person's bluff by taking actionable steps. For example, you can ask the group for their input in how to proceed. There are three possible outcomes: the group will side with you and ask the disruptive party to stop; the group will side with the difficult person and you will get some very valuable feedback about your presentation style, the group dynamics, or both; or the group will suggest a solution that will allow both you and the difficult person to agree by changing or improving the presentation and each of you will also be able to save face.

Please note: Just as in medicine, the higher the level of the medical intervention, the greater the likelihood of side effects. The same is true when using increased muscle level as a presenter. The good news is, the more you present and the better you know your material, the less likely it is that a participant will try to give you a hard time. If they persist, you can then, in good conscience, move up to Muscle Level Four.

Muscle Level Four: At this point, the situation is intolerable. You have tried everything you can to make it work and clearly it is not. You are clearly in your right to ask the other party to leave. If he or she refuses, you still have a number of choices. You can say that either he or she will have to leave or you will. Please note that this will rarely happen, if ever. In fact, it has never happened to Brad or to David. However, it is important to have a strategy in place just in case it becomes necessary.

Each of these strategies is risky, but so is continuing under intolerable circumstances. Another alternative is to call a break, then call a colleague and ask for his or her help in processing the situation and your alternatives.

Master Presenter David Foot had this to say about dealing with difficult participants:

> I have found that the best way to deal with difficult audience members is to let the audience deal with them. For example, I teach at several senior executive management programs. Sometimes the participants aren't used to listening, but there are subtle ways that if they violate the group norms or the group's wishes, the group can deal with it most effectively—the worst thing you can do is to become arrogant. For example, if they start pontificating about general management, I say something such as, "I'm not in general management. What I am interested in is the effects of demographics on retail or policy or...(fill in the blank)." If they continue, I suggest that they can cover whatever they are interested during a different session. In other words, I try to put very clear boundaries on what my session is about and what it is not about and suggest that we concentrate on what today is all about. Then I relax the boundaries in the question and answer period.

One strategy David finds effective when faced with a persistently difficult participant is to say: "You have a good point and one that probably deserves further discussion, but our schedule won't allow me to address it fully at this time. However, if you wish to stay after the program ends, I'll be glad to continue our discussion." This sends a signal to the participant and the rest of your audience that you are moving on and it implies that line of discussion is now closed. David also finds it interesting that often the person whom he invites to stay for further discussion either offers some great insights that deepen his understanding of the subject at hand, or the person is the first to leave at the end of the program because that person was only interested in seeking attention.

Dealing With Difficult Situations

Occasionally, a presenter can become too complacent. He or she has mastered the art of self-management and knows the material so well that no difficult participants would dare to "mess with him." At this point, it may be tempting for this presenter to say that he or she has seen it all. However, all of the Master Presenters that we interviewed warned about complacency. It seems that, just as soon as they have said to themselves that they have seen it all, difficult situations and unforeseen circumstances arise to humble even the most seasoned presenter. In the final section of this chapter, we will look at how Master Presenters have learned to deal with difficult and unforeseen circumstances.

The first scenario deals with a noisy hotel renovation that was taking place just below the seminar room. To make matters worse, the hotel staff was trying to pretend that the noise of jackhammers emanating from the room below wasn't really interfering with the presentation. In this case, our presenter had to use the concept of Muscle Level with the hotel staff as the following example demonstrates.

Paul was presenting to a group of contractors about the new Safety Act that had recently come into effect. He had the audience's attention right from the start by telling them that 90 percent of accidents are preventable and predictable and how by judiciously applying the safety standards, there had been 25 percent decrease in industrial accidents in the past five years. He was about to continue when the sounds of construction began intruding into the room from the floor below.

The first thing that Paul did was to validate his perception that the participants found the noise distracting and they confirmed they did. Paul then called the hotel operator to report the problem from the phone inside the room. He was told that someone from maintenance would be sent up immediately. Five minutes went by and the sounds were getting louder and louder. Paul called again and was again told that someone would be there immediately. Five more minutes went by, and it was very difficult to keep anyone's attention. Paul was told that the construction workers would do their best to keep the sounds to a minimum but the construction had to be completed for a large convention that was coming to the hotel the following week. The sounds were becoming more and more intrusive.

Next, Paul called the hotel manager and asked him to address the audience of his presentation because they were all having difficulty doing the work that the session was designed to accomplish. The hotel manager addressed Paul's group. They told the manager that it was impossible to concentrate in the room. Paul pointed out the cost in terms of the hourly salaries of the attendees that were being lost as well as to the hotel's reputation as a meeting/convention site.

The construction was halted. The session was a success and the participants not only appreciated the content of the session, but also Paul's assertiveness. Through Paul's use of Muscle Level, he made sure that his attendees were treated as well as possible.

In addition to having to deal with circumstances you can control, Master Presenters have to learn how to minimize distractions that they cannot control.

Minimizing a Distraction You Cannot Control

One of the most amazing presenters that Brad has had the pleasure of hearing was Yvonne Dolan.[4] There were about 50 people attending her presentation and for some reason, the audio system started making strange high-pitched noises. The technical people went to work, but the noises persisted. Yvonne was completely nonplussed as she asked the attendees to think of the sound as baby whales calling to their mothers. Although the sound persisted, the intrusiveness of the sound did not. Eventually the technicians located the source of the problem and corrected it. In all his years of giving and attending presentations, Brad has never seen anyone deal with an uncontrollable distraction so brilliantly.

A colleague, Jim Comer, suggests: "Acknowledge the obvious. Whether it's a distraction or a disaster, don't pretend it did not happen. Acknowledge it, address it, and if possible, use it. If you ignore it, people will think you are oblivious to your surroundings. And if they think you are oblivious to your surroundings, they may infer that you are oblivious to your audience, and maybe even to your subject matter, as well."

Master Presenter Terry Paulson recommends that we have a few "saver" lines that we can use when things go wrong. In relation to too much noise or the microphone not working:[5]

> How many of you in the back of the room read lips?
>
> Whatever that noise is, it's getting closer!
>
> You know, I'm actually starting to like that squeal.

Another favorite example is from an interview with Master Presenter Janet Lapp. She was speaking at a conference in San Diego.

The venue was a large tent, which had a huge echo, and there was absolutely nothing the technicians could do about it. Janet's response to the echo was to say to the audience, "It's actually a better deal because you can hear me twice." Janet added, "It's important that we give our audiences permission to relax, knowing that we are handling it."

It is also important to remember not to get angry, no matter how frustrating the situation or circumstance may be. Amateurs lose their tempers; professionals do not.

David: I had a circumstance in which just about every piece of equipment I was using failed. The LCD projector wouldn't project. The sound system cut out intermittently. The lighting couldn't be adjusted. The easy thing to have done was to blame someone, or make disparaging remarks about the facility. But I knew that would be a bad reflection on me. Instead, I laughed off each problem as a "new learning opportunity." The audience understood my frustration, but they appreciated my poise. Whether the problems that arise are your fault or not does not matter. What does matter is the grace with which you handle them.

Roz Usheroff, who teaches etiquette, says the sign of a real host is that he or she makes his or her guests feel comfortable. Master Presenters make their audiences feel comfortable—even under the most trying circumstances.

Hidden Agendas

Hidden agendas can be some of the most difficult situations with which any presenter has to deal. However, if you handle them correctly, you have a great opportunity to enhance your credibility as the following two examples illustrate.

David: One of the communication courses I teach is Business Writing Basics. Though some people will admit they are not good writers, almost everyone comes in with an attitude of "I already know this stuff." Aware of that prevalent attitude, I acknowledge the obvious: "I know that you are effective writers or you wouldn't be here today. It's the people who sent you who really should be here, right?" This gets a modest laugh and lets them feel superior. Then I say, "But even effective writers can be better if we eliminate a few blunders that even careful writers make. So let's take a quiz to see just how careful you are." Then I give them a quiz on the common writing and grammatical issues that confuse most people. It's a fair and relevant quiz, but a hard one. We grade the quiz as a group and then I say, "If you scored 100 percent, you don't need this class—go home, you're finished for the day. So who gets to leave?" No one ever raises their hand. Then I ask, "How many of you made an A?" Rarely does anyone score this high. "How many Bs?" Perhaps 25 percent fall in this category. "How many Cs?" The majority scores in this range. And then I ask, "And how many of you don't want me to ask the next question?" Nervous laughter follows. Then I say, "So we've found a few of you who need a little refresher on some of the basics, right? And that's what we're here for today—to remind you of what you already know and to help you be just a little bit better." The purpose of this activity and exchange is to emphasize two key points: 1) to acknowledge that attendees know a lot already, and 2) to assure them that I can supply them with at least a few tips to make them even better. It effectively diffuses the "I know all this stuff" attitude that can be so counterproductive if left unchallenged.

Brad: It was mid-August, and the organization I was working for at the time had secured a contract to do a workshop on Participatory Management to a group of mid-level managers for the federal government. When I began the presentation, I couldn't help but notice that the audience was incredibly hostile. I had a room of 20 apparently very angry participants staring at me in defiance. When I asked them for their expectations, the answers were non-existent, hostile, or sarcastic. I immediately stopped the presentation and asked what was going on. Boy, did I get an earful.

Paradoxically, although it was a workshop on Participatory Management, the participants had been told by their manager that they would, in no uncertain terms, attend the

workshop in mid-August. The fact that many of the participants in the room had already asked for and were granted
this time for their summer vacations—including one family's
trip to Disney World that they had saved for more than five
years—seemed to make no difference to this group's manager. The irony of forcing people to take a workshop on
Participatory Management would have amused me, if I had
not been tasked with teaching the workshop.

I then asked the group to look at the options we had regarding the workshop. Although many of them would have liked
to cancel the workshop, this was not a viable option. After I
allowed them to vent and they could see that I was not part
of the problem, they agreed to learn as much as they could
and deal with their manager in another way. To this day, I
am still very appreciative of the maturity of the participants
who were in that workshop.

Always Expect the Unexpected

Sometimes even if you work at being as well prepared and as well
informed about the audience as possible, things will happen or be
announced at the last minute that will put a pall over the group to
whom you are presenting and there is nothing you can do but go with
the flow and salvage as much as you can from the presentation.

Brad:　At one point, I did a lot of staff training at a local university.
The staff had never had training in the past and was very
appreciative of the training, which made them a pleasure to
teach. Imagine my surprise when I entered the room to teach
a course on Improving Personal Productivity and was met
by a sullen group with hostile stares.

It seems that it had been announced the day before that the
vice president of operations for the university had just hired
a consulting firm to do a time and efficiency study on the
university's staff. Both the staff and their union felt that the
process was very intrusive, would lead to staff reductions,
and would produce poorer levels of service at the university. The fact that the time and efficiency studies would only

be conducted on staff, and not on the university's administration, was particularly galling to the staff. The fact that I was being introduced to give a presentation on improving productivity by this same vice president of operations also added to my less-than-welcoming reception.

Master Presenter Bill Carr, a humorist, talked about being asked to give a humor presentation to a particular group. Just a few minutes before Bill was to present, the company's CEO announced that one of the company's most cherished and youngest employees had just been killed in a tragic car accident. The CEO then asked for a moment of silence before Bill was supposed to start his "humorous" presentation. Another example is that of an accountant who had to give a presentation to the company's employees telling them that the company's chief financial officer had just been found to have embezzled most of the employees' pension funds. As Bill Carr says, "Sometimes it doesn't matter how prepared you are, you can't recover and you just have to ride it out."

Unforeseen Circumstances

Barbara was giving the most important presentation of her life. Not only were her boss and boss's boss there, the entire board of directors of her company was in attendance. Barbara had never prepared a presentation so carefully in her life. She conducted numerous dry runs, and then the big day finally arrived. What Barbara hadn't planned on was that her laptop would die just before she began her presentation.

Unfortunately, she didn't have the presentation on a disk, if she had, she could have just borrowed someone else's computer. Because she had never had a single problem with her laptop, she hadn't thought to make transparencies. What she did do, however, was to make detailed handouts. Like a true pro, she started her presentation with some humor that she had a slightly used laptop for sale and then began her presentation as if nothing out of the ordinary happened. Because Barbara was so composed, her audience didn't notice that they didn't have the planned version of the slides to look at. You can also be sure that now Barbara never travels without a back-up disk or CD.

There are other unforeseen circumstances that are impossible to ignore.

Brad: I was teaching for Michelin in South Carolina, on September 11, 2001. We started at 8 a.m. We took our first break at 9:45 a.m. I was in the process of organizing some of my materials when one of the participants came up to me and said that there had been a terrible accident—a passenger plane had crashed into one of the World Trade Towers.

We decided to continue the class until the second break at 11 a.m. At that time we heard that another plane had hit the second World Trade Tower—that it was probably a terrorist attack—that several other planes had been hijacked—and that the potential loss of life in New York was horrendous. There was a surreal sense in the room. Could what we were hearing really be true? There were no television sets in our training complex; however, the participants were getting both similar and sometimes quite different information from their cell phones. As a group, we decided to work until noon and take an hour off for lunch to fully assess the situation and see if this unbelievable chain of events could possibly be true.

When the participants came back at 1 p.m., we knew that the unbelievable stories were true. We determined that no one in the room had relatives in New York so we decided to proceed for another hour, which would give me time to assign a short homework assignment and end the course for the day at 2 p.m.

It was a difficult choice. If I continued the course, it would be disrespectful of the thousands of people who lost their lives, and I wasn't sure if any of us could pay attention to the course material. If I had cancelled the course outright, it would seem like the terrorists had achieved their goal of disruption even more. So I decided what could be left out and still give the participants the best course possible under these terrible circumstances, and asked the participants if they could work for an additional hour. They agreed that this was the best option under the circumstances.

I started the next day with a minute of silence for all of those who lost their lives in the terrorist attack. It felt like we were under the weight of a heavy burden. However, the participants worked hard and we made the best of a very difficult situation. On the third day of training, it was announced that Michelin would donate $1 million to the American Red Cross disaster relief fund, supply unlimited technical support to keep all rescue and recovery vehicles running, and donate a quarter of a million new tires to aid in the rescue and recovery efforts. At this, everyone in the room felt proud to be associated with Michelin. There was something that their company was doing that was concrete and tangible. It also helped us focus on the work at hand.

I was surprised that the course evaluations were as good as they had always been. There was, however, one particular piece of feedback that I will always cherish: "A special note of 'Thanks' and a big 'well done' too for recognizing the impact of the bombings on Tuesday's class and for having the professionalism and skills to not only salvage the course, but to make it worthwhile."

Master Presenters have the seasoned judgment to know when to recognize that there are circumstances that are affecting the participant's ability to learn. They have also learned how to deal with these types of situations as sensitively and tactfully as possible. They also know when to ask for feedback from the group that will aid in making the best decision possible about if and how to proceed.

At this point, you have developed a dynamic presentation, have done your homework so you know your audience, developed superior organization, and made your presentation memorable, actionable, and transferable. You have also practiced so much that you know your presentation cold. You have also mastered how to deal with yourself, difficult participants, and difficult situations. You are now miles ahead of most presenters. However, there is still one critical difference between you and the Master Presenters we have interviewed in this book. The Master Presenters we interviewed don't stop here. They constantly engage in the process of total quality improvement, and that is the subject of our next strategy.

STRATEGY

7

Total Quality Improvement

The future belongs to those who prepare for it.

—*Ralph Waldo Emerson*

It takes time to get [it] right. I don't want it to look anything but accomplished and if I can't make it look that way, then I'm not ready yet.

—*Fred Astaire*

The world's best manufacturers have developed an excellent reputation based on Total Quality Improvement. Master Presenters have also developed their presentations and their reputations by using Total Quality Improvement. In this chapter you will learn how to take your presentations to the next level by maximizing the benefits from practice sessions and salient feedback. You will also learn how to develop the deep structure of your presentation and how to develop command (stage) presence—all of which are designed to lead the way to becoming a Master Presenter.

The Benefits of Practice Sessions

Practice! Practice by videotaping, audiotaping or role-playing with friends and colleagues. Be so comfortable with what you are going to say that you don't have to think about it. This frees your thoughts to be totally in tune with your [audience].

—Bill Bachrach, author and Certified Speaking Professional

Most presenters overprepare on content and underprepare on delivery. To counteract this natural tendency, we will explore five principles for effective rehearsals:

1. Test early, test often.
2. Simulate the setting and audience as closely as possible.
3. Conduct dry runs.
4. Test on mixed audiences.
5. Look at the presentation from a fresh perspective.

1. Test Early, Test Often

Too often, presenters find that they have perfected a part of their presentation that shouldn't be in the presentation at all. Often, this comes as a result of overrehearsing component parts, without considering the presentation as a whole. A better strategy is to listen to the presentation from start to finish, even if it is in rough form. In fact, you may even want to tape record an early version. The purpose of the taping is to get an overview of the presentation to determine what should be in it as well as what should not. By listening to an early version, you can begin to hear the central theme and the questions that the presentation should be answering. Because even the first draft of a presentation is enough to make people anxious, Harvard University's Joan Bolker[1] uses the idea of "the zero draft" to help people with writer's block. In her book, *How to Write Your Dissertation in 15 Minutes a Day,* Bolker, like many other writers, says there is no such thing as a good writer; there are only good rewriters. Likewise, James Michener said, "I have never thought of myself as a good writer. Anyone who wants reassurance of that should read one of my first drafts. But I am one of the world's best rewriters." In fact, most experts agree that the better the document, the more likely it has been revised numerous times. It is the same with presentations. The better the presentation, the more times it has been practiced, and that means practicing early and often. However, the hardest practice session for many of us to get around to doing is the first practice session, and this is an all-too-common mistake. One of the best ways to get around this is to do "the zero practice session."

We developed the idea of "the zero practice session" from Joan Bolker's recommendation to take the anxiety out of writing the first draft of a written document. Joan calls this "the zero draft." The purpose of the zero draft is to get words on paper or a layout of your presentation. The intended audience for the zero draft is you. So get something—anything—down on paper. Give yourself something to edit. You are purposely working out and clarifying your own thinking about a particular topic. Once you have a better idea of what you want to say, you can then decide if the material suits your intended audience. In other words, you have to figure out the answers to your own questions first. Then, and only then, do you work at figuring out the answers to questions your audience will likely have. Many times your questions and the audience's questions will be the same. Sometimes not. However, we often can't answer an audience's questions until we answer our own questions first.

We have found that the concept of the zero practice session has taken a lot of the anxiety out of the preparation process. It has also helped us by giving permission to write and develop presentations in a manner that is more in tune with how presentations are naturally developed, and we have confidence it will do the same for you.

Another way to ensure that you practice early and benefit from early feedback is to enlist selected friends and colleagues to listen to and give you feedback on your zero practice session. In this case, you should tell your audience that this is as much of a brainstorming session as it is a feedback session. You need to tell your audience that you want their ideas as to what should and what should not be included in the presentation as well as any other ideas they have, regarding both content and delivery. For example, the participants in our *Seven Strategies of Master Presenters* courses are amazed at how much more quickly they improve and how much better a job they can do when they develop and practice their presentations in small groups. Why is this true? They can test early and they can test often. This immediate feedback gives the presenter an idea much earlier as to whether an idea will work or not. When we ask our participants to give us an idea in percentages as to how much more effective this is, the normal estimate is 50 to 90 percent. Based on their experience in class, the participants are sold on using the "test early and test often" technique in the future.

Testing early and often is a proven strategy, yet you may think it difficult to find a live audience to practice in front of. Not so. Master Presenters know that there are numerous places when you can practice. For example, you can recruit a group of friends or family members, or even practice in front of the family pet or a tape-recorder. There are also organizations where you can find a willing and eager audience such as Toastmasters. There you not only have an audience to speak to, but the listeners will give you immediate feedback. This allows you to evaluate your presentation from your perspective as presenter, and to let the audience evaluate your presentation from their perspective as listeners.

2. Simulate the Setting and Audience as Closely as Possible

One of the reasons airplane simulators work so well is that they simulate actual flying conditions as closely as possible. Similarly, Master Presenters should simulate the setting and the audience as closely as possible. For example, Brad saw Master Presenter Patricia Fripp present a closing keynote on the last day of the Global Payroll Conference in San Antonio, Texas. Earlier that morning, Patricia had practiced her presentation in the empty room where she would give it later that day—you just can't simulate the setting any better than that. Of course, you won't always have the opportunity to practice in the same room in which you will give the final presentation, but if you can practice in a room of similar size and setup, your performance will be better as a result.

You may also want to consider practicing with an audience that will be as similar to your actual audience as possible. If you are presenting to professional engineers and you know several professional engineers, invite them to be your test audience. If you don't know people in the exact profession to which you will be presenting, find a practice audience that is as similar as possible to your target audience in terms of age, education, or interests.

3. Conduct Dry Runs

Dry runs are practice sessions and as such they can occur in a variety of settings. Dry runs will give you the time you need to make necessary corrections or to find and/or update any data, quotes, or statistics that you may be using in your presentation. Dry runs will also give you a sense of what is working and what is not working, and if there are any holes in your presentation. Also, after letting the outline sit for a while, you may be able to see that another way to organize your presentation makes more sense. Also, as discussed in the previous chapter, coming to the presentation fully prepared will help to alleviate much of the anxiety that plagues many presenters.

Dry runs also give your subconscious a chance to work on the presentation when you are consciously not thinking about it. For example, you may be going for a run, folding the laundry, or driving your children to their activities, when presto, right in the middle of not thinking about the presentation, you have a terrific idea about how to use a story, a prop, a metaphor, or an analogy that makes your presentation twice as good as it would have been without the insight. Because the subconscious doesn't work on a fixed schedule, if you leave too little time between the preparation and the delivery, it is much less likely that you will benefit from any of these important insights.

4. Test on Mixed Audiences

Different types of audiences will see and hear different things. For example, Brad had prepared a case study to be presented at a meeting of the Roundtable on the Economy and the Environment. The audience would be made up of members from government, the business sector, and environmental groups.

Brad: I found a perfect case of an asphalt company that was located in a small community. The plant either met or exceeded all of the current environmental standards. The problem was that when the wind blew under five miles per hour, particles landed on a nearby elementary school and the students and staff complained that their clothes picked up the odor. A number of students complained of headaches. The mayor promised to move the plant before the next municipal election, but it was not determined who would pay for the move. Lastly, the head of the town's industrial park had asked for a vote, and the board of directors had concurred that the asphalt plant would not be allowed into the "high tech" industrial park. It was a perfect case because it was current, on-going, and seemed to have no solution that was agreeable to everyone.

We had interviewed all of the constituents and made sure that we understood the case and all the proposed solutions. We painstakingly wrote up each party's instructions and made sure that we understood everyone's role as carefully as an FBI profiler and we developed a true scale map of the town and everything within the town limits and had verified with the town manager that our map was indeed accurate.

However, there was one more step and that step was to do a dress rehearsal. I invited a group of friends over for dinner and, after dinner, asked our guests to try the case study with the directions for role-playing as we had written.

I subsequently found out that my instructions, which were crystal clear to me and the people in the town whom I interviewed, were less clear to the people I had invited over to test the case.

The dress rehearsal saved me from asking the members of the Roundtable to try to resolve a case where the instructions were less clear than I had thought. The moral of the story is to do a dress rehearsal and find out if there are any problems with your information, exercises, case studies, etc., before, not after, you give the presentation.

5. Look at the Presentation From a Fresh Perspective

It is a common experience to spend so much time looking at the material from the same perspective that we can't see any other way to present the material.

Brad   This is analogous to me losing my glasses. I know they are somewhere in the house, and I have searched high and low and can't find them. I then ask one of my children if they have seen my glasses and they find them almost immediately because they are approaching the subject from a fresh perspective.

If you have a neutral outside party look at your presentation, that person may be able to see things that you don't see. This is especially true if you are presenting to mixed audiences where some of the members are very familiar with the material and others only have a slight understanding of the material being presented. Your material has to be so masterful that it reaches audience members who are extrinsically on different levels.

You can maximize the value of your practice sessions by harvesting maximum salient feedback—our next topic.

Maximizing Salient Feedback

Oh, that God would give us the gifts to be able to see ourselves as others see us.

—Robert Burns, Scottish poet

Salient feedback is feedback that is so personally meaningful that we actually change our behavior. The problem is that even though we live in a feedback-rich world, most of us do not harvest the feedback necessary for total quality improvement. We will present 12 methods to ensure that you are getting the feedback necessary to put you squarely on the road to becoming a Master Presenter.

There are many techniques that will help you get the feedback you need from those who have seen you present. A good evaluation form given right after the presentation will give you some indication of how well you presented. If you use the same evaluation form over time, you can gauge progress and the effect of changing an element of what you present or how you present.

There are almost as many types of presentation evaluations as there are presenters, however, many presentations are not evaluated at all. Presenters who fail to evaluate their presentations miss out on valuable feedback. We have found, as have the Master Presenters that we interviewed, that even presenters who have a great deal of natural talent will eventually present less well than their less talented counterparts who have sought out and benefited from constructive feedback.

We favor using scaled items (to help measure between presentations) and open-ended items to get a deeper sense of how the participants reacted to the presentation and to individual differences. Two things to keep in mind when you use these types of evaluations: You can't please everyone, and extreme scores can bias the ratings.

The 12 techniques to increase the amount of salient feedback you receive are:

1. The 3 × 3 Feedback Form.
2. The Presentation Evaluation Form.
3. The "A Penny for Your Thoughts" Evaluation.
4. The Post-it Note Evaluation.
5. The Daily Evaluation Form.
6. Highly Focused Feedback.
7. Audio/Video Feedback.
8. The Component Parts Analysis.
9. The Instant Component Analysis.
10. Be Vigilant for Opportunities to Maximize Feedback.
11. Seek Feedback from Spouse, Children, and Significant Other.
12. The Results Achieved Over Time Evaluation.

1. The 3 × 3 Feedback Form

The 3 × 3 Feedback Form is designed to help you get more systematic feedback on what you do well as a presenter, in addition to providing targets for improvement. It solicits feedback in threes: three things done well and three areas in which to improve. Research has proven that we tend to be poor observers of our own behavior and that we become much more accurate when we have a systematic method of data collection. In addition, we get much more accurate feedback by asking at least three different people to rate us. There are a number of criteria to consider when choosing the people who will respond to the form. You need to choose someone who is both free to and capable of giving you honest, direct, and straightforward feedback.

There are three reasons for starting with positive feedback: 1) It is important to be acknowledged for what we do well—no one in any of our training sessions has admitted that they suffered from too much positive feedback; 2) Behavior that is acknowledged and reinforced tends to occur more frequently; and 3) Positive feedback is often instrumental in helping us develop the focused motivation necessary to work harder in areas where we want to improve.

Figure 7-1: The 3 × 3 Feedback Form

Name _____

Please list three specific things I do well as a presenter.
For example, "Pat is a good presenter," is not specific. "Pat uses creative and unexpected visuals to anchor her points both aurally and visually," is specific.

1._____

2._____

3._____

Please list three specific targets for improvement. For example, "Paul needs to add more impact to his presentation," is not specific. "Paul needs to develop high-impact introductions and test his introduction with a focus group," is specific.

1._____

2._____

3._____

Lastly, an alternative method of data collection is to ask a neutral third party to collect the data for you and then present you with a summary of the data in such a way that no specific respondent could be recognized.

2. The Presentation Evaluation Form

The most common evaluation is an evaluation given immediately after the presentation. The evaluation will vary in length and level of complexity depending on the extent and intricacy of the presentation. We like evaluations that are both quantitative and qualitative. Quantitative evaluations allow you to see if you are making progress over time. Qualitative evaluations allow you to get information that is more idiosyncratic about the content of the presentation, what your audience enjoyed, what they learned, and specific targets for improvement. An example of this type of evaluation is presented in Figure 7-2 below.

FIGURE 7-2: PRESENTATION EVALUATION FORM

Please rate this presentation on the following seven scales:

The goals of the presentation were:

Unclear						Clear
1	2	3	4	5	6	7

The presentation was:

Disorganized						Organized
1	2	3	4	5	6	7

The presenter was:

Poorly prepared						Well prepared
1	2	3	4	5	6	7

The presentation was:

Dull						Lively
1	2	3	4	5	6	7

The presenter was:

Boring						Dynamic
1	2	3	4	5	6	7

I found the presenter (Difficult/Easy) to interact with:

Difficult						Easy
1	2	3	4	5	6	7

My overall evaluation of the presentation was:

Poor						Excellent
1	2	3	4	5	6	7

Please list three specific things you enjoyed about this presentation:

1. _____

2. _____

3. _____

Please list three specific things you learned from this presentation:

1. _____

2. _____

3. _____

Please list any suggestion you have for improving this presentation.

_____

_____

What other presentations could we offer to support your continuing professional development, follow-up on this program, or apply what you have learned?

_____

Thank You

3. The "A Penny for Your Thoughts" Evaluation

Each participant is given five pennies. At the end of the presentation, or possibly at the end of the first day of a multiple-day presentation, the participants can rate the value they derived from the presentation by putting a portion of their five pennies into a jar. For example, if they got relatively little from the first day, they would put in one penny. If they received a great deal of value, they could put in four or five pennies, and so on.

The following day, the instructor can either report the total number of pennies he or she collected in the jar, or work it out proportionally out of 100. As an example, assume there are 15 participants, each with five pennies, and at the end of the day there are 60 pennies in the jar. The instructor could say that on day one, the participants received 80-percent value (60 out of 75). Participants find this a fun activity. It also gives the instructor a good use for his or her "leftover pennies." The only drawback from this form of evaluation is that it does not tell the instructor what is working and what is not, but it can be used to start a conversation on feedback, for what worked well and what needs improving.

4. The Post-it Note Evaluation

The Post-it Note evaluation can be done by itself or in conjunction with the "A Penny for Your Thoughts" evaluation. For the Post-it Note evaluation, you will need two different colored Post-it Notes no smaller than 3 × 3 inches. Let's assume that the first color is green. Each participant is asked to write down on the note up to three things that worked well in the speaker's presentation. If the second color is yellow, the participants would write down up to three suggestions for improvement on the yellow Post-it Notes. On the way out, each participant can put his or her notes in a designated area such as on a flip chart. This evaluation gives specific feedback on what worked and what needs improving.

5. The Daily Evaluation Form

If you are giving a multiple-day program, you can use a form that is similar to The Daily Evaluation Form found in Figure 7-3.

Figure 7-3: Daily Evaluation Form

1. List several points/items you found useful today.

_____

_____

2. List any areas that require clarification or need to be reviewed.

_____

_____

3. Additional comments:

_____

_____

These evaluations can be used to start off the next day's session as a review, by highlighting items that the participants thought were particularly important, and by discussing those items that needed further clarification.

6. Highly Focused Feedback

An excellent way to get highly focused feedback is to do an e-mail survey where you ask only one or two questions. For example, you can e-mail 10 to 20 people who have heard you speak and ask them to tell you what they perceive as the most unique aspect of your content. Or you can ask them to tell you the most unique aspect of your presentation style. The purpose of this exercise is to receive as highly focused and specific feedback as possible, and for that reason it is better to ask only one question at a time.

For example, Brad asked 10 people what they most liked about his presentation style and five factors came back. One of the most interesting was the feedback he received from Jonathan. Jonathan said that he was very impressed with the way Brad used analogies, that is making something more understandable by relating it to something that is already well understood. The example that Jonathan related was using a trim tab (Figure 7-4) to help people better understand the leverage that can be gained from better understanding one's negotiating style.

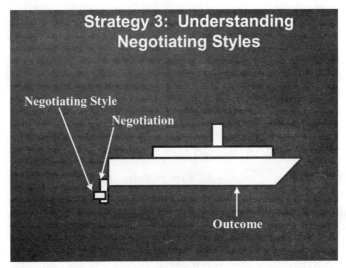

Figure 7-4

Brad: Although I realized that I used analogies, it wasn't until Jonathan pointed it out that I realized how powerful they were. I also vowed to improve my use analogies more consciously and to ask audience members for more specific feedback as to whether the analogy I used to help answer a specific question was helpful.

When soliciting highly focused feedback, it is easy to vary the question. If you use a lot of humor, you can ask them the most unique aspect of your humor, or what they most like about your voice, your use of props, transitions, or PowerPoint slides, and so on. The value of this question is that it focuses entirely on one aspect of your ability to present: the feedback is highly focused and decidedly useful.

In doing this exercise most people chose to ask the same questions, such as how dynamic, humorous, or memorable the presentation was. We encourage you to ask a large variety of different questions. For example, Master Presenter Tom Stoyan directly solicited feedback as to his trustworthiness. The following statements are among the responses he received:

- "Demonstrates confidence."
- "Shows genuine concern and interest."
- "Identifies and focuses on reducing our worry list."
- "Demonstrates thoughtfulness."
- "Demonstrates commitment."
- "Looks for opportunities to empower us."
- "Establishes and maintains a non-threatening environment."
- "Looks for opportunities to provide and get feedback."
- "Says what he is going to do and then does it."
- "Tells stories that demonstrate and reinforce trust-building."

As you can see, it is easy to vary the question. If you use a lot of humor, you can ask your audience what is the most unique aspect of your humor, or what they most like about your voice, your use of props, transitions, or PowerPoint slides, etc. The value of this type of question is that it focuses entirely on one aspect of your ability to present, and therefore, the feedback is highly focused and decidedly useful.

EXERCISE
7-1

Design a question on which you would like to get highly focused feedback. Then list the people you can solicit this feedback from.

7. Audio/Video Feedback

Taped feedback is one of the best sources of feedback presenters can get. The problem is, no one likes the way they look or sound on tape. A frequent comment is, "But I don't sound like that!" Yes, you do. The tape is a more accurate indicator of how you sound to other people. Remember, the voice that you hear when you speak is how it sounds in your head. You are "hearing" the subtleties and nuances that your brain intended. The audience is not privy to those intentions, so all they hear is the sound waves that fall on their ears. Our advice is to tape yourself, grit your teeth, and listen to it. If you don't like what you hear on tape, there is a good chance that the audience may be thinking the same thing.

No matter what you think about how you look or sound, what you see and hear is honest and accurate. In addition, taping yourself affords these advantages:

- You can play it for others to obtain their feedback and impressions.
- You can try various presentation strategies and techniques and compare them.
- You can capture not only what you say, but also how you say it.
- You can immediately see if your body language is congruent with your verbal presentation.

Audio and videotaped feedback is important for all aspects of the presentation, and it is especially important for the beginnings and endings because they carry such weight in the presentation. Remember, 25 percent of the impact from any presentation is from the beginning, and 25 percent is from the ending.

Brad: One night, as I was preparing for a presentation, I asked my son to videotape the beginning, the ending, and one section from the middle that I was not happy with. Based on seeing the tape, the beginning was excellent. I saw clearly how to strengthen the ending. But I was still stuck on how to make that troublesome point in the middle work. I tried three variations before deciding on a fourth (which combined elements of the other three) before I was happy with it. As an added bonus, my son now has a much better understanding of what his Dad does for work and his younger sister has already volunteered for the next time I need a cameraperson.

If the cameraperson also knows a great deal about presentations and/or the content of your presentation, you can also benefit from his or her expertise. One point to remember is that you also benefit from feedback from people who don't know the content area, especially if you will have people attending the presentation who are not familiar with your topic or content. In other words, to increase the validity of this exercise, you should consider asking your "coach" to be as similar to the presentation audience as possible.

Another advantage of taping every presentation is that you can capture those special moments when something wonderful happens by surprise. Victor Borge, one of the great entertainers of all time recorded every single performance. Why? He said, "Because I never know when I might say something funny."

8. The Component Parts Analysis

The component parts analysis is an evaluation of the individual components that make up your presentation. The component parts analysis will help you get a good sense of what parts of the program are working well, what parts need to be improved, and what ones need to be eliminated. Examples of component parts are: exercises, activities, stories, and visual aids.

The beauty of a component analysis is that it will save you from erroneous assumptions. For example, Brad has been giving a presentation on dealing with difficult people for more than 10 years. In the presentation, he shows a film that he was getting tired of using and had planned to remove from his presentation. However, when he performed the component parts analysis, participants rated it as one of the most highly rated parts of the presentation so it remained as an integral part of the course.

What will be very helpful is how the components are rated. You may find that the participants in general do not rate one of your favorite exercises nearly as favorably as you thought they would and you may, in fact, make the presentation much more effective by eliminating that exercise and replacing it with something that the participants find much more effective. Conversely, you may find that a part of the presentation that you don't like or, as in Brad's case, have grown tired of, is rated as one of the most valuable aspects of the presentation.

Warning! Our experience indicated that there is usually more discrepancy in how well or how poorly individual components are evaluated than there is when the participants evaluate the presentation as a whole. That is to say, the ratings of the components are usually significantly lower than the rating for the course as a whole. We believe this is because different components have a greater or lesser appeal to the participants than does the course as a whole—so don't be surprised or put off if the ratings for the components are lower than the ratings for the full program.

An example of a course component parts evaluation appears in Figure 7-5. Note that this is a components evaluation that was designed for our particular course. You can build your own form by removing our examples and substituting your own.

FIGURE 7-5: COMPONENTS PARTS EVALUATION FORM

Please rate the following course components on their usefulness on the following scale, where 1 is not useful and 7 is very useful:

1. Exercise 1-2: The characteristics of the best and worst teachers I had in school.

| 1 | 2 | 3 | 4 | 5 | 6 | 7 |

2. Understanding the four learning styles: theorists, reflectors, activists, and pragmatists.

| 1 | 2 | 3 | 4 | 5 | 6 | 7 |

3. Identifying your purpose and the film clips used to illustrate ITEM: to Inform, to Touch the emotions, to Entertain, and to Move to action.

| 1 | 2 | 3 | 4 | 5 | 6 | 7 |

4. Mastering one-minute talks.

| 1 | 2 | 3 | 4 | 5 | 6 | 7 |

5. Mind mapping using the TRAP model to reach each of the learning styles of your audience members.

| 1 | 2 | 3 | 4 | 5 | 6 | 7 |

6. Developing powerful beginnings.

1	2	3	4	5	6	7

7. The use of games to make it both fun and memorable.

1	2	3	4	5	6	7

8. The two-voice exercises: Moses Supposes and "This is the best presentation I ever attended" exercise.

1	2	3	4	5	6	7

9. Would you recommend changing any of the components? If yes, which ones? How would you recommend changing them?

_____

10. Do you have any additional suggestions regarding the components of the course or the way in which they are structured?

_____

Thank You

_____

However, you don't have to wait for the end of the presentation to do a component analysis. You can do an instant component analysis.

9. Instant Component Analysis

There is an easy and fun way to get feedback on any of the components, new or old. For example, Brad introduced a new exercise to a group of participants in *The Seven Strategies of Master Presenters* course. The exercise was to develop a mind map for one section from this book. Participants then developed a presentation based upon their mind map and applied the TRAP model (theorists, reflectors, activists, and pragmatists) to their presentation in order to make the presentation applicable to the learning style of the members of their audience. They were instructed to use a different colored marker for each learning style.

The beauty of using different colors is that the presenters get immediate feedback on how balanced their presentation is. For example, if green is the color that represents ways to involve the theorists, and there is hardly any green on the page, then the presenters know that they may need to develop more ways to involve the theorists in their audience. The participants then explained their mind map to the whole group. For example, one participant explained how he would make "the buddy system" attractive to theorists as well as to reflectors, activists, and pragmatists.

After completing this exercise, Brad suspected that his instructions were not clear enough nor was the time that had been allotted for the exercise sufficient. So he decided to do an Instant Component Analysis. He then asked each participant to fill out a yellow 3 × 3 inch Post-it Note on what worked in the exercise and to rate the exercise on a scale from 1 to 10 where 1 "didn't work" and 10 "worked very well." He also asked them to fill out a pink note on what would have made the exercise better. When they finished, they were asked to affix their Post-It-Notes on the flip chart paper that had "What Worked?" at the top and "What Would Make It Better?" written in the middle. After the exercise, they took a break. When the class started again, Brad reviewed the feedback. The average rating for the effectiveness of the exercise was 8.6. Typical comments of what worked and what would make it better are illustrated in Figure 7-6 starting on page 226.

Figure 7-6

What Worked?

Reading the assignment as homework and then designing the presentation as the first task in the morning. Got everyone interested and involved.	How the map helps with actual presentation.	Combining the techniques forced us to understand rather than just recite the elements.
Moving from practice or theory into reality.	Implementing TRAP and mind mapping helps in organizing ideas in presenting.	Seeing how different teams approached the problem.
Seeing how to get ideas across visually.	Teamwork in preparation and relating brainstorming ideas to the TRAP definitions.	Team participation, hearing other people's views on the same topic. Reinforced the TRAP model.

What Would Make It Better?

More specific instructions. Add 10 minutes more prep time for the in-class exercise.	More time to prepare a suitable presentation, that is, the last thing you do on Day One is the mind map—first thing we do on Day Two is the developing and presenting the presentation.	More rehearsal on our part.
Using the techniques to solve an actual problem (case) would be more effective.	A second exercise to enforce what we have just done. Although, I think this exercise worked well.	

There is one more way to use an instant component analysis. If the presentation has 10 parts, and if you give the presentation frequently, you can evaluate a different component each time you give the presentation. By the time you have given the presentation 10 times, you will have evaluated each component. Both the quality of this feedback and the quantity are absolutely guaranteed to improve your presentation content and style of delivery. In summary, instant component analysis is one of the easiest, more immediate, and most fun ways to elicit that feedback. And as presenters, we learn how to make the presentation more interesting for both the participants and ourselves.

10. Be Vigilant For Opportunities to Maximize Feedback

There is a scene from *The Sixth Sense* in which Haley Joel Osment plays the role of Cole, an 8-year-old boy, and Bruce Willis plays the role of Malcolm Crowe, a renowned child psychologist. The scene opens with Cole standing in the entryway of his house and Malcolm sitting in the middle of the living room. Malcolm tries to get his young patient to open up to him by wisely asking Cole if he would like to play a game (games are the natural language of children). The essence of the game is that Malcolm will try to guess what Cole is thinking. If Malcolm guesses correctly, Cole will take a step closer, and if Malcolm guesses incorrectly, Cole will take a step back. If Malcolm guesses correctly enough, Cole will sit down and they will have a conversation, if he does not guess correctly enough and Cole reaches the front door of his home, both the game and the session are over.

One of the many things that is so intriguing about this scene is that Malcolm has set it up so that he gets immediate feedback as to the accuracy of his perceptions about Cole. Likewise, Master Presenters are vigilant for opportunities and develop methods to maximize the feedback that they receive. This ability is clearly demonstrated in the following two examples.

For Master Presenters there are no obstacles or excuses that stand between them and their goal of maximizing salient feedback. Brad was presenting a keynote at the Year 2000 Millennium Conference in Ottawa. He was the keynote speaker on the second day. Janet Lapp was the keynote speaker on the first day. Brad had arrived a day ahead of his presentation to get a good sense of the conference and to tie his remarks into both the conference in general and to Janet Lapp's comments in particular.

Brad: I was waiting to talk to Janet at the end of her presentation. There was a long line ahead of me, so I decided to listen to the questions and Janet's answers as I waited. Three things particularly impressed me: 1) the number of people who stood in line to speak to Janet; 2) the quality of her answers; and 3) how aggressively she asked for salient feedback at the end of the presentation. I used the word "aggressive" here in a very positive sense. I also heard the quality of the feedback that Janet received. Watching Janet reinforced my dictum that we live in a feedback-rich world. Most of us do not "harvest" the feedback that exists.

David: I have found audience feedback has risks as well as rewards. The rewards come in the form of affirmation that you connected in the manner in which you intended, coupled with legitimate suggestions of how to make your points better. Every Master Presenter depends on this kind of feedback. This is how we grow.

Yet there are risks in processing feedback as well. Some people are simply poor listeners. Therefore, if you try to adjust your presentation based on the comment of someone who clearly misheard or misinterpreted you, you could end up trying to fix a problem that doesn't exist, except in the mind of one poor listener. This is another reason why taping yourself is so important. If an evaluation that says you said something, you can go to the tape to verify or refute the feedback in question.

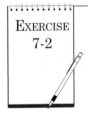

EXERCISE
7-2

Write down three opportunities that exist for you to receive more feedback about your presentations.

11. Seek Feedback from Spouses, Children, and Significant Others

It was potentially one of the most important presentations of Brad's life. He was flying to Toronto to give a presentation to Meeting Professionals International. MPI is the world's largest association of meeting professionals and one of their primary responsibilities is to organize meetings and conventions. If he did a good job it would increase the likelihood that he would give more presentations and keynotes. To add more pressure, the potential publisher of his newest book was coming to hear him present. If he presented well, it would dramatically increase the likelihood that he would get the contract; if he did not present well, the contract was history.

Brad: I had already booked our family's annual Easter weekend retreat at Nova Scotia's beautiful White Point Beach Lodge. There were many wonderful activities that the children could engage in and there would be lots of time for me to refine my presentation, practice it, and record it. Although I really liked the introduction, exercises, the transitions, and the ending, there was a part in the middle that I just wasn't happy with.

I asked my children—Katie, age 10, and Andrew, age 13—to listen to parts of the presentation, which included the part I wasn't happy with. Surprisingly, they both thought it was quite good. However, when it came to the part in the middle, Katie suggested that I change the order of a few of the words and that I add some increased emphasis and vocal variety to the parts I was having the most trouble with. Her feedback was right on. This once again proves that we live in a feedback-rich world, but most of us, however, do not do enough to harvest the feedback that exists.

David: Seek advice from many; accept advice from few. I learned this as I prepared for the World Championship of Public Speaking. As I went to various Toastmasters clubs to practice, on two specific points I heard constant and unanimous criticism. I had learned that the quickest way to please no one is to try to please everyone, so with each rehearsal when criticism on those two points was raised, I thanked the evaluator for his comments and then promptly told myself, "This is not negotiable." I then turned to my most trusted advisor, my wife, Beth. She, knowing me better than anyone else, said, "Yes, this is who you are, and this is right for you." The lesson was clear: Turn to people who know you best for the best advice.

12. The Results Achieved Over Time Evaluation

It is all well and good to find out that the participants enjoyed the presentation and that all of the presentation's components worked. However, the acid test is whether the presentation had a long-term impact on the "bottom line," the corporate culture, or whatever the desired goal was of the presentation. This is the most important and the most difficult-to-measure form of feedback. But measure it we must if we are to objectively determine the ROI (return on investment) for doing the presentation.

One way to get some of this data is to survey the people who attended the presentation and ask them for tangible proof that the materials that were presented have, in fact, been put into practice and have made a positive difference to the attendees and/or to their organizations. To better determine the long-term effects of the presentation, conduct a survey three months, six months, or a year after the participants have attended the session. You can ask some general questions about what the participants remember and what they have been able to use, but you should also ask specific questions regarding how well the material presented has transferred to the participants' actual work setting. The following figure is an example of a post-presentation evaluation form.

FIGURE 7-7: SIX MONTHS TO ONE YEAR POST-PRESENTATION EVALUATION FORM

Presentation: _____

Presenter: _____

Date of Presentation: _____

As a follow-up to your attending this presentation, please rate its long-term effectiveness:

The overall effectiveness of the presentation was:

Poor						Excellent
1	2	3	4	5	6	7

Please list one to three specific things you have been able to apply from the presentation session in your place of work and/or home life:

1. _____

2. _____

3. _____

Please list one to three specific benefits in your place of work and/or home life that have been derived from your attending this presentation:

1._____

2._____

3._____

Please estimate the ROI (return on investment) from your attending this presentation:

0%	25%	50%	75%	100%

Please explain:

_____

_____

At this point, do you have any suggestions for improving the presentation or its effectiveness?

_____

_____

Thank You

A Word of Caution About Feedback and Evaluations

David uses what he calls the 10-80-10 rule: 10 percent of any audience will like anything you do, and 10 percent will dislike anything you do. It is the 80 percent in the middle to whom you are really speaking. If you focus on either of the 10 percent groups at the extremes, you will likely not connect with the majority of your audience.

If you give too much emphasis to those in the 10 percent segments, the feedback you receive may be skewed. For example, at the end of the spectrum in which the "negative" 10 percent reside, though their suggestions for improvement may be valid, it is possible that the motives behind their criticism are mixed or mean spirited.

We have found that the best way to deal with the latter type of criticism and still maintain or enhance your credibility is to summarize the evaluations and ask the meeting planner to send out a copy of the evaluations to all of the participants. This allows the dissenters to see how their criticism stacks up with the majority of the participants.

One excellent technique to mitigate against the effects of extreme scores is to use Olympic scoring. In Olympic scoring, you throw out the highest and lowest scores and then average the remaining scores. Olympic scoring eliminates the fact that one unusually high or low score can bias the average, which gives a result that is closer to the true mean score (see Figure 7-8). For example, if there are fewer than 30 participants, and if one score is either much higher or lower than the average, then that score can radically skew the average ratings for any particular question. It is for this reason that we recommend Olympic scoring with groups of 30 or fewer. To use Olympic scoring, you simply list all of the scores for any particular question and then cross out the highest and lowest scores for that question. By using this process, you get a truer approximation of what the real rating should be and it is not subject to extreme scores as demonstrated below.

FIGURE 7-8

Overall evaluations of the presentation were:

    5   6   7   7   6   6   5   6   7   2

Average = 57 / 10 = 5.7

Using Olympic Scoring:

Overall evaluations of the presentation were:

    5   6   7   7   6   6   5   6   ~~7~~   ~~2~~

Average = 48 / 8 = 6.0

Change the Questions Periodically

The advantage of asking the same questions all of the time is that you have a consistent yardstick to evaluate how you are doing. The advantage of changing the questions is that you can receive different information, which can be very informative. You can also ask questions you previously had not thought necessary to ask or didn't have room to ask. Our best advice is to be consistent in your evaluation questions until you get relatively consistent feedback. Then consider varying the questions from time to time to see if you can elicit different feedback on different aspects of both your content and your style.

Send copies of the evaluations to the participants. Whenever possible, we send directly or ask the organizer to send participants copies of the evaluations to reinforce the learning and to show the participants that we take their remarks seriously. A copy of the letter we use is reproduced in Figure 7-9.

FIGURE 7-9

Dear_____:

    We have enclosed the evaluations from *The Seven Strategies of Master Presenters* course as an attachment to this document. We were pleased with how hard the participants worked at mastering the material. We ask that a copy of these evaluations be sent to each participant as it helps to reinforce what was learned during the presentation and it also demonstrates that we take their feedback seriously.

    Lastly, we must tell you that we are impressed with the professionalism of the participants and the feedback they gave us for improving the course.

Thanks again for all of your help.

Sincerely,

Brad McRae/David Brooks

Ask for Feedback as the Session Ends

Brad: In terms of asking the participants for salient feedback as they leave the session, I have never seen anyone do it as well as Janet Lapp. As I was in line waiting to congratulate Janet on her phenomenal presentation, I couldn't help but notice that she asked the people who were waiting to talk to her how they liked the presentation and what she could do to improve it. The amazing thing was that Janet really meant it. For her, it was not just a perfunctory remark; she deeply and sincerely wanted their feedback on how to improve the presentation. Remember that a vague comment like, "Should there have been more examples?" is not as helpful as asking specifically what kind of examples the person would like to see in the presentation. Also, ask the person's advice as to what should be taken out. Lastly, you can't incorporate everyone's feedback. By trying to please one person, you many displease three others or as David says, "If you try to please everyone, you'll please no one." Therefore, all of this feedback needs to be balanced.

It is also important to find out what the audience liked about the presentation and to note what you should do more or less of. These evaluations can also be used to start off the next day's session or your next presentation to the same group as a review, by highlighting items that the participants thought were particularly important and clarifying or discussing those items that needed further explanation.

In addition to maximizing their use of salient feedback, there are two last characteristics that differentiate Master Presenters from their less accomplished counterparts: 1) knowing the deep structure of your presentation, and 2) stage presence or command presence.

The Deep Structure

The best way to understand what we mean by deep structure is to use an analogy of stem cells. Stem cells have the amazing ability to transform themselves into any type of tissue or organ. Similarly, knowing the deep structure of your presentation means that you know your subject so well, and how each segment of that subject relates to each part of your presentation at the deepest level possible, that the presenter has the ability to change the presentation "on the fly" based on the immediate feedback he or she is receiving from the audience. For example, if the presenter perceives that there are more pragmatists in the audience, the presentation automatically becomes more pragmatic. This is called "attunement"—the audience and presenter are mutually attuned to each other's needs, wants, goals, and desires. Then, for example, when you are asked a question, you are able to come up with just the right example, story, simulation, metaphor, and/or research study to best answer that question.

When the deep structure is just right, all of the elements of the presentation work together perfectly. Master Presenters also use the deep structure to help make their sub-audiences into one unified whole as the following examples point out.

In Olympic figure skating, a perfect score from the judges is 6.0 in two categories: technical merit and artistic impression. Les Brown achieved perfect 6.0 from all those in attendance in both technical merit and artistic impression at the National Speakers Association 2000 convention in Washington, D.C. Not only was his presentation one of the most masterful presentations that Brad has ever had the pleasure of seeing, Les stopped at critical points in the presentation and told the audience exactly how he crafted each element of his presentation and then fully explained the "why" behind the "how."

The first lesson Les Brown taught was that our audience is really made up of sub-audiences and that your job as a presenter is to make that audience into one unified whole. When you, as a presenter, enter a room your audience is divided by the amount of energy they have, their ability to attend to the presentation depending on how many other things they have going on in their lives, by gender, by income level, by race, and by how predisposed or prejudiced they feel towards you and the topic you are presenting. As presenters we have to make that collection of sub-audiences into one unified audience—and transforming disparate audiences into one audience is Les Brown's forté.

The three techniques that Les had mastered to making disparate audiences into one audience are: the use of quotes and affirmations, making a commitment, and affirming that commitment by shaking the hand of the person sitting on your left and right.

Early in his presentation, Les asked the audience to speak aloud the words to a powerful quotation. Hearing Les's voice intermingled with the members of the audience's voices was very powerful. The words were powerful and the chorus with the audience hearing itself made them more powerful still. Think of the powerful words from Martin Luther King Jr.'s speech, "I Have a Dream." In your mind, hear Dr. King say those words. Now hear the same words spoken by Dr. King while being echoed by the thousands of people in his audience.

To connect with your audience rather than merely speaking to them, Les suggests that when you make a profound point, you hammer it home by asking the audience members to shake hands with the person on their left and state their intention to, for example, make a meaningful difference. Then ask the audience members to shake hands with the person on their right and again state their intention to make a meaningful difference. This has a wonderful effect of bonding each person with the person on their left and right. The audience members can also hear this same activity going on in the background all around them. What you can hear, if you listen carefully enough, is that all of the sub-audiences in the room are in the process of becoming one unified audience. We have never heard anyone do this better than Les Brown and you can hear it too by listening to his tape *Presentation Magic by the Motivator.*[2]

A second example is how Harold Taylor unifies his audience with humor, using his hilarious wit to poke fun at himself. Soon everyone is laughing, and at the same time hearing everyone else in the room laughing serves to unify his audience.

We use surveys and ask the audience to raise their hands in response to one or two pertinent questions such as, "How many of you would like to double your effectiveness as presenters?" or, "Raise you hand if you let your own personal fear keep you from being as powerful a presenter as you would like to be." When the people in the audience see that everyone is grappling with the same questions and concerns, it has a profound unifying effect on the audience. They can see that there is more that unites them than divides them. One note of caution: This technique can be overused. It only works well if you ask

EXERCISE
7-3

a powerful or profound question.

List any techniques that you have observed or used to unify an audience.

Next, outline at least one technique that you will use to unify the audience in your next presentation.

The result of knowing your deep structure, making sure that all of the elements in the presentation work together perfectly, and making your sub-audiences into one unified whole is flow. In summary, if you want to be a Master Presenter you must know the deep structure of your presentation—not only what elements are contained within, but how and why they fit together so well.

Command Presence

Command presence is a term that was developed in the military to describe someone who had the quality of a leader, especially those who would be leading soldiers into battle. The term has since been generalized to business and other settings. Command presence is an elusive quality, but you know it when you see it. Command presence takes place when you walk into a room, office, or any situation and you realize that there is someone who is in charge, even when he or she is not formally in charge. Command presence is communicated both verbally and nonverbally. It is an elusive quality, partly because the whole is greater than the sum of its parts. For people who have it, their personality and charisma fills up the room.

Brad: When my daughter was 8, she was in a ballet class. I remember going into the class and sitting down on the floor with some of the other parents. This ballet teacher had 16 8-year-old students and the attending parents' total attention. As I watched the ballet teacher demonstrate the steps she wanted her students to emulate, I remember thinking that not only did she have the attention of everyone in the room, but also, that she was a remarkably tall woman. I was shocked when I stood up at the end of the class, to see that this remarkably tall woman was in fact, rather short. Her command presence augmented both her physical and psychological stature.

Some political leaders, such as Winston Churchill were able to use command presence to help change the tide of history. Other leaders, such as Martin Luther King Jr. and Desmond Tutu, were able to use command presence to change society. Some movie actors have developed it. Watch *Paper Chase* with John Houseman or *Mandela and DeKlerk*, where Sydney Poitier as Nelson Mandela and Michael Caine as DeKlerk, give unbelievably masterful performances as examples of towering command presence. You can also watch Martin Sheen in the television show *The West Wing* where just the way he walks into a room demonstrates command presence.

For actors and presenters, command presence is called stage presence. You can get a strong sense of stage presence in the world of professional speaking by seeing or listening to Tony Campello, Jeanne Robertson, Marcia Steele, Les Brown, or Peter Legge who, within 10 seconds of beginning to speak, demonstrate command presence. In summary, command presence radiates a sense that the people who possess it are comfortable with themselves and they have a strong sense of who they are and what they represent. They also have the energy level, vitality, and ability to inspire people to dream of a better future by changing the way they think and moving them to action.

One of the most important things aspiring Master Presenters can do is to develop their command presence. One of the first steps is to do an honest inventory of where you have command presence and where you need to develop it. First, you can observe people who have command presence and notice how they behave. Second, you can interview people who have command presence and ask them how they developed it. Third, you can ask for feedback on your command presence and they must be honest enough to tell you the truth. The following exercise has been designed to help you develop your command

EXERCISE
7-4

presence.

Please make three specific suggestions of things you could do to increase your sense of command presence.

Total Quality Improvement is a continuous process requiring constant analysis, assessment, and adjustment. Just as the world's best manufacturers use Total Quality Improvement to improve their products, Master Presenters depend on the 12 techniques in this chapter to help them develop and implement their goals, and improve and enhance every presentation. However, there is one more thing that Master Presenters do to continually improve the skills and strategies as a presenter by setting a lifelong goal to become a lifelong learner. It is to this last factor that we will now turn our attention.

CONCLUSION

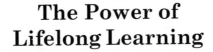

The Power of
Lifelong Learning

*The man who graduates today and stops learning tomorrow
is uneducated the day after.*

—*Newton Diehl Baker*

Master Presenters are defined by their deft use of the seven strategies examined in this book. They also have one additional overriding attribute in common: Master Presenters are dedicated lifelong learners. In fact, it is a dedication to lifelong learning that helps them become Master Presenters in the first place. We can define a lifelong learner as someone who first has the passion and dedication to learn from every source available. It doesn't matter if that source is personal experience, learning through the experience of others, or from books or courses. Second, everything that the Master Presenter knows is integrated with everything else they learn, which leads to growth. Third, becoming open to learning, in all its various forms and functions, makes growth possible and when you make room for growth, you make room for success.

In excepts from an article titled "From Training to Education,"[1] Master Presenter Nido Qubein describes one of the essential differences between Master Presenters and their less masterful counterparts.

Let me make a suggestion that at first may sound strange, coming from a management consultant. If your company has a training department, do away with it. Replace it with a Department of Education and Development. The reason: The new business environment needs fewer people who are trained to do things a specific way and more people who are educated to find new ways of doing things. As Stanley Marcus once said, "You don't train people; you train dogs and elephants; you educate people." What's the difference?

The word education comes from the Latin educo, which means to change from within. Training provides an external skill. Education changes the inner person. Training deals only with the doing level. Education teaches people how to think. Let me give you an example: I once ordered an apple pie and a milk shake at a fast-food restaurant. The server smiled and asked, "Would you like a dessert with that?" This young woman had been trained to act. She had been conditioned to smile and try to upgrade the sale by reciting her memorized lines. And she rehearsed them to perfection. But she had not been educated in customer interaction. She hadn't been taught to listen to the customer, to think about what the customer ordered and to acquire a feeling for what might appeal to the customer under the circumstances.

Training attempts to add on the qualities needed for success. Education builds them in. Now don't get me wrong. I'm not saying that you should never train people. Training is essential when a specific skill must be learned, or a specific procedure must be followed consistently in a manufacturing process. But training should be part of a broader educational process. One of my favorite proverbs conveys the wisdom that when you give people fish, they'll be hungry tomorrow; if you teach them to fish, they'll never go hungry. Training gives your employees a fish—a specific skill applicable to a specific task. Education teaches them to fish.

Corporations have no choice but to invest substantial resources in developing people. So it's best to invest in ways that let people grow; that teach them to think for themselves; that create a pool of solid candidates for promotion to higher positions.

In the same vein, Master Presenters don't just train people; they educate their audience and themselves—for today and tomorrow. In fact, Nido Qubein got it just right in describing this critical difference between Master Presenters and their less masterful counterparts.

To help you capitalize on the power of lifelong education, we will present seven critical methods that can help you become a lifelong learner:

1. Learn from experience.
2. Learn from mentors.
3. Learn from coaches.
4. Join a mastermind group.
5. Learn how to think like the experts.
6. Interview the best presenters you can find.
7. Learn from the best books to read, movies to watch, and courses to take.

There is an extraordinary book from the Centre of Creative Leadership titled *The Lessons of Experience.*[2] In doing their research for the book, the authors documented that 50 percent of what we learn, we learn from experience. We learn 20 percent from mentors and coaches, 20 percent from failures, and 10 percent from formal education. We have adapted and expanded this approach specifically for people who want to become more like the Master Presenters we interviewed in this book.

1. Learn From Experience

Darren LaCroix, the 2001 World Champion of Public Speaking, has a six-word mantra that helped him win this prestigious title. Darren's mantra is "Stage Time, Stage Time, Stage Time." In preparing for the World Championship, Darren spent as much time as he possibly could presenting before an audience. In addition to being a Master Presenter, Darren performs stand-up comedy. He said one of his comedy mentors asked him, "How can you expect to be funny in front of an audience until you are comfortable in front of an audience?" Darren says the only way you can be comfortable in front of an audience is by spending time in front of one. Experience comes from familiarity, persistence, and practice—in short—stage time. All of the Master Presenters we interviewed took advantage of every possible opportunity to speak. Where none existed, they created them. If you need more stage time, consider joining a Toastmasters club, speaking for local volunteer organizations, or your local Rotary or Lions club. For example, Darren LaCroix said when he was just getting started in comedy he searched for more opportunities to practice in front of a live audience. He said that because comedy clubs were only open at night, he had a limited window of opportunity. Then he found out about Toast-masters and the fact that many of them met in the day. So he immediately went out and joined four clubs so he could quadruple his stage time.

Many Master Presenters get some of their best stories from real-world experience as the following example illustrates.

Brad: I was offered the opportunity to consult with and facilitate a meeting with all of the stakeholders at the Sydney Nova Scotia Tar Ponds Toxic Dump Waste Site, which is the worst environmental toxic dumpsite in Canada. The stakeholders were the combined three levels of government—federal, provincial, and municipal; homeowners whose homes bordered the toxic waste site and were therefore worthless; environmentalists who maintained that this area was the cancer capital of Canada; and the soon-to-be unemployed steel workers who were adamant that the toxic substance be incinerated at the steel mill.

I hired a colleague who was very strong—both mentally and physically—to work with me. The steering committee had arranged for a two-hour meeting complete with Royal Canadian Mounted Police protection. We were told that it would be prudent for us to facilitate the meeting right in front of the exit doors, in case it became necessary for us to make a quick exit.

Eighty of the most angry people I had every met attended the meeting. The citizens of the area felt massively betrayed by a succession of governments over the last 20 years. Millions and millions of dollars had been spent and not one speck of soil had been remediated.

Although we had started the meeting by getting the participants to agree on ground rules, the first half of the meeting bordered on anarchy. After an hour of venting, the participants started following the ground rules and a great deal of progress was made in formulating criteria with which to assess the options, and a modicum of trust began to slowly develop.

I have been trained in negotiation, mediation, and facilitation skills at the Harvard Program on Negotiation. As invaluable as that training has been to my learning and to my credibility, there is no way that I could have learned as much at Harvard as I learned in preparing for and acting as a cofacilitator in that meeting. As part of my preparation, I read every newspaper article that was written about the tar ponds and conducted a number of in-depth interviews. I then wrote up this case from each group of participants' point of view. In so doing, I attempted to understand each participant group's point of view. I researched each participant's platform with the same depth and detail as an FBI profiler would use to try to understand their suspect. I firmly believe that you cannot attempt to change someone's mind if you do not know where their mind is.

Several months later, I modified and wrote up this case and I now have an absolutely terrific case study whereby the participants in one of my courses have to work in groups to decide how they would prepare for this same meeting. After the participants give their ideas on how they would prepare for the meeting, I debrief the session with how we set up the meeting in reality. Comparing their results with what actually happened is edifying both for the participants and for me.

Now that I have developed the case, tried it out, and know it inside out, I also have a terrific story that I can use in my presentations on how we can build our future with creative rather than wasteful solutions.

It was documented above that leaders and executives learn 50 percent of what they have learned about being a leader from experience. It seems reasonable then that presenters would also learn 50 percent of what they learn from experience. By judicially enhancing the types of experiences we have, we can enliven both our training and our keynotes while enhancing our credibility.

2. Learn From Mentors

If you have never experienced a mentoring relationship, we suggest you give it a try because whether you are the mentor or the "mentee," you will learn and grow from the experience. If you want to accomplish a task, learn from others who have gone before. They can help you farther down the road, faster, just by sharing their successes and their mistakes.

David: As a longtime Toastmaster, I have enjoyed a many mentoring relationships. At least once a week someone phones me to ask questions about speaking. I answer every one, because to teach is to learn twice. I find as I explain to others, sometimes the answer becomes clearer to me. I also always caution those who seek my help: "Just because I say it's so, doesn't mean it's so." And I encourage mentees to think for themselves after having picked through the advice I've offered.

How do you find a mentor? Look for someone whose skills or experiences correspond to your needs. For example, if you need assistance in developing a great opening, seek a mentor who begins presentations with dynamic beginnings. Then ask that person if they will be willing to help. Not everyone will say yes, but most will, because most people are honored that you thought enough of them to ask for their advice.

David: I am proud of the fact that I coached Mark Brown as he prepared for the 1995 Toastmasters World Championship of Public Speaking. Mark was the quintessential student. He was eager to learn and a good listener, but more importantly, he was a good questioner. I watched with pride as he went from a good questioner to a good thinker. By the end of our mentoring sessions, he was a well-reasoned decision-maker and had learned to teach himself. So as he stood on the stage in 1995 holding the World Championship trophy, I was every bit as proud of him as I was when I won the title. But the story doesn't stop there. Six years later, Mark mentored Darren LaCroix as he prepared for the 2001 World Championship. When Darren stood on the stage as World Champion, I felt that same sense of pride all over again, for the student had become the teacher.

3. Learn From Coaches

In the development phase, it was probably the additional training that I had taken along the way, theatre school, modeling, voice coaching, Toastmasters, and I had done a fair amount of professional theatre. It all helped in stage blocking and movement, in learning to fill a room, of creating a more powerful presence. The various coaches I have used for speaking have been tremendously helpful, at least when I could accept their feedback! Speaking is a performing art, where one constantly needs to improve, clarify, and enhance.

—Janet Lapp

Developing your own unique style through coaching is much like watching a master sculptor in action. By chipping away at the stone that shouldn't be there, a sculptor creates his or her own unique design. Almost all of the Master Presenters we interviewed had worked, either formally or informally, with one or more coaches or mentors who helped them chip away at the extraneous, irrelevant, and superfluous to unleash their own unique potential. Excellent coaches use all of their expertise to help you develop your own style; egocentric coaches work to develop clones of themselves. Excellent coaches can accelerate your learning and your career; egocentric coaches, ironically, can hold you back. Excellent coaches help to raise your self-confidence; egocentric coaches cause you to doubt yourself and your abilities. Excellent coaches give you options and the confidence to try them; egocentric coaches demand that you do your presentation their way and only their way.

In relation to her own coaching and the development of her style, Janet Lapp says:

> I got rid of everything I copied from other people—it is a process of becoming more and more of who you are, of deciding and making choices of who you are. It is like the story of Ghandi and sugar. A woman came to Ghandi and asked him how she should treat her son who was becoming obese. Ghandi asked her to come back in two weeks. At their second meeting, he suggested the boy stop eating sugar. The woman asked Ghandi why he didn't tell her that at their first meeting. Ghandi replied, "Because at that time I was still eating sugar." We need to use the same process in regard to the development of our style. We need to decide at a very fundamental level what to keep and what to eliminate or let go.

Almost every great athlete will tell you about the coaches who helped him or her develop his or her talents. Finding coaches who can help you move to the next level is one of the most beneficial things you can do for your career.

There are two ways to find a coach: on purpose or by accident. The first way is to look for someone who has the skills and abilities to be an excellent coach and then ask him or her to coach you. For example, Brad was going to give a showcase presentation in front of his peers at the annual convention of CAPS (Canadian Association of Professional Speakers).

Brad: I practiced and practiced; worked over the content and delivery, in addition to audio and videotaping the presentation. It was good, but not the excellent presentation that I wanted. I had the foresight to hire one of Canada's best speaking coaches, Fraser McAllan, to coach me. We spent two hours together. I was surprised that Fraser suggested very few changes to the content. The main focus of his suggestions was to increase the frequency of my dramatic use of hand gestures to help me tell the stories that I used to illustrate my points. My first reaction was that I wasn't comfortable with his suggestions and that I couldn't do them. Fraser suggested that I try them and eliminate them if I didn't like them. I had also brought along my video camera so we could see what they looked like. Although this was way out of my comfort zone, I agreed to give it a try. I had to admit that the gestures increased drama and poignancy of the story and made the point I was trying to make much more impactful and memorable. I would also like to point out that Fraser, unlike some of the other coaches I have had, puts equal emphasis on telling me the things that I do well in addition to targets for improvement.

The result was that the added hand gestures and more dramatic body language increased the effectiveness of my presentation by 100 percent. Not only that, but I learned to use gestures more effectively in all of my presentations and the coaching I had continues to help me teach my course on *The Seven Strategies of Master Presenters* and in the speech coaching I do with individual clients. All in all, it produced a huge payoff.

Whenever I am coached, I ask if I can videotape the session. There is simply too much feedback and this feedback is too valuable to risk not being able to remember it all. I also like to compare the "before coaching" version with the "after coaching" version.

The second way to find a coach is by chance. You may not be looking for a coach when you accidentally discover someone whose talents match your needs. The key to this approach is being alert to opportunities when they present themselves. Chris Beckett is the manager of a television studio at a local university. Brad hired Chris to produce his first video and audio demo tapes, and subsequently, a two-hour CD program.

Brad: While I hired Chris to produce my audio programs, what I didn't plan on was finding a voice coach at the same time. Chris has a naturally deep baritone voice, the kind of person who sounds like they were born to be on radio. What I didn't realize was how much voice training Chris had had, and he was willing to pass this knowledge on to me. I also learned a great deal about audio and video production, all of which will be immeasurably helpful to me in further developing my platform skills. It will also help me to produce even better audio and video recordings of my books.

A good coach's talent can best be described as being like a highly focused laser. He or she will hone in on the first part of your presentation and help you develop a "hook" to grab your audience's attention. An excellent coach should also have the ability to help you gain crystal clear clarity on what they are saying and on how to say it, in addition to focusing on vocal variety and projecting one's voice, when to stand still and when and how to move. Lastly, some coaches will gladly give you some time at no charge, but others who do this professionally will charge for their services. Coaching is worth paying for if you want to become a Master Presenter. If your coach is able to bring you from average to good, or from good to great, the cost for his or her advice is worth every penny.

Don't expect a coach, no matter how good he or she is, to transform you. The coach is not supposed to be a Henry Higgins, taking an Eliza Doolittle and molding her into something she was not. A good coach will help you identify the strengths you have and enhance them incrementally. But most importantly, a good coach will show you how to teach yourself.

In addition to using live coaches, consider getting some of the best audio and videocassettes of some of the best presentations. One of our favorites is Gene Griessman's presentation, *Lincoln on Communication*.[3] Gene Griessman is probably the best character speaker in the business and his video *Lincoln on Communication* is perfectly organized by topic. When we play parts of the tape to our audiences, they always want to see the whole tape. Another jewel is the audio- and videotapes of Les Brown from the 2000 National Speakers

Association's Annual Meeting in Washington, D.C. We don't think we ever heard a speaker speak with more intentionality. Mr. Brown told us exactly what he was doing as well as why he was doing it. Instructions on how to order these references appear on page 258.

4. Join a Mastermind Group

The purpose of a mastermind group is to assist in and support its members in accomplishing those activities that would serve as escalators to move the group members to the next level of success in their careers. Mastermind groups are groups of like-minded individuals who collectively help each other develop their abilities through peer mentoring and by holding each other responsible for achieving specific goals by specific dates. To be effective, the group should meet at least once a month. The group that Brad belongs to is occupationally diverse. It is made up of six individuals: three professional speakers, two CEOs, and a vice president of a successful company. Conversely, the mastermind support group that David belongs to is occupationally similar. His group is composed of six world-champion speakers.

Brad: One of the things that I wanted to develop were audio CDs. I had written four books, but only had one CD program. I had been talking about developing more CD programs for a long time, and it was well past time for action. Therefore, one of the goals I set with my mastermind group was to complete an additional CD program by a certain date. Because I set this as an important goal in front of people who are important to me, I would lose face if I didn't complete it, plus they would hound me—I mean, inquire—about the progress of the CD program. Likewise, one of my counterparts in the group is a very talented and eloquent professional speaker. Because he is the CEO of his company and is very active with his church and his family, he has not put pen to paper to develop written descriptions for his presentations. These are absolutely necessary to secure speaking engagements. This is something that two of us in the group do quite well, so when he set his goal to develop three first-rate seminar/keynote descriptions, the other members in the group acted as coaches and mentors. Another member most needs to work on writing a book. Her goal is to write a series of newsletters and then turn these newsletters into a book.

Yet another member wants to specialize in keynotes on leadership and the goal of the rest of the group is to make sure that he does everything in his power to achieve that goal.

David: The mastermind group I participate in operates similarly to Brad's in that we ask the others to help keep us accountable for our individual goals. Our group is different, though, in that all six of us are professional speakers and we all share a common achievement: We are all world champions of public speaking. Once a month, Mark Brown (1995 World Champion), Craig Valentine (1999 World Champion), Ed Tate (2000 World Champion), Darren LaCroix (2001 World Champion), Jim Key (2002 World Champion), and I meet via conference call. Because of the similarity of our businesses, we use our group meetings to exchange information that is of equal benefit to us all. For example, when one of us finds a product, service, or service provider that we like, we share it with the others in our group, saving everyone else the time it would take to research the same information individually. We share tips on product development and resource sales and we collaborate on projects that make us more effective collectively. To an outsider it may seem odd that we would give away information to others who could be perceived as "the competition." However, it's just the opposite. We know that all of us together know more than any one of us individually, so if we collaborate and cooperate with people who hold similar standards and goals, we all grow faster. It's just like the adage says, "A rising tide lifts all boats."

All of the members of our mastermind groups, each of whom is a highly motivated individual, stated that membership in the group has made them 20- to 30-percent more effective in those areas where they needed to grow. Warning! Other people will observe the effect of being in a mastermind group and will want to join, but you have to be incredibly selective. This is not a group to mentor people who are at a different stage in development than you are. That can be done in other venues. All of the people in your mastermind group need to be at approximately the same level of development. Of course, you will have different areas of strengths, and this is important because you can help each other develop those skills, and/or those skills can be applied to help each other achieve their goals. The easiest way to say this is that mastermind groups work best when made up of equally skilled peers.

5. Learn How to Think Like the Experts

Become a student of the world's best presenters. We can study the world's best presenters by listening to their audiotapes, viewing their videotapes, watching them on television, in movies, and, wherever possible, by observing them in person. For example, Winston Churchill became one of the most masterful presenters of the 20th century. However, he was not a "naturally gifted" speaker. In fact, as a child, he stuttered badly. Yet he became one of the world's greatest orators. The stories of how Churchill, Gandhi, John Kennedy, Barbara Jordan,[4] and Barbara Coloroso[5] came to understand and apply skills of other Master Presenters makes fascinating study and demonstrates that none of the eminent speakers who we might choose to emulate were "born speakers." Each had to work at it, just like master chess players or golf pros. To become a Master Presenter, we must learn from the experts. You can begin by researching excellent presenters on the Internet, in books, in movies, on videotapes, on CDs or audiotapes, and through in-person or telephone interviews.

EXERCISE 8-1

As shown below, make three columns. In the first column, list the names of several expert presenters and influencers you would like to know more about. In the second column, list what you would like to learn. For example, how they accomplished what they did and the strategies, skills, and methods they used to achieve their results. In the third column, list the resources you will use to research the expert(s) you have chosen. For example, you might want to learn more about powerful beginnings, storytelling, and the use of vocal variety. Some examples of the resources you could use are: the Internet, library, audiotapes, and/or videotapes of presentations and books of effective presentation skills.

Name of Expert	What I Would Like to Learn	Resources

6. Interview the Best Presenters You Can Find

Another proven method to continue the lifelong learning process of developing and delivering top-notch presentations is to interview the best presenters you know personally or those you do not know but would agree to be interviewed. You can select people who are well-known presenters, such as professional speakers, business leaders, entrepreneurs, politicians, community leaders, ministers, or advocates, and simply ask if you can set up a 10- to 15-minute appointment to gain information and insights. You can use both your time and theirs more effectively if you do some pre-interview homework. Find out as much as you can about a specific presenter's style and/or most accomplished presentation by preparing high-yield questions regarding strategies, methods, and techniques that they found effective. High-yield questions invite the person you are interviewing to share information at the most meaningful level possible. Examples of high-yield questions are: "What did you learn as you developed and delivered effective presentations that you would have liked to have known before you entered into your profession?" and, "What lessons about developing and delivering effective presentations would you want to pass on to someone who was entering your line of work?"

Alternatively, you can list three aspects of developing and delivering effective presentations about which you want to learn more. We used both approaches in interviewing the Master Presenters who contributed their stories and expertise to this book. We also learned and benefited greatly from their experience, and this increased the breadth and depth of our knowledge to a degree previously unimagined.

EXERCISE
8-2

Being very specific, list three aspects of developing and delivering effective presentations about which you want to learn more. Examples of topics are learning how to be more dynamic, more forceful, more creative, or some other aspect you want to develop. List up to three topics. Under each topic, list the names of three people who you could interview to learn more. Complete one set of interviews, learn all you can, document and record all that you have learned, and then apply some of those lessons before going on to the next topic.

Topic(s)	Person to Interview	Resource(s)

7. Learn from the Best Books, Movies, and Courses

After winning the World Championship of Public Speaking in 1999 in Chicago, I came back to the Baltimore–Washington International Airport, and the first thing I did was to get another book on the art of public speaking.

—Craig Valentine

Learning effective presentation skills is a lifelong process. In a very real sense, reading this book is only the beginning of that process. To answer the question, "Where do I go from here," we have listed several suggestions on how to find the best information possible.

Learning From Books and Films: A bibliography of more than 50 of the best books, and audio- and videotapes on presentations skills can be found in Appendix B. Each reference is described in enough detail to help you make an informed choice about whether it would be helpful to you in further developing your skills.

Learning From Courses and Speaking Organizations: Excellent courses of study, some programmed and some self-directed, are available through a number of organizations. We list some of them here:

Toastmasters International[6] is the world's largest organization to help develop speaking, listening, and leadership skills. At Toastmasters, members learn by speaking to groups and working with others in a supportive, encouraging environment. A typical Toastmasters club is made up of 20 to 40 people who meet once a week for one to two hours. Each meeting gives participants an opportunity to practice conducting meetings, giving impromptu speeches, presenting prepared speeches, and offering constructive evaluation.

There are many advantages to Toastmasters. First, they have been in the business of helping individuals present more effectively since 1924. Second, you can start at a level with which you feel comfortable and gradually and systematically move up to more complex presentations. Third, there is ample opportunity to practice, as most clubs meet two to four times a month. If you miss a meeting, you can attend a meeting on a different night or at another club in your area, or you can visit a club at another location if you are traveling. With more than 8,000 clubs internationally, finding a club is a relatively simple task.

At the *National Speakers Association* (NSA)[7] Annual Meeting, you can see presentations by some of the best presenters in the business.

Breakout and workshop sessions are designed to help you accelerate your skills. You can also attend the "Meet the Pros'" session, which is made up 10 individuals who get to sit down with a professional speaker for 20 minutes to discuss a specific topic on speaking. You can meet with three different pros and learn about three different areas of interest. It is amazing how much material can be covered in such a short period of time. Because the group is small and intimate, you can also get burning questions answered and make contact with an expert with whom you can talk to or correspond in the future. The array of topics presented is impressive. David has been attending NSA meetings since 1991 and Brad since 1997. We both agree that one of the biggest mistakes we made in our careers was not joining sooner.

The *NSA Youth Leadership Conference* is the best-kept secret at NSA. The program is open to children ages 10 to 16, and because it is set up as a parallel conference and run at the same times as the adult sessions, the children are completely looked after and their parents can take full advantage of the adult conference.

Brad: My children and I first attended together in 2000 in Washington, D.C. I thought the Youth Leadership Conference would be a good experience for them, to help them learn about the speaking profession, to be exposed to some of the best speakers in the world, and for us to have a first-class holiday all at the same time. When I explained what would likely happen at NSA, they said that it sounded too much like summer school, were afraid that we would spend too much time in Washington's museums—and therefore would prefer not to go. The end result, however, was that NSA was the highlight of our summer.

After a morning of sightseeing on the first day of the conference, my children and I attended the orientation session. The speaker for the opening session was the one and only Zig Ziglar. After the session was over, the parents were asked to leave, were told to relax for the rest of the afternoon, attend the opening session, and pick the kids up at 10 p.m. The children heard some of the best presenters in the world, including a visit from Abraham Lincoln, a.k.a. Gene Griessman.

The youth counselors and the people who directed the program were, in my children' words, "awesome." Their goal was to have a better conference than the adults, and clearly in my children's eyes, they did. In fact, these same children who originally did not want to go to NSA in Washington had such a good time that they couldn't wait to go to the next NSA Youth Leadership Program.

There are many good reasons for people who want to improve their presentation skills to attend NSA. If you have children, you now have another reason to go, because it is never too early to start learning.

The *National Speakers Association of Australia*[8] was established in 1987 and its foundation and evolution has been modeled on its U.S. counterpart. *The National Speakers Association of New Zealand*[9] was formed in 1994. These organizations exist to develop, promote, and uphold the highest possible standards of the profession for the benefit of their members and the public they serve. Any person who has an interest in the speaking industry is eligible to apply for membership.

The *Professional Speakers Association* (PSA)[10] is a an organization for professional speakers in Europe. PSA supports its members in developing their presentation skills, to share best practices, and to increase the awareness of the importance of professional speaking. There are currently seven chapters in England and one each in Scotland, Ireland, and Paris/Brussels.

The *Canadian Association of Professional Speakers* (CAPS)[11] is Canada's professional association for speakers, trainers, and facilitators. Just like NSA, CAPS has annual meetings where you can see and learn from the best speakers in Canada. CAPS currently has 11 chapters across Canada. Chapter locations and meeting times can be found on the CAPS Website. Just like the other national associations, CAPS offers tremendous value to it members.

Brad McRae and David Brooks offer basic and advanced courses on *The Seven Strategies of Master Presenters*. Custom-designed courses and individual coaching sessions are also available. *McRae and Brooks Seminars*[12] have trainers available across Canada and in the United States.

Lastly, most *colleges, universities*, and *local and national training organizations* offer courses in presentation skills. Nationally, *Dale Carnegie*[13] offers a presentations course as does the *Christopher Leadership Course*[14] As the quality of these courses is directly proportional to the abilities of the person teaching the course, use your research skills to find the right course and the right level of training to best meet your specific needs. Warning! Don't judge a course by its brochure. Use your research and networking skills to find the ones that offer the most value for your needs.

We all know from elementary school arithmetic that $3 + 3 = 6$. We also know that $3 \times 3 = 9$. Synergy is powerful. Synergy is based on the effects of combining some work in all of the areas listed above. Combining experience, mentoring, coaching, books, and courses results in compounded learning.

At this point it would be easy to congratulate yourself for having read this book and then put the book down. However, that would be a grave mistake. For Master Presenters and would-be Master Presenters, now is the time to take constructive action, and the action plan that follows is designed to help you do just that.

Helen Keller said that "life is either a daring adventure or it is nothing." In your presentation adventures, we wish you Godspeed.

—Brad McRae and David Brooks

ACTION PLAN

To overcome resistance to change, we must not only choose what to do, we must do it with persistence, commitment, diligence, and dogged determination. We must also be equally committed to what we are going to stop doing—in order to make room for that which we wish to start. Lastly, we must continue doing those things that have made us successful in the first place.

Start:_____

_____

Stop:_____

_____

Continue:_____

_____

APPENDIX

A

The Who's Who of Master Presenters

Richard Bolles, Best-Selling Author

Richard Bolles is one of the world's most innovative presenters. He is also the author of the phenomenal best-seller *What Color is Your Parachute?* (Ten Speed Press, 2003). This book, first printed in 1970, and rewritten every year since 1975, has sold more than 7 million copies. Richard's Website is *www.jobhuntersbible.com*.

Les Brown, CPAE, and Golden Gavel Award Winner

Les Brown is one of the world's most inspirational speakers. In 1989, he was the recipient of the National Speakers Association's highest honor: The Council of Peers Award of Excellence (CPAE). In addition, he was selected one of the World's Top Five Speakers for 1992 by Toastmasters International and has been awarded Toastmasters' Golden Gavel Award. To learn more about this outstanding international speaker, visit Les's Website at *www.lesbrown.com*.

Mark Brown, 1995 World Champion of Public Speaking

Mark Brown speaks to several thousand students each year. His ability to connect with children of all ages makes him in high demand by students, teachers, and school administrators across North America. To learn more about Mark visit *www.MarkBrownSpeaks.com* or *www.WorldChampionSpeakers.com*.

Bill Carr, Humorist

Bill Carr is one of Canada's most hilarious speakers who also helps his audiences see ordinary events in extraordinary ways. You can contact Bill at carrbill@ns.sympatico.ca.

Chris Clarke-Epstein, CSP

Chris Clarke-Epstein is one of the most respected speakers in North America and past president of the National Speakers Association. She is noted for being one of the most authentic and natural presenters in the world. Chris is also the author of several books including *The Instant Trainer.* Chris' Website is *www.chrisclarke-epstein.com*.

Warren Evans, CSP, HoF (CAPS Hall of Fame Member)

Warren Evans is a powerful blend of "facts, hope, and fun." His presentations combine statistics with common sense and humor to help his audiences make sense of the numerous trends swirling around us. Warren looks at the interplay between economics, corporate restructuring, demographics, globalization, technology, and psychographics to provide insights into social trends and the future of work. Warren is also a past president of the International Federation of Professional Speakers. Warren's Website is *www.wevans.com*.

David Foot, Author/Speaker

David Foot is an economic demographer. In most people's hands this would be a very dry topic indeed. Not so with David. David is one of North America's most creative thinkers on this topic. His sense of intellectual curiosity, passion, and sense of humor are infectious. David is known for both his outstanding content, his ability to customize his content to his audience's needs, and his rollicking good, fun style of delivery. Once you have heard David present, you will not forget either his message or his style. Articles that demonstrate the quality of David's content can be found at *www.footwork.com*.

Bob Gray, Author/Speaker

Bob Gray is among the most unique Master Presenters we have seen. Bob is the only person in the world who can speak backwards and write upside down at the same time. His memory feats and style are absolutely unique. Bob's mantra is, "There is no such things as a bad memory…only an untrained one!" Bob has appeared on *Ripley's Believe It Or Not,* ABC's *Live with Regis and Kelly*, NBC's *Today Show*, and on the CBC and BBC. You can learn more about Bob and see and his unique style on his Website *www.memoryedge.com*.

Rudolph Giuliani

Rudolph Giuliani was mayor of New York City at the time of the September 11, 2001 terrorist attacks. It is because of his leadership during that time that he became known as America's mayor. You can learn more about Mayor Giuliani's approach to presentation by reading his best-selling book, *Leadership* (Miramax 2002).

Gene Griessman, Author/Speaker

Gene Griessman is one of the world's best character presenters, and the character he brings to life is Abraham Lincoln. In fact, Gene has played Lincoln so frequently and studied Lincoln's life in such depth, that Gene's friends and colleagues are never quite sure if it is Gene Griessman playing Abraham Lincoln or Abraham Lincoln playing Gene Griessman. The CareerTrack video starring Gene Griessman titled, *Lincoln on Communication* is a classic in the field and one of the best instructional videotapes ever made. Gene's Website is *www.presidentlincoln.com*.

Lou Heckler, CSP, CPAE

Balancing wisdom, wit, and dynamic delivery, they just don't come better than Lou Heckler. Lou presents on Peak Performance, Customer Service, and Leadership By Example. Professional speakers throughout North America also ask Lou to help them create more effective presentations, focusing on speech organization and delivery techniques. Lou's Website is *www.louheckler.com*.

Jim Key, 2003 World Champion of Public Speaking

Jim Key is an example of persistence. He finished second in the World Championship of Public Speaking in 2001 and again in 2002. Many people would be discouraged when coming up short the first time, let alone the second time. But with determination and resolve, Jim went after his goal a third consecutive time becoming the 2003 World Champion. To learn more about Jim, visit *www.JimKey.com* or *www.WorldChampionSpeakers.com*.

Darren LaCroix,
2001 World Champion of Public Speaking

Darren LaCroix is not afraid to stand up and say "I failed, and yes, it hurt." This message is what propelled Darren to the top in the 2001 World Championship of Public Speaking by reminding the audience that we all have "ouch" moments, but that the most important moment is when we take the step after the "ouch." Darren illustrates his message with powerful personal examples. To learn more about Darren, visit *www.humor411.com* or *www.WorldChampionSpeakers.com*.

Peter Legge, CSP, CPAE, and Golden Gavel Award Winner

Peter Legge is a business owner, author, presenter, and volunteer extraordinaire. He is a Toastmasters International Golden Gavel Award winner, and is an acknowledged Master Presenter by such organizations as the National Speakers Association and the Canadian Association of Professional Speakers. Peter's Website is *www.canadawide.com*.

Janet Lapp, CSP, CPAE

Janet Lapp is one of the most sought-after speakers in the world today on how to adapt to an information society, and how to develop the skills to thrive with current and future change. Janet's Website is *www.lapp.com*.

Stephen Lewis, United Nations Secretary General's Special Envoy for HIV/AIDS in Africa

Stephen Lewis has held the offices of the Canadian Ambassador to the United Nations, special adviser to the UN Secretary General on Africa, Assistant Secretary General with UNICEF, and currently is the Secretary General's Special Envoy for HIV/AIDS in Africa. Mr. Lewis is a world renowned orator who uses words of eloquence to make the world, especially Africa, a better place. Learn more about the Stephen Lewis Foundation at *www.stephenlewisfoundation.org*.

Terry Paulson, CSP, CPAE

Terry Paulson is one of America's top-rated professional speakers who speaks on "Soaring on the Wings of Change." He is also a past president of the National Speakers Association. Terry is rated as one of the top 50 speakers in the United States in *The Speaking Industry Report 2002* by Lilly Walters. Terry's Website is *www.terrypaulson.com*.

Ian Percy, CSP, CPAE, HoF (CAPS Hall of Fame Member)

Ian Percy is an internationally acclaimed business and motivational speaker, registered organizational psychologist, author, Certified Speaking Professional, and member of both the U.S. and Canadian Speaker Halls of Fame. Ian has also been recognized as "One of the top 21 speakers for the 21st century!" by *Successful Meetings* magazine. Ian speaks about High Performance Leadership, Insightful Change, Corporate Vision and Purpose, Achieving Competitive Advantage, and Finding Meaning in Work. You can visit Ian's Website at *www.ianpercy.com*.

Bob Pike, CSP, CPAE

Bob Pike is the master of participant-centered learning. He is known for his ability to get the audience involved even before the presentation begins. Bob believes that participants learn best when actively engaged in the learning process, and his participant-centered model unlocks that power to learn and to dramatically increase retention and application. Bob Pike's Website is a must-visit at *www.bobpikegroup.com*.

Nido Qubein, CSP, CPAE, and Golden Gavel Aware Winner

Nido is a keynote speaker, seminar leader, corporate consultant, successful businessman, and author of many books and cassette learning systems. Nido doesn't just talk business, he lives it. He is an entrepreneur with active interests in banking, real estate, and advertising. As a "business insider" with extensive boardroom exposure, he's in touch with the challenges confronting today's businesses and organizations. You can visit Nido's Website at *www.nidoqubein.com*.

David Ropeik, Author/Speaker

David Ropeik is the Director of Risk Communications at the Harvard Center for Risk Analysis and is responsible for communicating the Center's approach of keeping risk in perspective to the press, policy makers, and the public. He is also the coauthor of *Risk: A Practical Guide for Deciding What's Really Safe and What's Really Dangerous in the World Around You* (Houghton Mifflin Co., 2002). With the world facing such challenges as West Nile virus, SARS, and terrorism, David and his research are in great demand. Prior to joining Harvard, he was a television reporter and news anchorman. He twice won the DuPont-Columbia Award, often referred to as the Pulitzer Prize of television journalism. Visit David's Website at *www.hcra.harvard.edu/ropeik.html*.

Jeanne Robertson, CSP, CPAE, and Golden Gavel Award Winner

Jeanne Robertson has been recognized by her peers with the top awards in speaking. In 1989, she became the first woman to receive the Cavett Award, the highest award of the National Speakers Association. In 1998, she became the first and still the only female professional speaker to receive the Golden Gavel Award, the top honor presented by Toastmasters International to non-Toastmasters. You can visit Jeanne's Website at *www.jeannerobertson.com*.

Mark Sanborn CSP, CPAE

Mark Sanborn is known internationally as a "high-content speaker who motivates." He presents 90 to 100 programs every year on leadership, team building, customer service, and mastering change. In addition to speaking, consulting, and training, Mark is president of Sanborn & Associates, Inc., an idea lab dedicated to developing leaders in business and in life. You can visit Mark's Website at *www.marksanborn.com*.

Martin Seligman, Ph.D., Author/Speaker

Martin Seligman is the Fox Leadership Professor of Psychology in the Department of Psychology at the University of Pennsylvania. He is also a best-selling author and was elected President of the American Psychological Association in 1998 by the largest vote in modern history. His main area of research and practice is Positive Psychology and his mission is to Using the New Positive Psychology to Realize Your Potential for Lasting Fulfillment." Martin's Website is *www.authentichappiness.org*.

Tom Stoyan, HoF (CAPS Hall of Fame Member)

Tom Stoyan has served is a Master Coach to sales and management professionals for more than 15 years. He coaches professionals to get the best out of themselves and others by breaking through the barrier from "knowing" to "doing." He is the founding president of the Ontario Chapter of the National Speakers Association that later became the Canadian Association of Professional Speakers (CAPS) and was the first inductee into the *Canadian Speaking Hall of Fame*. Tom's Website is *www.canadasalescoach.com*.

Ed Tate, 2000 World Champion of Public Speaking

Ed Tate is an "attitude-improvement specialist" who works with corporations and associations in transition. An international keynote speaker, trainer, and author, he has earned a reputation as a speaker who energizes, educates, and entertains. To learn more about Ed, visit *www.WorldChampionSpeakers.com*.

Harold Taylor, CSP, HoF (CAPS Hall of Fame Member)

Harold Taylor is the president and CEO of Harold Taylor Time Consultants Inc., and one of a very few and select people to be inducted into the Canadian Association of Professional Speakers' Hall of Fame. He is also one of North America's leading experts in time management, having written 13 books and hundreds of articles. Harold's Website is *www.taylorontime.com*.

Craig Valentine,
1999 World Champion of Public Speaking

Great presentations often use a metaphor. One of the best metaphorical presentations you will have the pleasure of listening to is *The Snake Bite* by Craig Valentine. Craig works with organizations on strengthening leadership and management in order to maximize effectiveness. His message stays with and inspires audiences long after he has walked off of the platform. To learn more about Craig, visit his Website at *www.craigvalentine.com* or *www.WorldChampionSpeakers.com*.

APPENDIX

B

References

Speaking and Speechwriting

Ailes, Roger, with Jon Kraushar. *You Are the Message: Getting What You Want By Being Who You Are*. New York: Doubleday, 1995.

Anderson, Dan. "How to Prepare for Presentations." *Training*, December 1983, pp. 98–108.

Arredondo, Lani. *How to Present Like a Pro*. New York: McGraw-Hill, 1990.

Booher, Dianna. *Speak With Confidence: Powerful Presentations That Inform Inspire and Persuade*. New York: McGraw-Hill, 2002.

Broad, Mary and John Newstrom. *Transfer of Training: Action-Packed Strategies to Ensure High Payoff from Training Investments*. Reading, Mass.: Addison-Wesley Publishing Company, 1992.

Brody, Marjorie and Shawn Kent. *Power Presentations: How to Connect with Your Audience and Sell Your Ideas*. New York: John Wiley & Sons, 1992.

Brody, Marjorie. *Speaking Your Way to the Top: Making Powerful Business Presentations* (Part of the Essence of Public Speaking Series). New York: Allyn & Bacon, 1997.

Carnegie, Dale. *The Quick & Easy Way to Effective Speaking*. New York: Pocket Books, 1962.

Charney, Cy. *The Portable Mentor: Your Complete Guide to Getting Ahead in the Workplace*. Toronto, Ontario: Stoddart Publishing Co. Ltd, 2000.

Cooper, Betty K. *Speak With Power: Six Steps and Eight Keys for Speaking Success*. Calgary, AB: Pow!-R Publications, 1994.

Dawson, Roger. *Secrets of Power Persuasion: Everything You'll Ever Need to Get Anything You'll Ever Want*. New York: Prentice Hall, 1992.

Decker, Bert with James Demey. *You've Got to Be Believed to Be Heard*. New York: St. Martin's Press, 1993.

Diestra, Diane. *Knockout Presentations: How to Deliver Your Message with Power, Punch, and Pizzazz*. Madison, Wis.: Chandler House Press, 1998.

Glickstein, Lee. *Be Heard Now! Tap Into Your Inner Speaker and Communicate With Ease*. New York: Broadway Books, 1998.

Henschel, Tom. "How to Talk so Your Audience Will Listen: Three Ingredients for Killer Presentations." *The 1996 Annual: Volume 1, Training*, San Diego, Calif.: Pfeiffer & Company, 1996, pp. 171–187.

Hoff, Ron and Barrie Maguire (Illustrator). *I Can See You Naked: A Fearless Guide to Making Great Presentations*. Kansas City, Mo.: Andrews McMeel, 1992.

Hoff, Ron. *Say It In Six*. Kansas City, Mo.: Andrews and McMeel, 1996.

———. *Do Not Go Naked into Your Next Presentation: Nifty Little Nuggets to Quiet the Nerves and Please the Crowd*. Kansas City, Mo.: Andrews and McMeel, 1997.

Humes, James C. *Podium Humor: A Raconteur's Treasury of Witty and Humorous Stories*. New York: Harper & Row, Publishers Inc., 1975.

———. *The Sir Winston Method: The Five Secrets of Speaking the Language of Leadership*. New York: William Morrow and Co., Inc., 1991.

———. *More Podium Humor: Using Wit and Humor in Every Speech You Make*. New York: Harper Perennial, 1993.

———. *Speak Like Churchill, Stand Like Lincoln: 21 Powerful Secrets of History's Greatest Speakers*. Roseville, Calif.: Prima Publishing, 2002.

Jeary, Tony. *Inspire Any Audience*. Tulsa, Okla.: Trade Life Books, Inc., 1997.

Leech, Thomas. *How to Prepare, Stage, & Deliver Winning Presentations*. New York: AMACOM, 1993.

Linkletter, Art. *Public Speaking for Private People*. Indianapolis, Ind.: The Bobbs-Merrill Company, Inc., 1980.

Mandel, Steve. *Effective Presentation Skills: A Practical Guide for Better Speaking, 3rd Edition*. Los Altos, Calif.: Crisp Publications, Inc., 2000.

Matekja, Ken and Diane Ramos. *Hook 'em*. New York: American Management Association, 1996.

Noonan, Peggy. *On Speaking Well: How to Give a Speech with Style, Substance, and Clarity*. New York: First Regan Books/Harper Perennial, 1999.

Paulson, Terry. *50 Tips for Speaking Like a Pro*. Menlo Park, Calif.: Crisp Publications, Inc. 1999.

Peoples, David A. *Presentations Plus (Second Edition)*. New York: John Wiley & Sons, 1992.

Robertson, Jeanne. *Don't Let the Funny the Funny Stuff Get Away.* Houston, Tex.: Rich Publishing Company, 1988.

Slutsky, Jeff and Michael Aun. *The Toastmasters International Guide to Successful Speaking: Overcoming Your Fears, Winning Over Your Audience, Building Your Business & Career.* Chicago, Ill.: Dearborn Financial Publishing, Inc, 1997.

Smith, Terry C. *Making Successful Presentations*. New York: John Wiley & Sons, 1991.

Spicer, Keith. *Winging It: Everybody's Guide to Making Speeches Fly Without Notes*. Garden City, N.Y.: Doubleday & Company, 1982.

Spicer, Keith. *Think on Your Feet: How to Organize Ideas to Persuade any Audience.* Toronto, Ontario: Doubleday Canada Ltd., 1985.

Stevenson, Doug. *Never Be Boring Again*. Colorado Springs, Colo.: Cornelia Press, 2003.

Thomas, Stafford H. *Personal Skills in Public Speech*. Englewood Cliffs, N.J.: Prentice-Hall, Inc., 1985.

Toogood, Granville N. *The Articulate Executive*. New York: McGraw-Hill, Inc., 1996.

Urs Bender, Peter. *Secrets of Power Presentations*. Toronto, Ontario: WEBCOM, 1991.

Walters, Lilly. *What to Say When…You're Dying on the Platform: A Complete Resource for Speakers, Trainers, and Executives*. New York: McGraw-Hill, 1995.

Wohlmuth, Ed. *The Overnight Guide to Public Speaking*. Philadelphia, Pa.: Running Press, 1983.

Wydro, Kenneth. *Think on Your Feet: The Art of Thinking and Speaking Under Pressure.* Englewood Cliffs, N.J.: Prentice-Hall, Inc., 1981.

Quotations/Anecdotes

Bartlett, John and Justin Kaplan, (Ed.) *Bartlett's Familiar Quotations: A Collection of Passages, Phrases and Proverbs Traced to Their Sources in Ancient and Modern Literature 17th Edition*. New York: Little, Brown & Co., 2002.

Simpson, James B. (Ed.). *Simpson's Contemporary Quotations: Most Notable Quotes from 1950 to Present*. New York: HarperResource, 1997.

Safire, William and Leonard Safir, (Eds.). *Words of Wisdom: More Good Advice*. New York: Simon & Schuster, A Fireside Book, 1989.

Prochnow, Herbert. *A Treasury of Humorous Quotations for Speakers, Writers and Home Reference*. New York: Harper Collins, 1969.

Language and Grammar

Bernstein, Theodore M. *Do's, Don'ts and Maybes of English Usage*. New York: Times Books, 1977.

Strunk, William Jr. and E.B. White. *The Elements of Style 4th Edition*. Upper Saddle River, N.J.: Pearson Allyn & Bacon, 2000.

Miscellaneous Reference

Wetterau, Bruce. *New York Public Library Book of Chronologies*. 1990. New York: Hungry Minds Inc., 1994.

Park, Ken. *World Almanac and Book of Facts*. New York: [World Almanac] Scripps Howard Company, 2003

Audio Tapes/CDs/Videos

Convention Cassettes Unlimited
74-923 Hovley Lane East, Suite 250
Palm Desert, CA 92260
Toll-free: 1-800-776-5454 Fax: 1-760-773-9671
E-mail: info@ConventionCassettes.com
Website: *www.ConventionCassettes.com*

Available from Convention Cassettes:

The Alfred Hitchcock Effect: Build Suspense into Every Story, Ann Bloch, NSA 2000 Annual Convention

Crafting Magical Moments, Jeanne Robertson, NSA 2000 Annual Convention

Kids Are Worth It, Barbara Coloroso, *www.kidsareworthit.com*

Lincoln on Communication, Gene Griessman, *www.presidentlincoln.com*

Making Time Work for You, Harold Taylor, *www.taylorontime.com*

Motivational PEG Session, Mark Victor Hanson, NSA 2001 Annual Convention

The Pause that Builds Applause, Lou Heckler, NSA 2001 Annual Convention, Tape #59

Presentation Magic by the Motivator, Les Brown, NSA 2000 Annual Convention

Presenting To Win: The Art of Telling Your Story, Jerry Weissman, March 2003

APPENDIX

C

The Master Negotiator's Preparation Form™

Interests	
Our Interests	Their Interests
1.	1.
2.	2.
3.	3.
4.	4.

The Prize: The Ultimate Outcome from the Negotiation	
Our Prize	Their Prize

Options at the Table	
Our Options	Their Options
1.	1.
2.	2.
3.	3.
4.	4.

Standards/Objective Criteria

(Objective standards or objective criteria help the parties look at the negotiation much more objectively and make it easier to reach an agreement)

1.
2.
3.
4.

Offers

• *Aspire to?*
  (The best arrangement you could get)

• *Content with?*
  (Satisfactory)

• *Live with?*
  (Acceptable minimal settlement)

BATNA (Best Alternative To a Negotiated Agreement)	
Our BATNA	Their BATNA

Leverage	
Our Leverage	Their Leverage

Possible Trade Offs/Concessions	
Our Trade Offs/Concessions	Their Trade Offs/Concessions

Type of relationship I would like to have during and after the negotiation:

My partner's negotiation style is:

The style I will use in this negotiation is:

Muscle Level: The amount of Power or Force I will bring to the table:
1.
2.
3.
4.

Our Opening Statement

APPENDIX

D

Checklists

Speakers are, for the most part, road warriors. Few of us have the luxury of speaking only in our home towns; the rest of us have to travel extensively to and from speaking engagements. And as every frequent flyer knows, it can be maddening to arrive at your destination only to discover that a key piece of equipment you *thought* you had packed is still sitting at home. The checklists on the following pages will help you think through your packing process.

Checklist 1: Don't Leave Home Without It

_____ Travel documents: airline tickets, government-issued ID, frequent flyer ID number for all airlines (in case you end up on a different airline than you intended).

_____ Hotel information: reservation confirmation number, street address, telephone number, and driving directions.

_____ Rental car information: reservation confirmation number, pick-up location, frequent-renter ID number.

_____ Cell phone, complete with fully charged battery, battery charger, hands-free earpiece for states that require them when driving.

_____ Pre-paid long-distance calling card for remote locations in which your cell phone won't work or is not part of your service system.

_____ Laptop computer, complete with fully charged battery, AC adapter/battery charger, telephone cable for modem, blank floppy disks and/or blank CD-R disks, remote control mouse.

_____ Handouts, including not only a printed copy but a backup copy of your handouts in your laptop computer and a second backup copy of your handouts on disk.

_____ Cables and wiring, including video cable to connect your notebook computer to an LCD projector, and a multi-outlet power strip.

_____ Essential office supplies, including legal pads, note cards, paper clips, pens, pencils, highlighter, mini-stapler, calculator.

_____ Large-display LCD travel clock to keep your presentation on time in rooms in which wall clocks are not visible.

_____ Resource material, including free items as well as items you may have to sell.

_____ Sales material, including credit card imprinter, charge slips, order forms, merchandise bags.

_____ Repacking material, including sealing tape and shipping labels.

Checklist 2: Preparing the Room, Both Front and Back

(Check the following well before the audience arrives.)

Microphone

_____ Is the volume and tone adequate?
_____ Are there feedback or radio frequency issues?
_____ Will you be sharing a microphone with the person who speaks immediately before you?
_____ If sharing a mike, how long you will have to make the transfer of equipment?

Lighting

_____ Does the lighting illuminate you in the best possible manner?
_____ Are there dark voids in the speaking area?
_____ If the lighting will be adjusted for your presentation, where are the dimmers/switches?
_____ If the lights will be adjusted as you speak, who will assist you with the task?

Introduction

_____ Have you supplied a printed, large-type printout for your introducer?
_____ Have you verified that the introducer can pronounce troublesome words?
_____ Have you determined if the introducer will wait center stage for you to arrive at center stage?

Room setup

_____ Is the room a comfortable temperature?

_____ Are the seats arranged for an optimum speaking environment?

_____ If you are the only speaker, have you arranged the room to suit your needs?

_____ Have you taped off the last few rows of seats to "encourage" attendees to sit at the front?

_____ Is your lectern properly set up with any material you may need as you speak?

Back-of-the-room setup

_____ If you have resources to sell, have you set the table in a high-traffic area?

_____ Do you have appropriate signage?

_____ Are prices clearly marked on individual items and multi-item packages?

_____ Do you have an assistant who can help with sales?

_____ Will an assistant be able to watch your table to prevent "five-finger discounts"?

_____ Do you have free items on the table to encourage traffic?

Checklist 3: Things You Don't Want to Leave Behind

In the crush of activity as you conclude a presentation, it is easy to overlook many items you brought in. We recommend you ask your host to assign one person to be responsible for gathering the following at the end of your presentation:

_____ Any item left on the lectern, including notes, clock, remote controller for mouse, any props or remaining giveaway items.

_____ Any speaker gift you may have been presented.

_____ Notebook computer, including your remote control receiver (attached to a USB port), LCD cable, multi-plug power strip.

_____ Unused handouts in the seats

_____ Unsold resource material from the back of the room, including resource order forms, credit card slips, credit card imprinter.

CHAPTER NOTES

Foreword

1. Bryan, William Jennings. *The World's Famous Orations.* New York: Funk and Wagnalls Co., 1906.

2. Ibid.

3. Ailes, Roger with Jon Kraushar. *You Are the Message.* New York: Doubleday, 1988.

4. Twain, Mark. From a speech titled, *The Babies*, given in 1879. This particular speech can also be found in a book titled *Mark Twain's Speeches*. New York: Oxford University Press, 1996.

Introduction

1. Galbraith, John Kenneth, *The Affluent Society.* New York: Houghton Mifflin, 1998.

2. Giuliani, Rudolph with Ken Kurson. *Leadership.* New York: Hyperion, 2002, p. 232.

3. Ibid. p. 224.

4. Ibid. p. 319.

5. Decker, Bert with James Denney. *You've Got to Be Believed to Be Heard.* New York: St. Martin's Press, 1992.

6. Susskind, Lawrence and Patrick Field. *Dealing with an Angry Public: The Mutual Gains Approach to Resolving Disputes.* New York: The Free Press, 1996, p. 89.

7. See Appendix A for a description of the Master Presenters we interviewed.

8. A copy of this newsletter is given to the participants regardless of whether the presentation is to 20 participants or to a keynote 500 people. You can view or download a copy of the annotated bibliography by going to the "Newsletters" section of Brad's Website: *www.bradmcrae.com.*

9. If you want to see a master at using self-depreciating humor to introduce a topic, we highly recommend Harold Taylor's videotape, *Making Time Work For You.* (See Resources for contact information.

10. Convention Cassettes Limited (see Resources for contact information).

11. Wydro, Kenneth. *Think On Your Feet: The Art of Thinking and Speaking Under Pressure*. Englewood Cliffs, NJ: Prentice-Hall, 1981, p. 18–19.

12. Ibid. p.17.

13. Swindoll, Charles, *The Tale of the Tardy Oxcart*. Word Publishing, 1998.

Strategy 1

1. Welch, Jack with Joan Byrne. *Straight from the Gut*. New York: Warner Books, 2001, pp. 105–106.

2. Video Arts UK and International Offices, 6–7 St Cross Street, London EC1N 8UA. Phone (UK): +44 (0)20 7400 4800 Fax: +44 (0)20 7400 4900, Website: *www.videoarts.co.uk*, E-mail: info@videoarts.co.uk.

3. Honey, Peter and Alan Mumford. *The Learning Styles Questionnaire*. Berkshire, U.K.: Peter Honey Publications, 2000, pp. 9–14. See also *www.peterhoney.com*. The Learning Cycle, which makes up these four learning styles, comes in order of stages, the order being, Stage 1: Activist, Stage 2: Reflector, Stage 3: Theorist, and Stage 4: Pragmatist. Therefore TRAP does not follow the sequence of the learning cycle upon which the learning styles are based, rather TRAP is used as a mnemonic device.

Strategy 2

1. Seligman, Martin. *Authentic Happiness*. New York: Free Press, 2002, p. 263.

2. Two Websites that document the power of the primacy effect and the recency effect are:
   www.ciadvertising.org/SA/fall_02/adv382j/easander/primacy.htm.
   www.ciadvertising.org/SA/fall_02/adv382j/easander/recency.htm.

3. In this case, Brad used PowerPlugs: Quotations by CrystalGraphics. This program has more than 45,000 quotes. With one click of the mouse you can import the quotation directly into Microsoft Word or PowerPoint. You can download a sample of the program by going to *www.crystalgraphics.com*.

4. Kouzes, James, and Barry Posner. *Credibility*. San Francisco, Calif.: Jossey-Bass Publishers, 1993, p. 197.

5. Augustine, Norman R. "Reshaping an industry: Lockheed Martin's survival story." *Harvard Business Review*: 1997, May–June.

6. Paulson, Terry. *They Shoot Managers Don't They?* Berkeley, Calif.: Ten Speed Press, 1991.

7. This case study was adapted from Michael Useem's *The Leadership Moment: Nine True Stories of Triumph and Disaster and Their Lessons For Us All*. New York: Random House, 1998.

8. Ibid. p. 11.

9. Kotter, John. *Leading Change*. Boston, Mass.: Harvard Business School Press, 1996, pp. 152–53.

10. Fisher, Roger, William Ury, and Bruce Patton. *Getting to Yes: Negotiating Agreement Without Giving In*. New York: Penguin Books, 1991, p. 148.

11. McRae, Brad. *The Seven Strategies of Master Negotiators*. Toronto, Ontario: McGraw-Hill, 2002, pp. 66–67.

12. Training Directors' Forum Newsletter, Vol. 11 (7), July 1995, p. 1.

Strategy 3

1. Alan Parisse, CSP, CPAE, speaks on Change and Leadership and has been rated as one of the top 21 speakers for the 21st century by *Successful Meetings* magazine, December, 1999.

2. Berstein, Leonard. *The Joy of Music*. New York: Simon and Schuster, 1959, p. 73.

3. Betty K. Cooper is a world-class presentation coach. She is one of a very few coaches who is repeatedly invited back to coach at the Million Dollar Round Table, a yearly meeting of insurance salespeople who sell a million dollars of insurance in a single year. She can be reached by phone: (403) 294-1313, or via e-mail: bkcooper@telusplanet.net.

4. Dr. Terry Paulson speaks about "Soaring on the Wings of Change."

5. David Paradi is an author and consultant. He publishes the *Communicating with Technology* e-zine and can be reached at *www.communicateusingtechnology.com*.

Strategy 4

1. Humes, James C. *The Sir Winston Method: The Five Secrets of Speaking the Language of Leadership*, New York: William Morrow and Company, 1991, p. 34.

2. Max Dixon is a sought-after speech coach who taught drama at the University of Seattle in Washington for 35 years. His e-mail address is maxdixon@televar.com and his Website is *www.televar.com*.

3. Covey, Stephen. *The 7 Habits of Highly Effective People: Powerful Lessons in Personal Change*. New York: Simon & Schuster, 1989.

4. Ann Bloch, Ann Bloch Communications, (413) 637-0958, e-mail annbloch@vgernet.net. You can order a tape of Ann's session titled: *The Alfred Hitchcock Effect: Build Suspense into Every Story*, available from Convention Cassettes Unlimited (see Resources for contact information).

5. Stevenson, Doug. *Never Be Boring Again*, Colorado Springs, Colo.: Cornelia Press, 2003, pp. 28–29.

6. Hoff, Ron. *Do Not Go Naked Into Your Next Presentation*. Kansas City, Mo.: Andrews McMeel Publishing, 1997, p 45.

7. If you have a great example of a prop and would like to share it, please send your ideas to us at brad@bradmcrae.com or dbrooks@texas.net.

8. *Toastmasters Magazine*, Mission Viejo, Calif.: Toastmasters International, March 1998.

9. Ibid.

10. Robertson, Jeanne. *Don't Let the Funny Stuff Get Away*. Houston, Tex.: Rich Publishing Company, 1998.

11. Ibid. pp. 15–16.

12. Wetlaufer, Susy. "Driving Change." *Harvard Business Review* (March/April, 1999). It can also be found in the book *Interviews with CEO's*. Boston: Harvard Business Review, 2000.

Strategy 5

1. The article, "Thinking Outside the Box" is found in *Negotiation Newsletter*, Vol. V, which can be downloaded by going to the Newsletters section of Brad's Website at *www.bradmcrae.com*.

2. Rubin, Jeffrey Z. "Caught by Choice: the Psychological Snares We Set Ourselves," *The Sciences* (1982) 22 :7, pp.18–21.

3. Robert Pike gave this presentation at the NSA 1997 annual meeting in Anaheim, California. His Website is *www.cttbobpike.com*.

4. Ash, Russell. *The Top Ten of Everything 1996*. Montreal, Quebec: Reader's Digest, 1997.

5. Marcia Steele's presentation was titled *Flying Deep*. The presentation was given at the National Speakers Association's 2001 Annual Meeting in Dallas, Texas. Copies of the video and the audio (#NSA 01061/3) are available from Convention Cassettes Unlimited (see Resources for contact information).

6. The idea for this exercise came from an exercise used by Michael Aun in *What to Say When…You're Dying on the Platform* by Lily Walters. New York: McGraw Hill, 1995.

7. Pike, Robert W. *Creative Training Techniques Handbook: Tips, Tactics, and How-To's for Delivering Effective Training, 2nd ed*. Minneapolis, MN: Lakewood Books, 1994.

8. See *The Negotiation Newsletter*, Volume XI, which can be downloaded by going to the Newsletters page of Brad's Website (*www.bradmcrae.com*).

9. McCall, Morgan, Michael Lombardo, and Ann Morrison. *The Lessons of Experience: How Successful Executives Develop on the Job*. New York: Lexington Books, 1988.

10. See Appendix C.

11. *Personnel Psychology*. Bowling Green, Ohio: (1988), 41, p. 63.

12. Wetlaufer, Susy. "An Interview with Ford Motor Company's Jacques Nasser," *Interviews with CEOs Driving Change*. Boston: *Harvard Business Review*, 2000, p. 4.

13. Broad, Mary L. and John W. Newstrom. *Transfer of Training: Action-Packed Strategies to Ensure High Payoff from Training Investments*. Reading, Mass.: Addison-Wesley Publishing Company, Inc., 1992, p. 108.

Strategy 6

1. Howard, John, David Cunningham, and Peter Rechnitzer. *Rusting Out, Burning Out, Bowing Out: Stress and Survival on the Job*, Toronto, Ontario: Financial Post Books, 1978. p. 87. This book is currently out of print, however, you may be able to find it in your library or order it from a used bookseller.

2. Meichenbaum, D.H. "Enhancing Creativity by Modifying What Subjects Say to Themselves." *American Education Research Journal*, Vol. 12, 1975, p. 129–145.

3. Waldo, Kenneth. *Think On Your Feet,* Englewood Cliffs, N.J.: Prentice Hall, Inc., 1981.

4. Yvonne Dolan is an author, presenter, and therapist. She has specialized in helping people overcome the devastating effects of sexual abuse.

5. Paulson, Terry. *50 Tips for Speaking Like a Pro.* Menlo Park, Calif.: Crisp Publications, 1999, pp. 82–3.

Strategy 7

1. Joan Bolker is the co-founder of the Harvard Writing Center, which offers invaluable suggestions for "blocked" writers. Much of her information is also applicable for "blocked" presenters.

2. Convention Cassettes Unlimited (see Resources for contact information).

Conclusion

1. This article is published on Nido Qubein's Website at *www.nidoqubein.com*. We highly recommend that you visit his Website and read the rest of the article as Nido goes on to eloquently discuss how to identify the learning style of your organization and the importance of being proactive in pursuing educational opportunities.

2. McCall, Morgan, Michael Lombardo, and Ann Morrison. *The Lessons of Experience: How Successful Executives Develop on the Job*. New York: Lexington Books, 1988.

3. A video or CD version of this masterful presentation is available from Gene Griessman at 127352 Sunset Blvd., Suite D604 Pacific Palisades, Calif. 90272. *www.presidentlincoln.com*.

4. Barbara Jordan was a United States Congresswoman who became the voice of moral authority during the Watergate hearings. She was also the keynote speaker at the 1976 Democratic National Convention and the first black woman from the south to be elected to the U.S. House of Representatives.

5. Barbara Coloroso is the award-winning expert on parenting and the author of the book *Kids Are Worth It!* (New York: HarperResource, 2002). *Kids*

Are Worth It! is also available as a videocassette and an audiocassette titled available from *www.kidsareworthit.com*.

6. Visit the Toastmasters Website, *www.Toastmasters.org*, to find out about the organization and the clubs that are nearest to you. Like all large organizations, each club has a personality of its own. You may want to do some research first to discover the club that would be most compatible with you. You may also want to visit several clubs to see for yourself which is the most comfortable and best suited to your specific needs.

7. *www.nsa.org*. The National Speakers Association (NSA) became a partner in the formation of an umbrella organization created to support the growing importance of the speaking profession globally in 1997. By making its resources available to existing international associations for professional speakers, NSA is able to enhance the value of those association memberships, encourage the formation of new associations for professional speakers, and set the benchmark for platform excellence worldwide.

8. *www.nationalspeakers.asn.au*.

9. *www.nationalspeakers.org.nz*.

10. *www.professionalspeakers.org*.

11. *www.canadianspeakers.org*.

12. You can visit McRae Seminars at *www.bradmcrae.com* and Brooks Seminars at *www.DavidBrooksTexas.com*.

13. *www.dalecarnegie.com*. Dale Carnegie Training® has helped individuals become successful professionals for nearly a century. They offer a comprehensive catalog of courses, seminars, and training products that enable participants to grow and prosper both professionally and personally. The course they offer that is most germane to the topic of this book is *High Impact Presentations*.

14. *www.christophers.org*. The Christopher Leadership Course helps participants gain self-confidence and learn speaking skills through a 10-week program. It is especially helpful for those who need to overcome their fear of speaking in front of a group. Participants begin by presenting silly prepared poems, which helps participants relax, release tension, and feel more comfortable. Participants eventually move on to present their own prepared speeches. As the program progresses, the speeches become longer and participants are asked to work on a project that puts them in the position of leadership, allowing participants to further develop confidence.

INDEX

ABOUT THE AUTHORS

BRAD MCRAE has a doctoral degree in psychology from the University of British Columbia. He is a registered psychologist, consultant, and author and is the president of McRae and Associates. He has lectured across Canada, the United States, in Mexico, and Africa. He was trained in negotiating skills at the Project on Negotiation at Harvard University and gives more than 100 presentations a year.

Brad has earned the Platinum Level Speaker designation from Meeting Professionals International. As such he is one of only 50 in North America, and three in Canada. He is a member of the Canadian Association of Professional Speakers and the International Association of Professional Speakers.

Brad is the author of four books: *How to Write a Thesis and Keep Your Sanity*; *Practical Time Management: How to Get More Done in Less Time; Negotiating and Influencing Skills: The Art of Creating and Claiming Value*; and *The Seven Strategies of Master Negotiators* and is the editor and publisher of *The Negotiation Newsletter*.

Brad lives in Halifax, Nova Scotia, with his two children, Andrew and Katherine.

DAVID BROOKS is the 1990 World Champion of Public Speaking. He has coached, advised, and mentored five subsequent World Champions and dozens of finalists. His combined journalism and Toastmasters background have taught him the art of clarity and brevity. He has spoken in every U.S. state, every Canadian province, and in China, Hong Kong, the Philippines, Singapore, Thailand, Oman, Ireland, Sweden, Puerto Rico, and Jamaica. He was the top-rated trainer for three consecutive years with an international seminar company. In 1990, he triumphed over more than 25,000 initial competitors to become the Toasmasters World Champion of Public Speaking. Since that time, he has coached and/or mentored five additional World Champions and dozens of finalists. And, though he has spoken to multiple thousands of business communicators, David claims one additional distinction: over the past 13 years he has spoken to more Toastmasters than anyone else in the world. Major international corporations have brought David in to train their employees in effective presentation skills. He was the highest rated trainer with a multinational seminar company for three consecutive years, and he has appeared on nationwide television and radio broadcasts in the United States, Canada, and Oman.

McRae and Brooks Seminars:
Helping You Get What You Deserve

The Seven Strategies of Master Presenters Seminar

This highly interactive two-day seminar will help you master the Seven Strategies of Master Presenters. The seminar is taught by Brad, David, and our associates across the United States, Canada, and internationally.

Keynotes and Seminars by Brad McRae

Brad's presentations are powerful and professional. His most requested keynotes and seminars are:

- *The Seven Strategies of Master Presenters*
- *The Seven Strategies of Master Negotiators*
- *The Seven Strategies of Master Leaders*
- *Optimal EQ: Developing and Enhancing Your Emotional Intelligence*

Keynotes and Seminars by David Brooks

David's presentations are entertaining, informative, practical, and memorable. His most requested keynotes and seminars are:

Keynotes:

- *The Seven Strategies of Master Presenters*
- *Field of Dreams: How and Why I Caught a Game Pitched by Nolan Ryan*
- *Been There, Won That: How to Make This Your Lucky Day*

Seminars:

- *Don't Open with a Joke, but Get Laughs Anyway*
- *Business Writing for Busy Professionals*
- *Goof-Proof Grammar*

CD Programs:

- *The Seven Strategies of Master Presenters*
  This 4-disk audio CD album covers each of the strategies used by Master Presenters and is illustrated with examples from some of the world's best speakers. As retention is critical to learning, this set will help you master the strategies and skills taught in this book.
- *The Seven Strategies of Master Negotiators*
  This CD contains a 45-minute keynote on the Seven Strategies of Master Negotiators by Brad McRae, 18 Negotiation Newsletters, a copy of the annotated bibliography and a copy of the Master Negotiators Preparation's Form and detailed instructions on how to fill it out.

- *Speaking Secrets of the Champions*
  Produced by David Brooks, this 6-disk audio CD set features six hours of instruction from six Toastmasters World Champions: David Brooks, Mark Brown, Craig Valentine, Ed Tate, Darren LaCroix, and Jim Key. It illustrates six different, but proven, ways to be a more effective presenter.
- *Elements of Eloquence*
  In this 4-disk audio CD set, David illustrates how to find and use your own personal stories, how to make your message memorable in as little as seven minutes, and how *not* to use PowerPoint.

You can contact Brad at:

5880 Spring Garden Road, Suite 400
Halifax, Nova Scotia
CANADA, B3H 1Y1
Phone: (902) 423-4680 or Fax: (902) 484-7915

E-mail: brad@bradmcrae.com
Website: *www.bradmcrae.com*

You can contact David at:

6300 Wallace Cove
Austin, Texas 78750

Phone: (512) 343-8000

E-mail: dbrooks@texas.net
Website: *www.DavidBrooksTexas.com*